THIEF PRINCE

By Cheree L. Alsop

Believe ~

Cheree Alsop

ISBN9781479135721

Cover Design by Andy Hair

www.ChereeAlsop.com

To my husband, Michael Alsop,
My own knight in shining armor,
Who has believed in me
Every step of the way.

To my family for their support,
For the laughter, love, and the
Endless adventures.

I love you!

Chapter 1

I stood out like a moth caught in a flight of butterflies. I accidentally stepped on my partner's foot again, and he rolled his eyes. I wasn't cut out for this crown princess stuff. By the end of the song, I'd managed to crush Crown Prince Trevin's toes three more times. I couldn't blame him when he turned without a word and made a beeline through the other dancers to where his sister, Kaerdra, and Princess Nyssa waited. Both princesses glanced at me and then laughed. I turned away before they could see my red cheeks.

The room was stuffy even though the dancing had just started. The Eskand servants had stoked the fires to a roaring ferocity before the royal gathering entered the ballroom. It was a relief to slip behind the thick, gold-embroidered curtains to one of the many balconies. My breath fogged in the chilly night air. It wasn't surprising that the balcony was unoccupied. Behind me, a violinist played the beginning chords for a brisk waltz. The tune was quickly taken up by the other string players. Laughter and footsteps in time to the music followed.

I sighed and tried not to feel sorry for myself. A snowflake landed on my cheek and I brushed it angrily away. It was hard not to feel awkward around the beautiful, proper, perfect, stuck-up, shallow princes and princesses gathered for the winter celebration. It wasn't their fault I didn't fit in. It was mine.

I was the one who spent the summers making rounds with the healers and playing in the gardens instead of studying and training like my brother Rory. But back then, Mother and Father hadn't seemed to mind that I ran as wild and free as the fillies in the fields below the castle. Because back then, everyone knew Rory would be Crown Prince. It was alright for them to look the other way when I hid from my tutors for the hundredth time so that I could learn swordsmanship from the guards. Captain Rurisk had even fashioned a sword my size.

I traced the calluses that had begun to fade along my palms since Rory got sick. I clenched my hands into fists, then dropped them to my sides, blinking rapidly to chase away the tears.

A brief rise of music and laughter announced that someone had entered the balcony. I didn't have to turn around to recognize Father's soft chuckle. "Here you are, Kit," he said. He reached out to smooth my ruffled hair. "I missed you in there."

I nodded but didn't trust myself to speak until my emotions were under control.

Father guessed my thoughts. "Thinking about Rory?" he asked gently. At my silent nod, he squeezed my shoulder. "He's going to be alright." He sounded like he was trying to convince both of us.

For his sake, I didn't argue. "It got stuffy in there," I said, changing the subject.

He chuckled again. "The room or the people?"

This time I laughed. "That's a bit harsh. It's not their fault I don't fit in."

"It's not yours, either," he replied. At my unconvinced glance, he ran a hand through his thick chestnut hair. Despite the latest fashion, he refused to tie it back. Shoulder length, it reminded me of a wild horse's mane. He also hated to wear his crown for other than extremely formal occasions, so despite the fact that the other kings and queens wore their golden crowns with the jewels bearing their country's colors, Father's was still packed in his room. He shrugged, slightly abashed. "I should have followed your tutoring more closely, but I liked to see you without rules, especially when there wasn't any reason to keep you in a schoolroom for hours on end."

"No reason until now," I said quietly. "Maybe I wouldn't embarrass you and Mother if I'd been more attentive to my studies."

"You're not an embarrassment, and no one knew what the future would hold. Rory will get better, and then you won't have the weight of a kingdom on your shoulders." His expression brightened; his brown eyes, a shade lighter than mine, crinkled at the corners. "You should come back to the ballroom. There's been an interesting turn of events."

At his bemused expression, curiosity rose in my chest. "What turn of events?"

"The Antorans have arrived."

Surprised, I stared past him at the purple curtain, wishing I could see through it. "How do they dare show up after all the raiding they've done?"

Father shook his head. "They shouldn't have. If it wasn't for honor, Crown Prince Andric's entire party would have been killed the second he stepped into the room. He and his father have made plenty of enemies." His eyebrows rose. "King Fayne didn't come, but Prince Andric doesn't seem too fazed by it. He's very collected for someone his age." He glanced at me. "He can't be more than a year or two older than you, eighteen at the most."

I nodded, remembering Tutor Farnon's rushed course in social history. "He's an only child, and lost his mother to sickness when he was twelve. The Antorans have been raiding the other countries for the past two years, and no one can catch them once they reach the mountains."

Father held out his arm. "It's a pity to waste such a beautiful evening out here in the cold and miss all the excitement. With your mother home tending to Rory, I need someone to keep me company." He smiled down at me. "And there's no other company I'd rather have."

When we walked back into the ballroom, I saw the group of princes and princesses clustered in a circle talking and pointing not-so-discreetly at the other end of the room. A look in that direction revealed the one who had to be Prince Andric. He stood near the wall, his arms folded across his chest and his dark-eyed stare nonchalant as he gazed around the room. His dark brown hair was tied back in a simple warrior's tail, and he wore loose robes of Antoran black and green. His eyes darted to us when we entered the room and lingered briefly on Father's dress knife before dismissing us with the rest of the gathering.

Father's surmise of Prince Andric seemed accurate. Though the other royalty in the room were obviously perturbed at his presence, he merely watched the dancers and sipped the honey-laced wine set out for refreshment.

His guards wore the same robes of Antoran black and green; the only difference between their attire and that of their prince was the gold medallion around Andric's neck. The medallion held the biggest elder diamond I had ever seen. Considered one of the most prized possessions of Denbria, kings had gone to war for diamonds smaller than the one he wore.

The arrival of the Antorans created a chink in the festive evening. The ball wound down just past midnight, and I saw several dark stares thrown toward the prince as subdued partiers left to seek their rooms in the spacious palace. It seemed that though honor prevented them from physically making their hostility known, the kings and queens of Denbria weren't about to pass up a chance to make him uncomfortable.

***

I couldn't sleep. Though the huge bed could easily have fit ten girls my size, and the sheets and the feather mattress were very soft, I couldn't get comfortable. The night sounds of the palace were foreign, and the wind whistled in different places than my room back home. I missed our gardens, though the snows had them locked in frozen beauty. I missed Phantom, the great black wolfhound that slept beside Rory's bed waiting for him to get better. More nights than not I rested with my head pillowed on the faithful dog's side as I waited with him.

I rose to dash away the escaped tears on my cheeks with lightly perfumed water from the pitcher on the side table when a knock on the door caught me by surprise. I grabbed an evening robe and hurried to the door. The servants slept in the smaller room between Father's and mine, but I didn't think it made sense to wake them just to answer the door. I pulled it open and looked down the hall, only to find that it was empty.

Confused, I turned to shut the door again when I noticed the small envelope at my feet. 'Princess Kirit' was written across it in an elegant hand. I frowned. Nobody who really knew me called me Kirit. Father had taken to calling me Kit when I was little and the name stuck.

I shut the door, took the envelope back to bed, and opened it in the light of the moon that shone through the glass windows. The message was simple, but in the same elegant handwriting from the front of the envelope. "An Invitation to All Crown Princes and Crown Princesses of Denbria: Prepare for a Night of Adventure and Meet beneath the King's Living Spire."

I smiled. It wasn't a very hard riddle. King Trand's great grandfather, son of the original ruler of Denbria, had planted an evergreen tree the day his son was born. The tree, now sheltering the same son's final resting place from the merciless weather, towered above the other trees at the edge of the King's Forest. Not too tricky, but considering the other princes and princesses, I figured that was probably a good idea.

A small burst of excitement filled me while I pulled on a pair of loose riding pants and a soft blue shirt with sleeves that were too big, as was the fashion. Fashion was never very convenient. At home, I would have just rolled them up, but I just shook my head and decided to live with it. I already doubted my choice to wear the riding pants. The other princesses would probably wear their frillery since the princes were also invited.

That was something I didn't have to worry about, as attested to by the night's dancing. Though I had been asked to dance several times by the princes, it was out of royal courtesy. Only the title of Crown made us the same. Before, I wasn't destined to inherit one of the eight countries of Denbria. Now that Father had given me the temporary title of Crown Princess as Rory's sickness worsened, the other Crowns didn't know how to respond. It didn't matter that I accepted the title grudgingly, believing and hoping that I would be giving it back to Rory as soon as he got better. They treated me like an imposter, and I felt like one.

For a moment I questioned whether I should accept the invitation at all. Then I argued that I would probably miss out on the only excitement the festival had to offer. My heart pounded faster as I fastened my blue cloak with the gold palm leaf clasp that was the symbol of our country.

Chapter 2

Kenyen and Danyen, the twin seventeen year old sword fighters from Tyn, were there before me, along with Landis of Faer and Tisha from Maesh. It was rumored that Landis' and Tisha's parents had already reached an agreement for their arranged marriage; they were holding hands when I stepped into the light of Danyen's lantern. My breath fogged and I shivered in the early morning chill. We waited for the rest to appear, saving our questions until everyone was together.

The beautiful, fair skinned and auburn-haired Brynna of Eskand was next, followed closely by Nyssa in Veren's royal purple and silver. Trevin and Kaerdra were last, siblings from Cren and duel heirs of the Crenian crown. It wasn't often that a king granted both of his children heirships, but it was no secret that he planned to split his kingdom when the brother and sister were old enough to take over.

"What is she doing here?" Kaerdra asked; her tone indicated me even though she refused to look in my direction.

"She's a Crown Princess, too," Tisha said quietly. She threw me tentative smile. Landis gave her a pained look and brushed a stray strand of her curly blond hair behind her ear.

"She's an imposter Crown," Brynna said with a glare in my direction.

"Not by choice," Tisha replied, her voice uncertain.

"Doesn't matter," Trevin said. His sister nodded in support. "She doesn't have the training or the knowledge to lead her country properly. Rory knew what he was doing."

A dark figure within the shadow of the pine caught my attention as I turned away to hide my cheeks that were bright red with embarrassment. My eyes adjusted from the shifting light of the lantern to starlit darkness, and I made out the form of the Prince of Antor watching us.

"What is the thief doing here?" Kenyen asked coldly when the Prince's presence was noticed.

Andric walked toward us; the darkness separated slowly from his black clothing as if loath to relinquish him to the dim light. Only the gold medallion stood out against his chest. No outward expression betrayed any emotion he felt at what the Tyn Prince called him.

Nyssa sniffed and swept her hair back. "It's not right that your father allowed this thief and his band of bandits to attend the winter festival," she said to Brynna.

"Funny," Andric replied with a wry twist of his lips.

"What is?" Nyssa was forced to ask when Andric didn't embellish.

The Antoran Prince shrugged. "That you were so willing to accept my invitation."

My heart slowed at the implication, but Nyssa merely stared at him.

"What are you talking about?" Landis growled.

The Prince's dark eyes gleamed. "That's my handwriting on the invitations you hold."

A knot formed in my stomach and I glanced down at the card in my hand. The writing I had thought elegant before now looked ominous.

Andric caught my expression. "My mother felt that good penmanship was one of the qualities of a proper king." He gave a simple gesture with one hand and dark shadows separated from the night to surround us. "My father stressed the importance of the element of surprise."

I stared at him, unwilling to accept what my eyes saw. The dark shapes were soldiers in Antoran black and green, armed with swords and wicked-looking serrated daggers. "Are you kidnapping us?" I asked in amazement.

Andric nodded, his expression calm. "In a manner of speaking." Another gesture and horses walked from the darkness. They were short and rugged with thick dusky fur that grew long around the hooves. They were already saddled but didn't have bridles or any form of leading harness that I could see; they stopped beside us and waited.

Andric swung onto the mount closest to him. He then looked back at us. "It'll be a much longer journey if you walk." He spoke quietly, but in a tone that carried no room for argument.

I looked at the waiting guards and saw that we had no choice. I could fight them, but I was unarmed and couldn't take down a dozen soldiers by myself. I highly doubted the other princes and princesses had any battle training. My best bet would be to survive and find a way to escape along the way. I gritted my teeth and took a step toward the nearest horse.

"You don't really think we're getting on those horses just because you say so," Kaerdra snapped.

"Kaer," Trevin said softly with a nod toward the guards. "I don't think this is a good time to argue."

Kaerdra turned to glare at the soldiers around us, her chest heaving. She looked like she wanted to argue, then gave up in a huff of breath that showed white in the night air. "Fine, but you'll be sorry when our father finds out about this."

"I intend to be long gone by then," Andric replied. His jaw tightened as his eyes searched the darkness of the palace walls.

I looked around at the guards and fought back a wave of panic when a soldier stepped toward me. I took a deep breath and leaped onto the closest horse. His hooves shifted under my weight, then he turned his head to sniff my fur-lined boots. They were soft and thick for short walks in the slight skiff of snow that covered the ground, definitely not meant for riding. I settled them in the stirrups and wondered how long they would last. The horse snorted softly as if he read my thoughts and I gave him a small smile.

"At least pretend like you're unhappy about this," Brynna said icily to me as she mounted the next horse. She tossed her auburn hair back. "Unless," she said with a slight twist of her lips, "You want to run away. Goodness knows your country would be better off."

I looked past her and tried to ignore the burning that reddened my face. The guards were already in their saddles and awaiting Andric's orders. He nodded. "Let's move."

The horses started with a quick jolt that caught us by surprise. With no bridle for guidance, we were forced to hold onto the horses' thick manes until we got used to the strange cadence of the mountain mounts. They didn't gallop, but settled into a bone-jarring, mile-eating trot from which they didn't seem to tire. I felt rattled after the first few minutes; I was used to the horses of the plains, the long-legged, smooth gaited striders that Father bred as a hobby and raced against Faer's swift steeds.

My horse was fast and eager, but maintained his place in line without any guidance from me. I wondered who had trained them to obey so well. The other princes and princesses rode before and behind me in silence as they, too, struggled to adjust to the rugged animals.

We covered more ground than I would have thought possible by the time the sun started to rise. The forest grew thicker the further we rode from the castle; soon, trees were the only thing we could see in any direction. I wished I had grabbed my riding boots; my feet were already sore from attempting to soften the fall of the horse's hooves with my weight in the stirrups. My legs shook from the stress of holding myself off the horse's back.

"Loosen up," a voice said.

I looked over to see Prince Andric riding beside me, his face expressionless.

"I don't think now is the time to criticize my flaws," I replied crossly.

The briefest smile quirked at the corners of his mouth, then vanished. "No, I mean you ride too stiff. That might work for your grassland horses, but for these you need to loosen up and grip with your knees instead of putting your weight on your feet. You'll be a lot less sore that way."

I tried to come up with a cutting reply about how it was impolite to give advice to someone you just kidnapped when Kenyen spoke.

"So what's to keep us from riding off with your horses back to the palace?" the Prince of Tyn asked.

"Yeah," his twin put in, "You couldn't catch all of us."

"Try it if you'd like," Andric challenged, "But you won't get anywhere." He and one of the guards riding toward the front of the column exchanged a look. "The horses listen to Drade, and only to Drade."

Kenyen frowned. "Well," he finally said, "Then what's to keep us from jumping down and running away? It wouldn't take long to lose ourselves in the trees."

As if on cue, a shadow ghosted through the forest next to me; there were two more close behind. I glanced over my shoulder to see another two on our other side.

"Wolves," Landis said in a hushed voice. He threw a worried look at Tisha.

15

Andric gave a grim smile. "You wouldn't get far." He urged his horse forward and rode to the front of the column.

"Animal magic," Danyen said in a low voice to his brother. "Father was right. They're demons, all of them."

"My mother told me that they bewitch the animals into listening to them, that they make them do cruel and horrible things," Tisha said.

I glanced back and realized she was talking to me. We rode near the end of the column, with four soldiers trailing behind. The one who brought up the rear attempted to mask our passing the best that he could, but it was nearly impossible to cover the tracks of two dozen horses. The guard just behind Tisha met my eyes and glanced away. A shiver ran down my spine.

"Maybe. . . maybe it's not like that, we don't know," I guessed in an attempt to appease them both.

"All I know is that Mother won't be happy with me letting myself get kidnapped. She'll be furious when she sees I'm gone." Tisha's eyes glistened with tears.

"We'll be alright," I tried to reassure her despite the tightness in my own chest. "I don't think they mean to harm us."

"Faster," Andric commanded from the front of the column. His was the firm tone of someone used to giving commands that were obeyed without argument.

Our horses sped up without any urging from their riders. Their ears pricked forward, their eyes on Drade as we loped through the forest. I swallowed my pride and tried Andric's advice, forcing my legs to relax and tightening my knees at the horse's sides instead. Immediately, my body fell into a gentle swaying rhythm that matched the rise and fall of the horse's hooves. My legs ached from the released tension. I wouldn't have held up much longer the way I had been riding. The horse's steps softened too, as if he realized I was no longer fighting him.

The wolves kept pace easily, loping alongside the column with a quiet grace. One wolf, a huge, dark gray animal, ran beside Andric's horse. When we stopped, all of the wolves went to the Antoran Prince as though to wait for their next assignment. I wondered if Tisha's comment that the animals were under some sort of spell was true.

***

We stopped three times the first day to rest and water the horses. Andric's guards gave us rolls, hard cheese, and dried beef with mint-flavored water to wash it down. The small meal tasted like a feast after the hard ride, though Brynna, Nyssa, and Kaerdra complained and refused to eat. By the end of the day, though, they devoured their portions as quickly as the rest of us.

Four of the guards with pack horses rode ahead and had a camp set out by the time darkness caught us. It was a relief to see tents ready with lined mattresses and plenty of blankets to fight off the night's chill. The guards served a hot, spiced soup with the same hard rolls to dip in it, along with warm, sweetened pumpkin milk.

We ate in silence, the other Crowns too tired for once to even argue, though they had done their fair share at each of the stops throughout the day. By the time I was finished with my meal, I could barely keep my eyes open. I crawled gratefully into the tent a guard pointed to, and was asleep before my head hit the small pillow.

Chapter 3

I dreamed of Father that night. He would know by then that I was missing, and would ride at the head of his troops bent on reaching us before we made it to the mountains. Throughout the dream, Father yelled, "Stop them before they reach the pass!" and "Kit, don't go through!" I wanted to go to him, but I couldn't get my body to respond. I was stuck on my horse while he trotted faithfully along in the column, his eyes forever on Drade's back.

I awoke to the sound of someone shaking my tent. Dim light filtered through the cloth to announce the sunrise. "Time to go," a gruff voice said, then his footsteps moved to the next tent.

An argument followed. "I'm not going anywhere, and you can't make me."

"We aren't in a position to negotiate right now, Brynna," Kenyen replied tiredly.

"My father will be here any moment. You'll be sorry. All of Eskand will be with him," she threatened; her voice wavered slightly, betraying the emotions she tried to hold back.

Andric gave a low reply, but I couldn't make out the words. I poked my head outside my tent in time to see Nyssa and Brynna standing arm in arm, Kenyen and Danyen a few feet away. The rest of us were in various degrees of awake as we struggled out of our tents and watched the guards pack them up quickly and efficiently and load them onto the backs of the horses. Another guard handed out more cups of warm, sweet pumpkin milk. I sipped it and felt my mind wake up as it chased the chill from my aching bones.

With the taste of cinnamon lingering in my mouth, I made my way to the horse I had ridden the night before. He stomped as if impatient to be on our way, and shook his mane when I neared. I held out my hand and let him smell my fingers. His hot breath fogged in the early morning air, reminding me of my own Fray, a black mare Father had raised from a filly just for me. She was sleek and fast, built for speed, the exact opposite of this shaggy, short, impatient animal. He nudged my chest with his nose; I rubbed his forehead and then leaned against his side.

The scent of horse made me miss Father with such an ache that I felt a stabbing pain just below my heart. He would be worried, more than worried, terrified for me. He didn't know if we were safe or hurt. He always assumed the worst. Mother, his calm counterpoint, was home with Rory and wouldn't be able to help him.

Rory wouldn't have gotten himself into this situation, would he? I missed him more than anything, because deep down I didn't know if he would still be alive when I returned. I knew that was why Father decided to take me to the Winter Festival while Mother stayed home. Rory and I were so close, and it was killing me to see my brother slowly get worse. Rory was my best friend.

A tear slid down my cheek and I wiped it away before anyone could see it.

"Mount up," Andric ordered. I wondered when he had appeared; he hadn't been in the small clearing a moment ago. The dark gray wolf waited beside him; the Prince's hand rested on the wolf's head as he watched us prepare to leave. I should be afraid of the animal, but I was too tired to feel fear, only sorrow at the situation I had gotten myself into and the disappointment and hardship it would bring my parents.

I forced my aching muscles to respond and clambered onto my horse's back, feeling much less agile than I had the night before. I was amazed to think that it was only last night that the Prince of Antor and his guards had forced us to leave the warmth and safety of Eskand castle. The protest of my sore joints felt like we had already done weeks of riding.

"I can't do this," Tisha said. I looked back and saw her standing next to her horse with tears in her eyes. Landis was beside her, his hands held out in a helpless gesture.

I glanced ahead and saw that Andric had mounted and was riding toward us. I gritted my teeth and slid off my horse, fighting back a wince when my sore feet hit the ground. "It's alright, Tisha." I put an arm around her shoulder. Landis hesitated, then gave me a surprisingly grateful smile and hurried back to his horse.

"It's not alright, Kit," she said with a sniff. Then her eyes widened and she looked at me. "I'm sorry I called you that. It's just that I remember Rory talking about you so often that it's the name I think of when I see you."

"It's fine," I grinned at her, relieved to feel a bit of humor in the dismal situation. "I prefer Kit anyway. Everyone back home calls me it. Though," and I felt the dark cloud settle again, "I don't think anyone will take me seriously with a name like Crown Princess Kit."

She gave me a reassuring smile and wiped the tears from her cheeks. "It's alright; at least you sound like an adult. Crown Princess Tisha will always sound like a little girl's name." She smoothed her curly blond hair away from her wet cheeks.

I grimaced as I helped her with her stirrup. "Princess Kirit doesn't sound so grown up. It sounds more like ruler of the vegetables." That was a sore spot with me, and the reason I preferred Kit. It sounded a lot less like carrot to me. At least I didn't have orange hair!

Tisha swung her leg over the horse's back. "Ruler of the vegetables? Now that would be an easy job." She gave me a small, self-conscious smile. "Thanks, Kit."

"Anytime," I replied and turned back to my own horse. He snorted as if to tell me to stop taking my pleasant time. "Why are you so eager to get going?" I asked him when I was on his back. "You're the one that has to do all the work." He shook so that the saddle swayed on his back and I had to grab his mane to stay on. "Moody creature," I mumbled. He nickered in reply.

I looked up and met Andric's gaze; a gleam of humor showed in his dark eyes. I glowered at him and he turned his horse away. I glanced back at Tisha, and smiled to see her weaving her fingers through her horse's hair. Landis gave me a nod from where he sat on his horse. Before I could respond, my horse jolted into a trot. I turned back around, reminding myself to move with the animal instead of against it. The tiredness eased from my muscles as my body remembered the rhythm from yesterday.

"How much further is it?" Nyssa asked from up the line. The whiny twist to her voice set my teeth on edge.

"A couple of days," Trevin replied when Andric didn't answer. He twisted back in his saddle to look at her. "It depends on the time we're making. We're moving at a pretty good clip."

"Shut up," Kaerdra replied crossly behind him.

"I hate horses, I hate nature, I hate bugs, I hate the cold," Brynna ranted, "I hate camping, I hate being dirty, I hate bathroom breaks behind trees." I wasn't the only one who chuckled. "I hate tents, I hate snow, and I hate you," she said to Andric's back.

He rode on as if he didn't hear her, his back straight and his body swaying with the cadence of his horse's hooves. A wolf trotted on either side of him; their long legs ate up the ground as swiftly as the horses'. The other wolves paced the group at a further distance through the trees. They watched the path around us, alert for signs of attack.

I needed to leave a note for Father. He would be extremely worried about me, and the other Crowns' parents were probably just as worried about them. Though I didn't know Prince Andric's plan, I also didn't think he would harm us. He didn't seem like that type of person, and he could have done it last night instead of listening to all of the whining through another day. Of course, the wolves that ran on either side of him didn't boost my confidence at all.

When we stopped, exhausted, for the night, everyone ate dinner in silence and retired to our tents without a word to each other. I was almost asleep before I remembered my vow to leave a note for Father. I felt a pang of guilt at the lack of homesickness I had felt today, but exhaustion blanketed every other emotion. I wasn't used to this kind of journey, and neither were the others. Even Prince Andric and his Antorans conserved energy by conversing only when necessary and retiring to their shifts the same time we went to our tents.

I grimaced when I thought of Andric, so cold and sure about what he was doing. I didn't know how he justified kidnapping nine princes and princesses, and what he planned to do with us, but he had no right to push us so far. I worried about Tisha. She looked like she was ready to drop midway through the day. I don't think she touched much of her dinner before going to her tent. Landis looked as worried as I felt, and turned his frustration on Prince Andric, but Andric didn't seem bothered by the Prince of Faer's angry outbursts. He brushed off the rude names and cruel words echoed by most of the other Crowns.

I guess he expected it, which filled me with regret I couldn't explain. How would Rory have responded in the same situation? The others never mentioned him after our first encounter, except for when Tisha said that he had spoken of me. For some reason, that made me miss him even more. It meant so much to know that he had thought of me even when he had been with the other Crowns.

I swallowed the lump in my throat, stepped into my boots, and climbed out of the tent into the snow that covered the ground. That was another disheartening thing on our trip; the snow was getting deeper and the ground was starting to rise. I knew if we could see through the thick forest of trees, the mountains would be on the not-to-distant horizon. I had overheard Andric's guards say we would reach the mountain pass tomorrow if we pushed hard enough. I just hoped the others could take that much pushing.

I didn't know what to use to leave a note. One of the Antorans glanced at me from where he leaned against a tree on the first night watch. When I sat by the fire and stirred the embers with a stick, he turned back to his vigilant scrutiny of the darkness beyond our camp. Small sparks rose as I traced shapes into the gray ash left from our dinner fire. The trees hid any light from view, so the Antorans didn't worry about the kings of Denbria seeing our campsite.

Another stick poked out of the fire beside the one I had just put in. On impulse, I removed it and smiled when I saw the blackened point. I rose, mentioned in passing that I was going to relieve myself, and disappeared through the trees.

I kept close enough to camp that the guard could see where I was, but had a low bush between us so that he couldn't see what I was doing. As we neared the mountains, the ground had changed from the soft, loamy, snow scattered earth of the King's Forest to icy slates of snow-covered rock that made the horses stumble if they weren't paying attention. I cleared the snow and undergrowth from a patch of rock, then sketched a brief note.

"Father, we're safe. We are being taken to Antor. No one is hurt, Kit."

I surveyed my work. It was rough, but it would have to do. It didn't seem like enough, but I was out of room and I couldn't think of anything else to tell him anyway, since I didn't know much more myself. I only hoped Father would find it.

When I went back to my tent, the guard merely glanced my way and then back out at the forest again. I slept fitfully that night; images of Father hunting through the snow and underbrush inches from my note but unable to see it kept waking me in frustration. I saw fear on my father's face. He had no way of knowing we were alright; but when I thought about it, neither did I. What if we didn't make it through this safely? I forced the thought aside and grabbed a last few minutes of sleep before my tent was shaken.

We rose even earlier that morning. Gray hadn't even touched the horizon before we were rudely accosted from sleep and forced out into the below-freezing temperatures. I felt dazed after the night's restless dreams, and barely acknowledge it when Prince Andric handed me a thick cloak of soft woven wool. The warm oatmeal and hot pumpkin milk failed to chase away the early morning chill. I shivered as I climbed onto my horse's back and wrapped the wool cloak over the blue one I already wore.

Kenyen and Danyen muttered a few choice words in Andric's direction when they mounted up. Tisha didn't say a word as Landis helped her onto her horse. He shot me a worried look before climbing onto the one behind her. Kaerdra argued, but it was with less energy than normal. In the end, she accepted her brother's assistance and mounted her horse in a sullen silence.

The ride felt long and as the trees thinned, the thud of my horse's hooves on the rocks and hard earth jolted me to the core. By noon, the sun had soaked through our cloaks and we were feeling a little more energized. The Tyn twins used their energy to insult Andric, his guards, the snow, and pretty much everything Brynna had mentioned in her last rant. Nyssa and Brynna talked heatedly about what their fathers would do to Andric when they caught him, and Trevin and Kaerdra ran through ways to escape, mostly involving harming Andric and his guards in cruel ways in the process. Because the wolves were our constant companions and the horses truly did seem to listen only to Drade, their plans were mostly just talk, which was why they said them loud enough for everyone to hear.

The wolves kept my attention. Even though it was easy to think that the animals were bewitched, they certainly didn't act like it. At night, they ran off in pairs for what I assumed was their evening hunt. Even Andric disappeared right after dinner and seldom returned before we were all asleep. I wondered if he was checking our back trail to keep an eye on our pursuit.

The wolves took turns running beside Andric's horse during the day, but the dark gray one with blue eyes was his constant companion. He fed them scraps of his own food at our breaks, and they lounged beside him like he was one of them. It seemed more like they were friends than that they were under some spell, though the thought of humans and animals being friends on that level sent a strange chill up my spine.

I was lost in my thoughts when I heard a scream further up the column. They had just disappeared around a bend.

Jagged rocks jutted up toward the sky like massive daggers thrust up by giants from below the earth, and we wove through them in single file on horseback. The scream sounded followed by high-pitched shrieking, and my heart skipped a beat.

Forgetting the wolves entirely, I jumped down from my horse and ran past Nyssa, Kenyen, and Danyen. I rounded the corner to find Kaerdra bent over her horse with tears rolling down her cheeks. Trevin, Andric, and the guards were around her still on their horses.

"What's going on?" I demanded.

They all turned. Andric's eyes widened slightly when he saw me. I glanced around and the sight made my heart stutter. Two wolves, the huge dark gray one and a smaller one with light gray fur, stood on either side of me. Their heads were low and their eyes on the Prince as if they waited for his cue to attack. Andric gave a slight shake of his head. Immediately, the wolves walked away as if my life hadn't been hanging in the balance.

Kaerdra started to cry louder.

Andric's brow creased. "She got stung by a blue wasp."

"And it hurts so bad!" Kaerdra said with more tears.

I hesitated. "Can I help her?" I asked with a glance at the wolves who were hanging casually near.

I couldn't read the expression on Andric's face when he got my meaning. He turned his horse away, his words short. "They won't hurt you."

I hurried past the guards to where Trevin helped Kaerdra down from her horse. She held her arm close, careful not to touch the spot just below her wrist. Blue wasp stings hurt like crazy, but weren't serious if treated quickly.

"I'm a healer," one of the guards said as he dismounted from his horse next to me.

"Don't touch me," Kaerdra shouted.

She buried her head in Trevin's shoulder. Her blond-haired brother looked up and met my eyes. I lifted my hands in a gesture of offered help and he nodded. "Please," he mouthed. He whispered something to Kaerdra and she turned quickly toward me.

"Can you help me, Kit?" Her tone was pleading.

I nodded. "If the healer has some plantain leaves."

He nodded and handed over the leaves he had already withdrawn from his pack. I fought back a smile at the relief on his face that someone else was prepared to take care of the shrill princess.

I took her hand and studied the stinger that stuck from the small, red spot on her arm. Before she could protest, I pinched the stinger close to her skin and pulled it free with a short, quick jerk. She let out a yelp, but breathed a sigh of relief when she saw that the stinger was gone. I chewed up some of the plantain leaves, added a peppermint one the guard gave me, put the pulp directly on the sting mark, and covered it in the cleanest snow I could find.

The guard handed me strips of white cloth. "Thanks," I told him with a small smile.

"No, thank you," he replied with a hint of a smile in return.

I wrapped the sting securely, then tied the ends of the cloth and wrapped them under the other strips so they wouldn't snag on anything.

"You act like you've done this before," the guard commented.

I nodded with an inward cringe. "I was more interested in learning how to heal than in being a princess."

"It's a worthy pursuit," he replied.

I gave him a tired smile. "Thanks. There're others who wanted me to pursue more sensible pastimes."

"I'm glad you didn't," Kaerdra said softly.

I looked at her in surprise. She gave me a small smile, then her brother helped her back to her horse.

I stared after her for a minute, then walked back to my position in line. The others waited on their horses just in front of the corner of rock, wary of the wolves while they watched from what they assumed was safety. My horse, on the other hand, still stood obediently where I had left him. I walked around the corner to go to him when something below caught my eye.

We had worked our way up the foothills and entered the mouth of the mountain pass. At the edge of the forest that fronted the small hills we had ridden over just hours before, I saw riders.

"They've found us," I said in surprise.

I must have said it louder than I thought because Andric appeared around the bend on his horse followed closely by the others.

"Father!" Brynna shouted and waved her hand above her head.

"Shhh," Andric warned her sharply. "Do you want to start an avalanche?"

She glared at him. "Wouldn't be worse than what you've put us through."

"Yeah," Trevin snapped. "I wouldn't want to see what our fathers do to you when they get here."

The Antoran Prince stayed calm. "We won't be here when they arrive."

"You've lost," Danyen said, incredulous. "Give up!"

Andric merely turned his horse. His wolves stalked closer than usual. The rest of the horses followed the Prince, carrying their unwilling captives. My horse took an uncertain step forward, then looked back at me.

It would be easy to run. The wolves were there, but Andric had already promised that they wouldn't harm me. I looked back at him and saw that he regretted the statement. His regret made me more certain that the wolves wouldn't follow if I ran. A glance at the line of soldiers that rode from the forest line into the open clearing below showed more of them than I had thought there would be. I could escape. My heart began to race with the implications.

I looked back. The others watched me as if they realized what I contemplated. Tisha, more alert now than she had been through the last day, shook her head, her eyes pleading for me not to risk it. Nyssa and Brynna both nodded encouragingly, while Trevin, Landis, and Kaerdra waited for me to make my own choice. Andric's guards looked to him for his command. He merely watched me, his expression guarded and eyes calculating. I realized then that he expected me to go.

For some reason, that made up my mind. I kicked the snow from my boots and stepped back into the saddle. My horse snorted and took the few hurried steps needed to catch up to the rest. Andric threw me a last, puzzled look before he turned his horse to lead us into the heart of the mountain.

"Why didn't you go?" Tisha whispered.

"I don't know," I whispered back, but I did know. I didn't want Andric to be right. I wasn't going to run and leave the others to whatever fate he had set for them. If I could fight, I would. I wouldn't run away like a coward.

Chapter 4

We rode on in silence. Andric hurried us to faster paces whenever possible. The thick snowdrifts, up to the horses' knees in some places, covered layers of ice above the slate. The treacherous footing required the horses' full attention along the snow-covered path. Walls of stone rose to dizzying heights around us as we followed a gash in the mountain that stood out bare amid the fir-spotted, snow covered sides.

The walls closed in, creating a channel with only one direction to go, up. I fought off claustrophobia as we continued to rise. We sweated as much as our horses while they braved the trail.

After hours of riding, we finally reached a clearing near the top of the path. The walls spread out and created a sheltered cove in the mountain's height. We stopped to give the horses a much-needed breather. Drade and two of the other guards made a small fire to thaw snow for the horses to drink. I removed my horse's saddle and rubbed him with a handful of stubborn snow grass to help him dry.

"You take good care of him," a voice said.

I turned to find Drade behind me, a small pouch of grain in his hand.

"He's a good horse, and he's worked hard," I replied, embarrassed. He wasn't my horse; I wondered if I had overstepped a line tending to him.

"Trae's one of my favorites." He winked at me and lowered his voice. "Just don't tell the others."

"Trae," I repeated. The horse responded by bumping my shoulder with his nose. I turned and rubbed his forehead. "I like that name."

Drade smiled and handed me the grain sack. "Give him just a bit. It'll help him have energy for the trip down."

I nodded and took the sack. Trae sniffed impatiently at my fingers, then took an eager mouthful when I opened it for him. He munched happily and bits of barley fell off his whiskery nose to the snow below.

Drade checked Trae's hooves for rocks, re-saddled him, then took the grain sack and moved on to Tisha's horse. Trae bent and snuffed up the few remaining kernels on the ground, then sniffed me thoroughly for more. When he found none, he shook himself, then stamped a hoof, eager to begin our journey once more.

Everything fell silent. Before, the sounds of horses shifting their weight from hoof to hoof, people talking in low voices, packs creaking, and the occasional snort scattered through the air; but within the space of a few seconds, all sounds stopped.

I looked up to see that Andric had called his guards together. They talked in low voices, punctuated by gestures from his captain. "What's going on?" I whispered to Landis.

He shrugged, his eyes on Andric's back. "The guard said he saw Breizans."

"Breizans!" My heart slowed. All Denbrians are told stories of Breizans since we were little children. Mothers told warning stories about the ice men who wore the skins of savage beasts like their flesh to scare children so they didn't wander off at night.

The adults told horror stories on late winter evenings to frighten each other when they thought their children were asleep. I wasn't the only one who snuck in to listen to the stories, frightened but reassured by the thought that the Breizans weren't real.

"There's no such thing as Breizans," Brynna said with a snort; she flicked a strand of auburn hair behind her shoulder.

"They're just made-up monsters to scare children into obeying their parents," Trevin agreed loudly. "We're too old to believe in them now."

"He's just trying to scare us, right Nyssa?" Kenyen asked with a grin.

But Nyssa didn't smile back. She looked at the ground instead, the toe of one foot tracing a pattern on the snow. "I saw one once, close the castle," she said, her voice quiet. Her tone sent a chill down my spine. I knew I wasn't the only one who wished she wouldn't continue speaking and shatter the bubble of safety we thought we lived in.

She took a small breath and let it out to cloud the air. "It was winter and a friend and I sat on the wall throwing snowballs. I remember something separating from one of the trees. It stared at us with wild eyes, and didn't look human at all, but it stood on two feet and bared its teeth at us. It had on a mask made of a goat's head, with the eyes cleared out so that it could see through." She shuddered. "My parents said they didn't believe me when we ran back and told them, but they didn't let us near the wall anymore." The truth to her words sent another shudder through my skin.

When Andric turned back around, the whiteness of his face and the hardness of his eyes confirmed Nyssa's words. "We've got to ride. Now!"

Danyen shook his head. "Our fathers will make it with their soldiers. They'll stop the threat."

Andric shook his head. "They won't make it in time. We've got to ride through the pass. There's a clearing with a wall; we've used it before."

When he turned to give orders to his men, I looked back down at the soldiers who made their way into the foothills. They were little black dots in the white snow, not even close enough to distinguish the colors of their uniforms. Andric was right. If we were in danger, they wouldn't make it in time.

The stories danced through my mind. If Breizans were real, I wasn't going to sit around helpless while we were killed by flesh-eating, savage humans. "Give us some swords," I said; the authority in my voice surprised me.

Everyone turned and stared. I swallowed and kept my eyes on the Antoran Prince. "Andric, we can help."

He gave me a calculating look, then nodded to one of his guards. The man retrieved spare swords from one of the saddle packs and handed them out. The princes all took one, and the guard offered the final sword to me with a slight smile on his face that I assumed meant he was joking. His eyes widened when I accepted the weapon and swung onto Trae's back.

Andric commanded, "Jashe, guard our left flank, and Falen, your team to the right. My pack will cover our backs. Let's ride."

The horses leaped into a gallop after the Prince. I held on tight with my knees like Andric had instructed, and attempted to keep my heavy sword steady in one hand while my other knotted in Trae's mane. The horses ran at a breakneck speed over the dangerous footing of snow and ice. The mountains closed around us as we charged into the pass.

I saw them a few seconds later. Men flanked us through the trees and kept pace with our horses. I call them men because I don't know what other term to use. Like Nyssa's description, they ran on two legs and were the size of men, but if they had been on all fours, I would have considered them beasts too foul for a name.

They wore skins stained rust brown from the blood of the creatures from which they had been taken. The same blood tainted what I could see of their flesh, brownish red around their mouths, dark red fingers that looked more like claws. They held jagged-edged knives and other weapons made to injure, not for a clean kill. The sight of them sent a cold pit of fear in my stomach.

I leaned down on Trae's back. He responded by lowering his head to gallop faster. Gratitude washed through me for his sure feet on the uneven ground. The clearing rose ahead. The wall was there; I estimated it was at least six feet tall at the side that faced us.

Andric reached the clearing, two guards behind him. He spun his horse, his sword raised. Before he could escape, Breizans rose out of the snow around him, the wild, human beasts crashing up through the snow. The air shattered with high-pitched screams that froze my blood. Trae's steps faltered. Andric swung his sword and took out the two nearest creatures. The remaining Breizans sliced at his horse's legs in an attempt to bring them both down. The horse kicked out and caught one in the chest; the force of the impact smashed the Breizan into the wall. Andric's guards leaped their horses into the fight; swords flashed against the winter sunlight. We slowed our horses.

"Jump the wall!" Andric shouted back at us. He turned in time to slice down a spear thrown at his back.

Trevin sat near the mouth of the clearing; he looked back at us and his eyes went wide. "Behind you!" he yelled.

I turned to see Breizans rush out of the trees toward us. Andric's wolves leaped at them, pulling them down from all sides, but it was obvious the five animals wouldn't be enough to stop them. My heart thundered in my chest.

Trevin tightened his knees and his horse jumped into the clearing at almost a full gallop. The horse flew across the ground, barreling over the Breizans who stood in the way. Trevin blocked an axe flung at his head, and then bent down when his horse gathered his legs and leaped. They disappeared behind the wall.

"Let's go," Kaerdra said, her voice unsteady. Her horse ran forward and made for the clearing. Before she could reach the wall, one of the Breizans jumped in her way and swung. The sword sliced across her horse's chest. He whinnied and reared. Kaerdra tumbled in an ungraceful heap to the ground.

My heart slowed. "No!" I shouted. Trae leaped forward as if the very wind flowed through his veins. He galloped toward Kaerdra, then veered to one side when three Breizans with serrated swords barred the way. They grinned at me, their teeth bloodstained a dull rust color. Two more ran past to attack the others who waited behind me. Trae danced away from a spear point; I leaned down and chopped off the end of the spear with a quick slice of the sword. I had to hold on tight to keep from falling off the horse's back with the weight of the blade.

I looked up, expecting to see Kaerdra dead in the snow. I almost cried in relief at the sight of Andric standing horseless in front of her; he fought the Breizans with ruthless efficiency. His horse stood behind them and lashed out with his front hooves to stop a Breizan who ran toward the pair. Andric stabbed one in the stomach, then spun and sliced across the chest of another.

Kaerdra shrieked when one of the creatures escaped past the horse and ran toward them. Andric turned just in time, and his sword was driven deep into the Breizan's body by the beast's momentum. Three more creatures rushed them from the other side. Andric tried to jerk his sword free, but it was stuck in the Breizan's chest. I turned Trae to make a run for them, but two more ice men came at me from either side. I slashed at one and he jumped back; the other ducked in time to avoid Trae's bared teeth. I looked back at the pair in front of the wall.

Andric picked up a short sword from the ground and threw it. The point sunk deep into one attacker's stomach. The other two Breizans charged at them. The Prince pulled out a knife, parried one sword, then turned and shielded Kaerdra with his body. The other Breizan's sword sliced down the back of Andric's shoulder. The Prince's face was twisted with pain when he turned back, but he kicked before the Breizan could bring his sword down for another slice. Andric's boot connected with the ice man's hand; the sword flew from his grasp. Before the creature could retaliate, Andric ended his life with a quick slice across the throat with his knife. One of his guards broke free and lopped off the head of the other Breizan.

Relief filled me as Andric helped Kaerdra to the wall and hoisted her up to her brother; Trevin pulled her to the top, his face white and eyes tight.

Trae lashed out with a hoof and my attention returned to the battle at hand. Three Breizans circled us, wary of the horse's quick hooves. I cringed when a spear slipped past my sword to lay open a gash along Trae's flank. Trae let out a shrill cry and backed toward the sheer mountain wall near the entrance to the clearing. A Breizan on our right side threw an axe. It whistled by only inches from my head.

The Breizan laughed, showing crooked, pointed teeth, then hefted his other axe. From the look in his feral eyes, I knew he wouldn't miss this time. Fear shot through my heart. I ducked as low as I could as his arm came forward. He was about to let the axe go when a gray blur leaped through the air and pummeled him to the ground. Andric's wolf silenced the screaming creature with a quick flash of his jaws.

My heart pounding, I turned to see a mounted guard fight his way to my side. We urged our horses forward, covering each other through the fray. By that time, Landis, Danyen, and Brynna had all made it over the wall. I looked up in time to see Kenyen gallop by, his face pale.

Nyssa was the only one left at the entrance to the clearing. The wolves around her fought off four Breizans who tried to reach her with their spears. "Ride, Nyssa. You can make it!" I shouted.

But it was obvious by the terror on her face that she wasn't in control of her actions. She sat frozen on her horse, her hands motionless at her sides.

"We've got to help her," I said to the guard beside me.

He nodded without a word, and turned his horse toward Nyssa. Two Breizans attacked us. The guard's horse reared on its back legs and stopped them both with heavy hooves. Trae charged forward. His shoulder caught another ice man and trampled him underfoot. I swung low to defend his flanks.

When we reached Nyssa's side, she merely looked at us and shivered. The guard grabbed her around the waist and hoisted her in front of him on his horse. "Can you make it?" I shouted above the screams of the creatures around us. Several of the other guards fell back toward the wall to clear a path for us.

"We'll make it," the guard answered in a tight voice. He urged his horse forward. The animal galloped across the broken, blood-spattered snow and leaped across the wall. The horse's hooves cleared it by barely inches. Nyssa's horse followed close behind, unwilling to be left with the savage men. I galloped after them with two more guards behind me. I sliced at the Breizans who attempted to stop our escape, then leaned down as Trae's powerful muscles bunched underneath me. He soared over the wall and kicked up snow when he landed. We rode to the other end of the walled circle before I dismounted; the two other guards cleared the wall after us.

The soldiers lined the walls with Andric to fight off the Breizans who tried to follow. The Prince gave a short, sharp whistle. Seconds later, the dark gray wolf and a white one jumped onto the wall. The other three followed close behind. They paced back and forth, snarling at the ice men below. Andric and his guards threw knives into the fray. I could hear the shrill answering screams from those that met their targets.

Then the screams stopped. The sudden silence hurt my ears. I wanted to climb up with Andric and his soldiers, but I couldn't reach and I was afraid of what I would find. As quickly as the Breizan screams had stopped, they started again; it was louder this time and even higher than before. The voices mingled, creating a bone-jarring dissonance that rattled my teeth. I put my hands over my ears to shut out the noise, then glanced over to see the others doing the same thing.

"Get close to the wall," Andric shouted. He and his guards jumped down to join us.

The ground rumbled. I crouched and closed my eyes tight as the thunder grew louder. I forced my eyes to open just as a blanket of white shot over the wall. Horses screamed in terror, then ran toward us out of the way of the snow. Fur touched my hand and I looked down to see a slender white wolf crouched near me. I pulled her closer to the wall. She didn't fight me and instead crawled between my arms. Her heart pounded with mine as the avalanche poured around us.

Chapter 5

The rumbling finally stopped. The ground still trembled, but faintly, as we rose from our hunched positions against the wall. The wolf whined and shivered against my leg. I rubbed her head, my fingers numb from the cold.

Brynna stood next to me; Landis was on my other side, his arm tight around Tisha's shoulder. She stared at nothing in particular, her green eyes huge in her pale face. Kenyen and Danyen were a few feet away, wiping the blood from their swords on the snow. Horsemaster Drade assessed the horses' wounds, while Andric and two of his guards checked the perimeter of the wall.

Snow had piled along the far side where the avalanche dumped it after leaping the wall. Snow piled high past the wall on our other side, the side we had come from. I shuddered to think of the Breizans buried beneath.

"How are the horses?" Andric asked. He spoke quietly, though it sounded like he was shouting after the dead silence that followed the screams and the avalanche.

"Good enough, for the most part. They'll need some patching when we stop," Drade replied, his jaw tight.

Andric nodded. "Let's move. We can't be caught out here when the Breizans return."

"Return?" Landis cut in, his voice tight. "They have half the mountain on top of them now."

Andric gave him an understanding nod, then spoke to all of us in a gentle but firm tone. "There will be more of them, so we have to go now. There's a cave less than a mile from here where we'll be safe. We can make it before dark."

The thought of being caught in the open mountain pass at dark scared all of us into action. Drade had already climbed the wall to check the ground on the other side to see if it was safe for the horses to jump. Satisfied, it took only a low whistle from him for the animals to follow. Trae was last, the wound on his flank dark red against his light brown fur. My heart clenched. He wasn't the only horse carrying wounds from the battle, but it was one I felt personally responsible for.

The guards helped us over. My knees buckled when I hit the ground, but hands caught me before I could fall. I looked up to see Andric looking down at me. "Good call on the swords," he said with a slight, tight smile.

I straightened up, embarrassed. "Thanks for trusting me," I replied, then realized I didn't have my sword anymore. I turned back to the wall, but he stopped me.

"Don't worry about it; it'll be buried by now. You dropped it before Trae jumped the wall." He turned to help Brynna down. "And a good thing, too," he continued in a quiet voice. "You needed both hands to hold on."

I stared at him, and was surprised to see his eyes crinkle slightly at the corners when he looked back. He was making fun of me! I glared at him. "I'll have you know that I've been riding since I was five. I'm a competent rider."

He nodded, suddenly solemn. "Yes, you are, and I owe you my thanks. You're good with a sword."

My cheeks grew red and I turned away on the pretense of looking for my horse. Trae stood near a scraggly tree, his injured hind leg held so that the hoof rested lightly in the snow. I walked over to him and rubbed his neck. "Sorry, boy," I whispered. The warmth of his shaggy fur brought the feeling back to my frozen fingers.

I started to shiver as the adrenaline from the battle wore off. I saw the whole fight again from a neutral point of view. The Breizans rose in front of my vision in sharp, realistic form. I buried my face against Trae's side.

"We're going, Kit," Kaerdra said quietly behind me.

I turned to see her ride after Danyen and Nyssa, Trevin at her side. Four guards waited so that they could bring up the rear. I couldn't see the wolves, and wondered if they were already scouting the area for signs of more of the ice men. The thought made me shudder. "Come on, Trae. Let's get out of here," I said to the horse. He whickered quietly and limped behind me toward the guards.

"I think I'll walk," I said to them when I was near enough. "Trae shouldn't be carrying anyone in his condition."

Landis sat on his horse next them. He looked down at me and said in a worried tone, "Tisha wouldn't mind sharing her horse; she could use some company."

I looked up at Tisha's white face. The Princess stared off toward the front of the group with blank eyes. Her hands shook where they clung tightly to her brown horse's mane. "Tish," I said.

She didn't hear me until I repeated her name for the third time. Then she stared at me with wide eyes. "Is it alright if I ride with you?" I asked gently.

She nodded.

I looked up to where Drade sat on his mount nearby. He watched us with a concerned expression. "Can her horse carry two?" I asked him

He nodded. "Easily. Pantim can handle it."

When I swung up behind Tisha, Trae whickered and pawed the ground with a front hoof as if to prove that he was fit to be my steed. We fell in with the group and he limped behind us making little disgruntled sounds.

Everyone rode quietly. I wondered if their senses prickled with the same feeling of being watched that mine did. I saw Breizans in every shadow until my nerves were completely frazzled. The guards rode with swords ready; the wolves paced the perimeter of our group with ceaseless diligence. The few glimpses I had of Andric at the front of the column were of him giving silent orders to his men.

They obeyed him without question, treating him like a true leader instead of the way I had seen some soldiers take orders from regular crown princes. He was in charge and in his element, not some teenager trying to prove his worth. Andric showed no sign of the sword wound he had gotten protecting Kaerdra. I wondered how bad it was.

By the time we reached the cave, my legs were tired from gripping Pantim's wide sides and my arms ached from reaching around Tisha to hold onto the horse's mane. Tisha had fallen into a stupor and it was all I could do to keep her from falling off of the horse. I hoped that some rest and food would help her come out of her shock.

The cave loomed between two huge slabs of rock. The horses picked up their pace when they saw it, as anxious to rest in safety as we were.

Jesson, the healer, helped me lower Tisha down. He carried her into the black crevice that marked the entrance to Andric's cave. I followed him on wobbly legs and found to my surprise that the cave widened into a cozy chamber about three feet past the entrance, and separated into an even larger chamber through a hole in the back wall. The guards helped their injured into the larger cave where Jesson immediate got to work. Tisha settled numbly onto a pile of blankets in the first chamber, which grew warm from the fires Captain Jashe and Falen lit.

Drade led the horses to a small glade nestled against the side of the sharply rising cliff wall where they were protected from the wind by a thick grove of trees. He was already tending to Trae's leg when I found them. The Horsemaster looked up when I stepped into the glade, then turned his attention back to his work. Trae's ears were back, but he didn't move a muscle as Drade carefully stitched the long wound across his flank.

"He's a really good horse," I said.

Drade nodded. "You've taken good care of him."

I walked forward through the snow and ran a hand down Trae's shaggy forehead. "Not really," I admitted quietly.

Drade turned and stared at me for a moment, his expression unreadable. "You feel bad for this?"

I nodded with a lump in my throat.

The Horsemaster smiled, surprising me. "He'll live. And it's not your fault. These are the best horses in Antor. They've been through worse than this."

It was my turn to stare. "You mean you've fought the Breizans before?"

He nodded, but didn't comment further. I watched him tie off the thread, and then smooth a thick salve over the wound to seal it from the elements. Trae lowered his head to sniff at the ointment, snorted, and turned away with a shake of his head. The scent of evergreen, lavender, peppermint, and another plant I didn't recognize tinged the air.

"We don't brainwash them," Drade said.

His tone was quiet, and I looked up, caught off guard.

He must have taken my silence for disagreement, because he continued, "I know that's the rumor, but it's not true. I'd hate for you to think that of any of us, let alone Crown Prince Andric." The worried expression on the old soldier's face made me realize how important this was to him.

I tried my best to understand. "Then why do they follow you? It's unnatural." I blushed at the blunt words as soon as they left my mouth, but he didn't seem to mind.

"I don't think I could explain it in a way you'd understand." At my pensive expression, his eyes tightened.

"Not every Antoran has the ability to connect with animals, and no one can predict what kind of animal a person will match with. It's like we have a connection with them since birth, a sort of unique bond with that type of creature. And then it's up to the animal to accept us as well."

He glanced at me to gauge if I followed him. Though I had to force my tired mind to keep up, I nodded.

He smiled and continued, "For me, it was horses. Before I could speak, I was already drawn to the fields near our house. My mother told me one time she thought she lost me and had the whole town out looking only to find me hours later in the horse field playing with the foals." He smiled, his gaze distant. "She kept a closer eye on me, but knew what my inclination would be. By the time I was five, I had befriended every horse within four miles of our home. Farmers from leagues away brought their horses over for me to gentle."

I smiled at the thought of Father's horses back home. He could really use someone like Drade with the new racing stallion they were training. That horse didn't like anyone, and showed his feelings with his teeth. Homesickness and weariness that came from deep in my bones made my eyes prick with sudden tears; I buried my face against Trae's shoulder.

Drade pretended not to notice my sudden surge of emotion. "I was recruited by the King to train his horses," he continued, "And I bonded with Sorn and his mare." He indicated the brown horse he normally rode and the tawny colored mare Brynna had been using. "The rest of the herd naturally followed."

He patted Trae's side, then headed to the cave. I gave Trae's nose one last pet, then followed the Horsemaster inside. My eyes strained to adjust to the sudden darkness of the cave and I stumbled around one of Andric's wolves.

When I made it past the tight crevice, welcoming warmth seeped into my chilled skin. I went to the fire in the first cave to thaw out while Drade continued to the next one.

All of the Crowns were there. I was grateful to see that Tisha slept with Brynna and Kaerdra sitting close by. Kenyen held a cloth to his arm. I caught Danyen's worried glance. "Are you alright?" I asked on impulse.

Kenyen glared my way, but his anger wasn't directed at me. "I'd be fine if the thief hadn't kidnapped us. What right does he have to put us in danger?"

"We could've been killed," Danyen echoed in agreement.

I knelt down and looked at Kenyen's arm. He didn't resist and I felt a pang of guilt when I realized that the Crowns' hostility toward me had become temporarily replaced by their hatred for Andric. I knew I should be mad at him also, but I kept seeing the way Andric let himself get hurt to save Kaerdra. I kept telling myself he must have a reason for what he was doing.

Jesson looked in our cave and when he saw me tending to Kenyen, he brought some of his ointment and bandages. He already had his hands full taking care of the other soldiers' wounds and it was obvious he was relieved that someone else tended to the Crowns.

I cleaned Kenyen's arm, put salve on it, and wrapped it in a clean white cloth. His brother gave me a grateful smile when I finished and moved on to Landis. The Crown Prince of Faer had twisted his ankle quite badly, but hadn't noticed until Tisha rested peacefully. He winced when he eased off his shoe to show me that it was already swollen. I used the same numbing salve Drade had put on Trae; the oils would quickly absorb into the skin to ease his pain. I then wrapped it and told him to elevate it while he slept. He settled down near Tisha and propped his foot on a convenient outcropping of rock. It wasn't long before I heard him snoring softly.

When Nyssa made a fuss out of a small purple bruise on her arm, I humored her by rubbing salve on it, then turned away to make my bed.

It surprised me when Andric walked into the cave. I didn't know he had been outside all that time, and wondered if he had been scouting the area to make sure the Breizans hadn't followed us. The others grew quiet upon his entrance, but he didn't seem to notice any of us. He looked tired and pale when he leaned against the rocks near the crevice and stared out into the darkness, the ever-present gray wolf at his side. I then remembered the sword wound he had received protecting Kaerdra.

"Let me look at your back," I said quietly.

He didn't respond.

Kenyen and Danyen glared at me, but I ignored them and spoke louder. "Andric, let me see your back. Someone needs to take care of it."

This time, he turned his head to look at me, surprise clear in his dark eyes. I motioned for him to come over. He looked past me at the twins; then gave a minute shake of his head before he turned back to his watch. Exasperated, I glared at the Crown Princes of Tyn, then gathered up my supplies and made my way over to Andric. Even though he might be the enemy from their point of view, there were worse creatures out there and I wouldn't leave an injured person untended.

Andric turned to me when I drew near, a guarded expression on his face. I willed my beating heart to slow and set the supplies out carefully on the cloth Jesson had given me. I forced my tone to be light. "You won't be any good to us if you bleed to death or the wound gets infected."

He watched me. His jaw clenched and unclenched and I knew he debated whether to trust me. If he denied my offer, I would at least tell Jesson that the Prince was injured so the healer would take care of him.

The Antoran Prince surprised me when he finally nodded, knelt with his back to me, and eased off his shirt. He turned his attention back to the cave entrance. The white wolf that I had sheltered during the avalanche appeared for a minute, looked at him, then vanished again like a ghost into the darkness. I bit my lip and turned my attention to the Prince's back.

Blood caked the wound that ran from the top of his left shoulder to his mid back on the left side. The blood flowed in a steady trickle from the wound down to his pants. I imagined that it would have grown very uncomfortable during the ride to the cave, and wondered why he hadn't said anything or shown any sign of his injury. Concern filled me at how deep and long it was.

I glanced over my shoulder. Kenyen and Danyen no longer glared at the Antoran Prince. Their eyes were wide and they looked a bit pale where they sat across the fire. Nyssa turned away when she met my glance and straightened her cloak. Trevin and Kaerdra exchanged a look I couldn't read; Kaerdra bit her lip and the light from the fire showed tears in her eyes.

"You should have had this taken care of right away," I whispered to Andric so the others couldn't hear.

"Before or after the avalanche and the flight for our lives?" Andric replied as quietly with an unexpected chuckle.

I stared at his back for a moment, but was unable to come up with a response. Slightly miffed, I grabbed a damp rag and began to clean off the worst of the blood. "Blood loss can make a person dizzy and disoriented. It's your responsibility to take care of yourself so that you can lead your men."

Andric glanced over his shoulder, his eyebrows lifted. "Are you lecturing me?"

My cheeks turned red, but I nodded.

He gave a true laugh this time. "It's been a while since I've been lectured."

"Maybe it'll do you good," I replied curtly, the thought not far from my mind that he had in fact kidnapped all of us and put our lives in danger.

He turned back to watch the entrance. I threaded the curved needle, then smoothed some of the numbing salve over the wound. The ointment wouldn't stop all of the pain, but I hoped it would at least ease the bite of the needle. I flinched at the quick intake of breath I heard as I began the first stitch at the top of his shoulder, but Andric held himself perfectly still for me to continue.

The big gray wolf sat down next to me and watched my every movement. Self-conscious, I eased the smooth thread through the skin and began the next stitch. The wound was deepest at the top of the shoulder, and blood flowed down to pool on the floor where he sat. I used a rag to save what I could of his clothes, but they were already caked in dried blood from the ride to the cave.

The minutes stretched past, and the others turned their attention away. Kenyen and Danyen argued quietly, while Brynna braided Kaerdra's hair. Nyssa had already curled up under her cloak, but I doubted she slept.

The wound closed beneath the stitching and the flow of blood slowed. I could feel the wolf's warm breath on my shoulder.

"You're the first one to call me just Andric since my mother died," the Prince said so softly I almost didn't hear him.

His words surprised me. "What about your father?" I asked.

Andric didn't answer. He put a hand on the floor to steady himself. It was clenched into a fist, the knuckles white against the dark gray rock.

"How far is it to Antor?" I asked in an attempt to change the subject.

"Two days on a hard ride, but we'll probably make it in three. I don't want to push anyone in the shape the Breizans have left us."

"And the horses," I put in, thinking of Trae.

He nodded and his wavy dark brown hair brushed the back of my hand. His warrior's tail had pulled loose sometime during the battle; some of the strands of hair were darker where they brushed against his wound.

He fell silent and I thought our conversation was over, but he whispered again after a few minutes, "I saw the note you left for your father."

My heart skipped a beat. "Did you erase it?" I demanded louder than I meant to. We both glanced over at the others, but they were caught up in their own activities.

Andric shook his head. "No, I didn't. I'm glad you left it."

Confused, I asked, "Why?"

He shrugged, then winced when the movement pulled against my thread. "I don't want them to worry any more than you do. When we get to the castle you can send messages to your families to let them know that you're safe."

"So we can't go home?" Kenyen asked suddenly.

I looked over to see that he watched Andric with sparks of anger in his eyes.

Andric shook his head, his expression guarded once more. "Even if I wanted you to, you can't. The avalanche sealed the pass and it won't open again until spring."

Brynna's mouth fell open in shock. "So we're stuck here?"

"This is all your fault!" Danyen shouted; he rose to his feet. Commotion sounded from the next cave; Captain Jashe and Falen appeared, swords drawn. They moved toward Danyen, but Andric held up his hand and they stopped.

I finished the stitching and tied off the thread quickly. I moved to spread salve over the wound when Andric rose. "No, this is your fault, and the fault of your parents, the *honorable* Kings and Queens of Denbria," Andric growled back; his dark eyes flashed as passionately as the Tyn Prince's.

"And how is that?" Danyen threw back. He still looked defiant, but he had backed up slightly at Andric's unexpected outburst.

The Antoran Prince's face hardened. "They're the ones who turned their backs while my country starved to death. They take our jewels, then leave us to fend for ourselves with nothing." His tone darkened. "You are here to learn what following your own selfish pursuits can do to another country. If you don't learn to work together, then yours will fall the same way mine has. My country is starving to death."

"So you're going to ransom us," Trevin noted, his tone haughty as if Andric's words confirmed his suspicions.

Andric laughed, but it was a cold, hard sound. "My country's already lost. Even a prince's ransom couldn't save it now." His voice dropped softer, but his eyes were still as hard as iron. "This is a learning experience for you, nothing more. Forcing you to spend the winter in the last grips of a fading country won't save my people, but perhaps it will be the means of saving your own from a similar fate."

He grabbed his torn and bloodstained shirt from the ground and stepped out into the dark night without a backwards glance; the gray wolf followed faithfully at his heels.

I looked back at Captain Jashe and Falen. Captain Jashe glanced around the room once and then passed me to leave through the crevice after his prince. Falen turned back to his cave and left us in silence. One of the guards came in and handed around cups of steaming oatmeal sweetened with honey. I held mine for a long time. It chased the last of the chill from my fingers. The other Crowns settled on their beds and pulled the thick cloaks over them as blankets. I sat on my bed stared at the crevice through which Andric had disappeared.

***

The others had fallen asleep long before, but I couldn't quiet the whirlwind of thoughts that tormented my exhausted mind. I finally rose and stepped into the other cave. The guard Falen and Jesson, the healer, were talking quietly by the fire. Most of the other guards were asleep, some with bandages and salves covering wounds from the battle. One of Falen's hands was wrapped, something I hadn't noticed earlier when he and Captain Jashe had rushed in to help Andric.

The thought of the long sword wound down the Prince's back made me suddenly cold. At Jesson's welcoming nod, I crossed to the fire and sat down near them.

"You're not tired?" the healer asked with raised eyebrows.

I shook my head. "I'm exhausted, but I can't get the fight out of my head."

Falen smiled kindly. "That's normal for one who's seen their first battle. I remember the first time I was in a fight against Breizans. I was up half the night following it, retracing my steps to see if I could have done any better. My father, who was the captain at the time, finally gave up trying to get me to sleep and went through the fight with me. By morning I felt like I could take on a whole Breizan horde by myself."

He chuckled and I couldn't help but smile at his easy going manner. Then my thoughts flashed back to the bloodstained mouths and hungry eyes of the Breizan horde. I shivered and pulled my cloak closer. "Do you have to fight the Breizans often?" I asked. I hated how timid my voice sounded.

Falen stared into the fire. I had begun to wonder if he heard me when he spoke in a quiet voice. "Antor isn't like the other countries of Denbria. Where you have rolling green fields and lush plains as far as the eye can see, we have valleys of rocks the size of houses, mountain lions with claws longer than a man's hand, and snowdrifts so deep if you fall in, you'd never be able to climb out." He sighed and shook his head. "But the one thing Antor had that isn't found anywhere else was elder diamonds. It was our only resource besides the furs of the animals we kill, and it was our one downfall."

When the big guard fell silent, Jesson took up where he left off. "We've become poor because the one asset we had was also one so rare and high in demand that instead of trading for it, countries stole it."

I stared at him in shock.

He nodded at me, his gaze sad. "Greed overcomes common sense when it comes to riches and wealth. The other countries of Denbria aren't the only ones who steal from us. Countries from across the sea go to great lengths to attack our city and storm our mines. We've fought many battles to defend our one resource and support our country." He turned his gaze to the fire. "Only, that resource is gone now."

"Gone?" I couldn't imagine it. Father had always painted a picture that Antor was filled with the elder diamonds, that Antorans used them as chess pieces and shooters for marbles, that they spilled out of every cupboard and dowry chest like so much silk. I wondered if he said those things to justify the raids. I didn't know if the guilt that rose in my chest was for doubting Jesson, or for doubting my father. "So what do you do?" I asked at a loss. "How do you support your country?"

"We can't," Falen replied without looking at me. "The Prince has done what he can, but there's nothing left."

"Then where does everyone go?"

"When spring comes, we'll go wherever we can. But there's not much tolerance for people like us past the mountains." The guard stated it as a simple fact, which made it so much harder to hear.

We sat in silence for a long while listening to the sound of the flames and the quiet moans and whispers of the soldiers sleeping around us. I wondered why Andric hadn't returned, but remembered that Jashe hadn't either; I hoped the Captain was with his prince. Perhaps he could protect him from himself. His eyes had been so dark and stormy with the passion he felt for his country. It was obvious he blamed himself for his country's fate.

When I finally crossed back to the other cave and settled on my bedroll, I realized that Andric's men didn't blame him. I had seen them take orders from him with more respect than soldiers gave kings who had ruled for four decades. The words Falen and Jesson had spoken were blameless and only carried the same sorrow Andric felt for Antor.

Chapter 6

The unearthly screams rose again as the Breizans surrounded me. The rumble of the avalanche shook the earth, only I wasn't behind the wall with the others, I was in the open surrounded by the cannibal horde with only Andric's white wolf at my side. The Breizans charged. I screamed and woke up gasping for air.

Everyone still slept around the fire that now burned low in the cave. I realized I had only screamed in my dream, and forced my heart to slow. I glanced toward the front of the cave and saw a shadow near the entrance. It turned its head toward me.

"Nightmare?" Andric asked quietly.

I nodded, then realized he probably couldn't see the motion against the black backdrop of the cave. "How do you keep from having nightmares after a battle like that?" I willed my voice not to quiver.

"I don't go to sleep," he replied. I could hear a touch of humor in his voice and wondered if he was smiling.

The bedroll proved little cushion against the cold stone floor and my muscles protested when I rose and sat down against the wall near him. A dark shadow at Andric's feet lifted its great head and sniffed at me, then the big gray wolf turned back to watch the crevice opening. A light-colored phantom slipped through and licked Andric's hand.

"She's beautiful," I whispered.

Andric ruffled the fur on the white wolf's head. "Freis," he said, then frowned thoughtfully. "At least, that's what it sounds like out loud."

"How else would you say it?"

Andric looked at me, his eyes too dark to see in the dimly lit cave. "It's different in my head, how I talk to them."

I stared at him. "You talk to them?"

He nodded. His tone was careful when he continued, "Antorans communicate with their animals by thought. Some animals speak differently than others, but the essence is the same. Wolves use images as well as sound to convey meaning, which is why howling is so effective." He glanced at me. "So we don't control them, we work together, like a pack, for lack of a better term," he shrugged, then winced as the motion pulled at his fresh stitches. "It's hard to explain."

I couldn't think of a response.

"She showed me how you protected her during the avalanche," Andric whispered. "Thank you."

I hid my surprise and looked down at Freis to find her watching me. Her golden eyes reflected the flickering light of the low fire. She whined and nudged my hand with her nose; I smiled and petted her head. She settled down next to me with her head on my knee so that I could continue.

The gray wolf gave a quiet snort. Andric chuckled. "Bayn isn't one for open affection."

As if to prove his point, the huge wolf turned and stared straight at me. The intelligence in his eyes surprised me. I couldn't help but smile in surprise at the slight touch of humor in them. It was as though he and Andric shared some private joke.

Andric straightened his back against the wall, then winced when it brushed against his shoulder.

"You should be sleeping," I said. "You won't recover well without rest; you've lost too much blood."

"There'll be time to sleep when we reach the castle," he replied. "My men are out scouting to make sure we're safe. If they send a warning, I'll be ready." He rested his head back against the wall and his eyes closed for a brief moment. He opened them again and looked at me with a faint smile. "I haven't been told what to do in a very long time." His smile was sad.

Despite all he had put us through, my heart ached at the look in his eyes. "You miss her, don't you?" He nodded and looked back toward the entrance to the cave. How it would be to lose my mother? She did so much and shared love so freely with everyone. Father always said she was the counterpoint to a government of strict law. She helped make our peoples' burdens lighter.

I pictured her at home with Rory. She never left his bedside and took over where the healers normally worked. She confided in me once that I reminded her of her childhood when she, too, had traveled with the healers to learn their art. She had met my father tending to him after a brief battle with Tyn. He said she saved his life and stole his heart as payment. My heart throbbed at the echo of her laugh in my memory, and the way she always stood on her tiptoes to kiss Father lightly on the cheek.

I tried to picture Mother tending to Father, but only saw Rory sick in bed, pale, and wasting away. A tear rolled down my cheek. "I miss Rory," I said quietly.

I hadn't meant to say it out loud, and I think Andric knew it. "I know," he replied, his tone gentle. "You really didn't mean to be here at all, did you?"

I shook my head and more tears spilled down my cheeks despite my efforts to keep them from doing so. "I don't fit in here with the Crowns. I'm so different from them."

"Did you want to be a Crown?" Andric asked with a slight hint of curiosity in his voice.

I shook my head again and wiped the tears away with the corner of my cloak. "Rory is still the Crown Prince of Zalen. He knows exactly what to do, and he'll be the best leader for our country." I frowned into the darkness. "I don't know what to do at all."

Andric shifted against the cold stone. "Perhaps that's what can make you the best ruler."

I glanced at him. "Why is that?"

The Antoran Prince gestured toward where the other Crowns slept. "They've grown up knowing that they'll be rulers, and with everyone around them knowing that they'll be the next kings and queens. They've had to become suspicious and distrusting, looking for those who would use them or deceive them for a grasp at some of that power." He looked back at me, his dark gaze frank in the dim light. "You don't have that. You seem to take everyone at face value. You're not predisposed to assume that everyone you talk to has an ulterior motive. That would be a valuable trait for a king or queen to have."

He leaned his head back against the stone and looked up at the ceiling. "Imagine being able to accept the story of those who come for pardon or assistance and trusting the words of those who would be friends instead of searching for the hidden intent behind their efforts." He glanced at me out of the corner of his eye. "You'd have to be careful, though. There're many people not to be trusted."

I nodded. Bayn settled down again and without thinking, I reached over to run a hand through his hair. The gray wolf's fur was thick, a bristly, long outer coat over a heavy, soft undercoat to keep in warmth. Freis' fur on the other hand was silky and long, pure white and soft. Bayn rolled to his side so that I could rub his belly.

I smiled. "Not one for open affection, huh?"

Andric grinned down at the wolf. "Guess he couldn't refuse. You have a soft touch."

I stared at him, but he turned away before I could read his expression. I looked back down at the wolves that lay on either side of me. Bayn was well muscled and thick, tall enough to stand at Andric's height on his hind legs, and big enough to tackle a small bear. Freis was petite and slender, a graceful counterpoint to her mate's brawn. Her head was narrow and body sleek. I had already seen her run for hours without tiring. Her body was built for speed.

"When my father realized I had bonded with a wolf cub from the forest behind the castle, he started searching the world for a suitable mate for the wolf." Andric smiled, reaching down to run his fingers through Freis' fur. If the movement pulled at his stitches, he didn't let it show. "Eventually, there were five wolves in all. Bayn and Freis were the leaders of the pack, with me at their head."

"They must be getting old for animals," I replied, but the wolves looked young and fresh even despite the day's events.

Bayn nudged Andric's hand and he responded by rubbing the wolf's great head. "Animals who are bonded age with their human counterpoints, so it's normal for the animals to live the average human age." He traced a white scar on Bayn's chest and frowned slightly. "I think that's because it would be so unbearable to lose a companion who's even closer than a family member. You share your thoughts with them and trust them because it feels like you know them better than you know yourself."

He caught himself and gave an embarrassed smile. "Sorry. I guess I haven't had much time to think about it. I'm probably telling you more than you'd like to know."

"That's alright," I told him honestly. "I like hearing about it."

He looked doubtful. "You do?"

I nodded. "It helps me understand, and it'll hopefully help me undo some of the rumors about Antorans." My eyelids began to feel heavy and I leaned back against the cave wall.

"Tired?"

"More than I've ever been before," I answered with my eyes closed.

"Then sleep," he replied, his tone encouraging.

I tried to nod, but I was already drifting away.

***

When I woke up, my head rested on Andric's shoulder. He stared out at the black night beyond the cave entrance. The others were still asleep. I sat up quickly and mumbled an apology for using him as a pillow, then rose and went back to my spot by the fire. When I glanced back, he was watching me, his expression unreadable in the dark cave.

Chapter 7

The next morning they loaded the wounded guards who could ride onto horses and created stretchers for the two who couldn't. One of them had a stomach wound and had lost so much blood that even his lips were pale. Jesson walked beside him with a worried expression on his face. I asked once if I could help, but he shook his head and said he would let me know if he needed me.

One of the horses had such a bad wound that it wouldn't survive the trip to Antor. Drade was as pale as the wounded soldier, and looked shaken. I found out that he had spent the entire night out in the grove with the horses, tending to their wounds and trying to save the one. Andric pulled him aside the next morning and offered to put the animal down himself, but Drade shook his head. They both went together into the grove empty now of all the horses but one.

When we set off, the Prince and Horsemaster rode silently at the front of the column. I could see Andric speaking to Drade, both their heads bowed and faces solemn. An air of loss filled the entire company.

"All this is over a horse?" Kenyen mumbled once.

The looks of scorn and hostility on the faces of the guards around him silenced all of us for the rest of the ride. I sat behind Tisha on Pantim again, and was happy to see that she had recovered somewhat from the shock of the battle yesterday. I even saw her exchange a small smile with Landis.

We stopped that night under a stand of evergreen trees that made the air smell crisp and sharp. The guards cleared the snow the best that they could and pitched our tents on what was left. The snow wasn't quite as deep as it had been back at the cave, and I hoped that meant we would be off the mountain soon. I didn't know how much longer we could physically put up with being forced to ride for so many hours a day, though when Brynna complained, Andric mentioned that she could walk instead and give her horse a break from her incessant whining.

It was the first sign of a temper that he had displayed since the outburst in the cave. He hunched slightly on his horse and I knew his shoulder hurt more than he let on. When we stopped, he cradled his left arm after he swung off his horse. Jesson questioned him, but Andric shook his head and motioned for the healer to direct his concern to the wounded soldiers. Andric did the same and made sure they were as comfortable as possible before he pitched his own tent.

We ate a tasty meal of two turkeys one of the guards had surprised on the trail earlier and spirits rose. The bread, cheese, and dried meat we ate at the stops during the day provided energy, but the turkey tasted like Cook Mumphrey's own. They served potatoes on the side with a small dessert made of thick maple syrup on small wheat cakes.

We had been forced to stop a bit early for the sake of the wounded guards on stretchers. After dinner, even though we were exhausted, no one could fall asleep. Everyone settled around the fire except for the soldiers on guard duty. One of the guards pulled out a small riding flute and played a few quiet notes. The flute had a very low tone that was pleasant to ears in the way that the wind blowing around the eaves of a house makes one feel comfortable to be inside and warm. For that small space of time I felt safe; the cold, snow, weariness, and being so very far away from my family and anything even remotely familiar was forgotten, or at least pushed to the back of my mind. I let myself drift with the music, and felt as if I was the one weaving in and out of the trees.

I remembered Captain Rurisk's teachings of battle lore and woodsmanship and kept my eyes averted from the fire so as to save my night vision in case of an attack. I lost myself instead in the dark shadows of the trees that swayed gently from side to side as if in time to the haunting melody. Starlight chased itself between the branches, speckling the snowy ground with sparkling crystals, vanishing and reappearing like so many woodland fairies.

I wondered what my mother would do in the same situation, what would be the appropriate action for a princess. She had married into the Crown, as all spouses of Crowns do. It was against the law for the Crown of one country to marry the Crown of another and either take away their rightful heir or divide the countries. This was only done if there was another heir to take up the throne, and very seldom did the Kings and Queens ever give their consent for such a marriage to take place. So Crowns were required to select their spouse-to-be, or have them selected, by someone in their country, preferably of a royal bloodline. Often, younger siblings were given away to other countries as spouses for Crowns in order to unite the countries and resolve differences.

My mother, on the other hand, had been the daughter of one of the royal gardeners at the palace. She had taken up the healing art when it became apparent she had a talent for it. She and my father had fallen in love and he had refused the offer of a daughter of Tyn, much to his own father's disappointment. There had always been stressed relations between Father and the twins' father, because King Tirrot had taken the refusal of his sister's hand as an insult and had never forgiven my father for marrying Mother.

After they married, my mother spent as much time as she could in the garden as tribute to her parents, and left the healing arts to the healers until Rory became sick. Father built her enormous green houses so that she could keep her flowers and herbs year round. They even had bees kept by a beekeeper who lived in a cottage near the castle wall. I had often seen him and my mother in their bee outfits inspecting comb from the hives. The honey had a wild flavor to it that I preferred over the delicate honey Father bought from the beekeepers who ranged their bees on the clover of the plains.

My thoughts turned to Rory. He would know what to do in this situation, of that I was sure. Rory always seemed to know just what to do. My chest ached, and I wondered if he would be alright. I couldn't bear to lose my big brother.

I forced myself back to the present and realized that most of the others had gone to bed. Tisha and Landis held hands and whispered quietly, but other than the guard who played his flute, I was the only one still by the fire. The moon was high overhead and the stars shone bright through the clear night sky.

The guard nodded to me when I rose to go to my tent. I whispered a quiet thank you for the beautiful music before I turned to duck under the tent flap; then I noticed a dark form leaning against one of the trees and staring out into the darkness. The wolf shadow at his side would have told me it was the Antoran Prince even if I hadn't recognized his straight shoulders and easy stance that still commanded respect even in the depth of night. He could use the rest after the sleepless night before, but I shook my head and ducked into the tent. There was nothing I could do about it but worry, and I had plenty to worry about already.

***

The next morning, Prince Andric looked pale and drawn but determined. "If we make it to the valley, we'll be at the castle by midday tomorrow," he told us.

Kaerdra and Trevin exchange angry glances while Kenyen and Danyen muttered to each other out loud about what their father would do to Andric when spring came. Brynna began another list of things she hated about the trip, which now included Breizans, swords, campfire, stars, pine trees, flutes, soldiers, more snow, and being dirty.

I had to agree with her about the dirty part. It was quite a change from washing at least once a day in the warmed marble tub in the royal bathing chambers. The water was always scented with lemon in the morning and lavender before bed, in case a member of the royal family wanted a relaxing bath before going to sleep. Father usually used it after a day of training with his soldiers, and Mother if it was a particularly warm day tending to the garden.

But I could sure use a bath now, scented water or not. I felt like I had dirt caked on every square inch of my body, which wasn't pleasant to think about. My legs had been rubbed raw from the long hours of horseback riding, and my feet were wearing holes through my soft-soled boots. I hoped that somehow the Antorans knew we were coming and would have hot baths prepared the second we stepped through the city gates.

I didn't know the accommodations we would be given once we reached the castle, but I doubted Andric would forbid us the chance to clean the filth from the arduous ride. I looked forward to that almost as much as a bed to sleep in. I refrained from questioning whether he would have real beds for us.

The snow on the ground lessened as we rode down the gentle decline, making the way easier for the horses and the men on foot carrying stretchers. The Antorans traded off with the stretchers, and even Captain Jashe took a turn. I could tell that Andric wanted to join them, and realized by the way he treated his men that it was more his shoulder than his station which prevented him.

***

When night fell, we were in the valley, and we were surprised to find a roaring fire and tents already pitched and waiting. A small party of five soldiers met our company with grins on their faces and welcoming calls. Andric swung down and met them on foot to give them what I assumed was a briefing of the events that had befallen us in the mountains. They exchanged a few questions, then two of the soldiers mounted waiting horses and left into the night.

The other three took the night watch to give our guards a full rest. We ate a much appreciated dinner of roasted venison with thick gravy, apples cooked in the coals until they were tender and mushy inside their skins, and squash slow-cooked by the flames and sprinkled with butter and cinnamon. I felt full and exhausted after eating and was secretly glad that everyone would be able to get some much needed sleep; but after dinner, I saw Andric standing sentry again, watching our back trail from the shadow of a large tree.

On my approach, he glanced at me and then back into the night. Freis licked my hand in greeting, then scooted so that her head would be within easy reach of my hand. I ran my fingers absently through her soft fur, my thoughts on other matters. "You should be sleeping," I said quietly.

"I'll sleep when we're home," he replied in the same courteous tone he had used in the cave.

"How is your shoulder?" I asked. "You should let me put some of Jesson's salve on it."

The Prince fell quiet for a moment. "It's a bit sore," he admitted softly after a few minutes had passed.

I stared at him a second, caught off guard that he was actually being open with me now when he was so closed off during the day. I wondered how hard it must be to be in charge of all of this, knowing what he did about the state of his country. I couldn't believe that it was as bad as he said, but at the same time, I feared what we would find when we reached Antor. I didn't want to believe my father had a hand in bringing about the country's downfall.

Andric didn't protest when I lifted his shirt to inspect the wound. The fading firelight provided poor lighting, and I could see a faint trail of blood, but I couldn't tell if some of the stitches had pulled through. "We need to move closer to the fire so I can see better."

He shook his head. "We'll be at the castle tomorrow. It'll be taken care of then."

He moved to pull his shirt back down, but I held it firmly. "Fine," I said quietly in exasperation. "I'll take care of it here, but it'd be better by the fire."

He turned back to watch the darkness and let me apply the salve from the back of his shoulder down to his mid-back. Blood had leaked from the wound, but I couldn't tell the source. He held himself still as I cleaned it, flinching only slightly when I touched an overly tender spot.

It wasn't until I had dressed the wound in clean bandages and pulled down his shirt that he spoke again. "It's not that I'm stubborn," he said softly with his eyes still on the forest. "It's not good for soldiers to know that their leader is wounded. They need to know that he's fit to lead them, and capable of protecting them."

"I thought soldiers were supposed to protect their prince, not the other way around," I replied. I jumped when Bayn bumped my other hand with his nose, then obliged by petting his head also.

Andric shook his head. "A good leader never asks more of his men than he's willing to do himself. My men trust me because they know I would die beside them as readily as I lead them in battle."

I ran that through my mind a few times. I spoke before I thought about my words. "You sound so old."

Andric glanced at me, a small smile on his face. "I feel old sometimes."

I shook my head. "I don't. I feel foolish and fumbling, like a child trying to walk in her mother's shoes. I've got so much to learn and not enough time to learn it."

Andric nodded thoughtfully. "At least you can admit it. It's the people who feel that they've learned all the world has to offer that are truly foolish."

I laughed, unable to help myself. "Now you really do sound old."

He grinned and turned back to the night. "You're a strange girl, Princess Kirit of Zalen."

"And you are surprising, Prince Andric of Antor." I grimaced. "And please call me Kit. Kirit just sounds way too grown up."

He nodded. "As you wish, but you might be more grown up than you think."

I shook my head and walked back to my tent.

Chapter 8

The atmosphere the next morning sparked with excitement. The knowledge that we would be somewhere else by nightfall other than riding horses and camping on the cold ground filled us all with energy. By now, any change was welcome, even if we didn't know what to expect when we reached Antor.

I gave Pantim a chance to rest and walked next to Jesson and the soldiers on stretchers. Trae followed close behind me, limping slightly on his injured leg. Drade still rode silently at the front of the column next to Andric. It was obvious the Horsemaster still mourned the loss of his horse. I thought of what Andric had said about his bond with the wolves, and wondered if losing a bonded animal was truly harder than losing a family member.

I forced myself from that train of thought and concentrated on the landscape around us. We rode in the foothills now, and though the snow was still deep, it wasn't ice-packed like in the mountains. A shallow road ran through, which gave promise of civilization. The horses pranced with light hooves and the three younger wolves raced around the column like puppies. There was a light gray female, a smaller dark gray male, and a young black male. The three were long-legged and lanky, as if still growing into their limbs.

I wondered how they had come to bond with Andric and his pack. It was obvious they weren't as close to him as Bayn and Freis, but he still regarded them with close affection. They often gamboled around him and licked at his hands when he dismounted. Earlier in the ride he had disappeared often into the trees with all of the wolves at his heels; now, he stayed with the column and I wondered if he was as anxious to return home as the guards clearly were.

Tall, twisted trees with gnarled limbs covered the hills. The road was easy and smooth, and the ride went quickly. Finally, with the sun straight overhead, we topped the rise of the final hill to see Antor spread out below.

The city had been laid out defensively with two rocky hills on the north side, a massive wall on the west with battlements across the top, and a stone wall that lead to frozen docks at the seaside on the east. A separate road led toward the mountains we had just left and worked around to disappear at the base. I assumed it led toward the now vacant mines.

The castle caught my eye. Though it was also built for defense, with a surrounding wall and enough room in the courtyard to shelter all of the citizens if needed, the castle had a beauty close to magic. The walls had been carved of white marbled stone that caught the light and bathed the area around it in brilliance. It seemed to share its light with the city, to brighten it just by being in its center. The city itself looked cozy, houses clustered together with narrow streets and smoke rising from the chimneys. I could see people lining the road, and realized they were waiting for us. The thought made my stomach twist nervously.

The horses picked up their pace and outdistanced those of us who were walking. The cries of welcome and shouts of glad tidings from the Antorans as we neared the city made me glad I was toward the end of our group. It looked as if the entire city had come out to welcome Prince Andric and the soldiers home. People lined the snow-covered road all the way to the castle wall. They didn't seem to notice the cold as they greeted their prince and his guards.

Andric and the others had dismounted, leaving only the Crowns on Drade's horses. I watched Andric shake hands with the waiting men and receive hugs from the women, tousling the hair of the children as though he knew each one. I had never seen a member of any royal family greet his or her common citizens that way. I always assumed it was out of respect the citizens had for their rulers, but when I saw the way Andric's people welcomed him home, I realized there was more than one kind of respect.

I watched the crowd's reaction to the wolves and horses in amazement. Instead of ignoring them or giving them a polite pat on the head as would be courteous for a noble's pet, both the wolves and the horses were welcomed as warmly as the soldiers. Bayn, Freis, and the other three wolves licked greetings to the Antorans and received hugs and kind words from the citizens. The horses had winter flowers braided into their manes and tails and were given handfuls of warm oats that were more than welcome after the long, cold journey.

There were other animals among the crowd. Members of the great bird family, hawks, eagles, and osprey perched on rooftops or gloved arms and gazed alertly at the arriving company. Several dogs and a black fox darted between the feet of the horses who weren't spooked as would happen with normal animals. The smaller creatures played in familiar winding patterns around the shaggy horses' hooves.

A beautiful white deer stood next to a young girl with big blue eyes and a quick smile. Two rabbits played around a pair of twins near a street opening. A snowy owl blinked at us from the shoulder of an elderly man who was missing a hand.

When we entered the crowd, a ferret, wearing its white coat for the winter, ran up Jesson's cloak and perched on his shoulder. "My wife's," he explained as he rubbed its furry head in greeting.

At my stare, he smiled. "Don't worry, you'll get used to it." A lady with long, beautiful black hair separated from the crowd and threw her arms around Jesson's neck. He laughed and spun her around. The ferret ran from shoulder to shoulder. After he set her down and kissed her soundly, he turned back to me with a wide smile. "My Love, this is Crown Princess Kirit of Zalen. Princess Kirit, this is Isea."

She gave me a graceful curtsy which I returned. "Please call my Kit. Everyone else does."

Isea's eyebrows rose in surprise and she gave me a warm smile. "Welcome to Antor, Princess Kit," she replied.

"Thank you," I said. "Antor is more beautiful than I imagined." I then bit my tongue, hoping they didn't take it to mean I had imagined Antor to be ugly.

"It's our little piece of heaven," Jesson said. He exchanged a glance with his wife. Sadness crossed both of their faces. Jesson shook his head and nodded toward the group that was already halfway to the castle. "Looks like we're getting left behind."

"If you have a chance," Isea said to me, "We would love to have you over for supper one of these nights." She looked at her husband. "I hope I'm not being too forward."

Jesson glanced at me, his eyebrows slightly lifted in question. I nodded and hoped I didn't look too anxious. I didn't know what would happen now that we had reached the castle. Who knew where the next few moments would find me? Andric might treat us all as prisoners and lock us in the dungeon as penance for the cruelty of our kingdoms. I swallowed the knot of uncertainty in my throat and gave her a smile. "I would be honored," I said.

Isea smiled back and bid farewell to her husband, reminding him that he would have a warm meal waiting when he returned home that night.

"She's beautiful," I said honestly.

Jesson nodded. "She's my life," he replied, looking back at her. "It'll be hard to leave the city we love, but as long as we're together, it'll be alright."

He fell silent and I didn't press him. The crowd welcomed us as warmly as it had the others, and I was glad to see that they didn't seem at all angry at the appearance of visitors from below the mountains, even visitors who seemed to be at least partially the cause of their dire situation.

We were swept toward the castle with the others; laughter and questions were exchanged by Jesson and various members of the party who had attached themselves to us. The young girl with the deer was on my right, and she caught me looking at the animal.

"Her name is Lilis," she told me without a hint of shyness. The deer sniffed my fingers and permitted me to run my hand through the thick, soft fur at its neck.

"I'm Kit," I told the girl.

She smiled, her blue eyes bright counterpoints to the white cloak she wore. "Sare," she replied. "Lilis says we can trust you, that you smell like a friend."

I looked back at the deer. The animal met my gaze, its eyes soft and trusting like the girl's. "Thank you," I said to both of them. We walked to the waiting gates in companionable, if unusual, silence.

Guards bowed us between the gates and down a long walkway through the courtyard lined with black and green uniformed soldiers who held their fists to their hearts in salute. The warm reflection from the castle seemed to light up the entire courtyard. As we drew closer, I could see that the rocks were huge solid stones bigger than I was tall. I wondered how they had been stacked together. The mortar between the stones seemed to capture the light of the walls and glow with warmth.

The Antorans left us at the castle gate with well wishes and promises to meet together again. We passed under a black iron portcullis and through a thick door of lightly colored, thick wooden beams followed by another gate. The soldiers who were around us turned away down a side hall lined with green tapestries to what I assumed were their own quarters. We had finally caught up to the others in time to hear Danyen say in a voice too loud for just Kenyen's ears, "Geesh, do you think they went a little overboard on the security? I mean really, soldiers living *in* the castle?"

Jesson shook his head but didn't say anything. The four soldiers who carried the stretchers turned off at a smaller white stone hall lined with maroon tapestries. I paused to say farewell to the healer.

"Thanks for your help back there," he told me. He glanced up the hall at Andric. No matter how casually the Prince acted about his wound, I wasn't the only one who had been concerned. The healer read my hesitation to head up the hallway after the others. "Don't worry," he said with a reassuring smile. "Everything's going to be just fine. I look forward to seeing you again soon."

"Hopefully under better circumstances," I replied.

He gave me an appreciative smile. "Definitely."

I watched him walk with the soldiers down the hallway, then steeled myself and turned to follow the others.

We crossed through another doorway and my feet were grateful for the thick, soft carpet that covered the stone floors. I fought back the urge to take off my worn boots and walk down the hall barefoot. It was like I had already forgotten such luxuries and was hard pressed to remember that I had lived on thick carpets my whole life. But that life seemed very far away.

I wondered if Father had gone back home to tell Mother what had happened, and hoped they didn't tell Rory. He didn't need to worry about me while he was sick. The first thing I wanted to do was get a message back to them to let everyone know we were alright. I hoped Andric remembered his promise to let us write home.

We were led up a set of richly carpeted stairs to the second floor, through an arched doorway, and into a grand gathering chamber. Multiple doorways led off from the room lined with the luxuries and comforts we were used to back home. My legs threatened to give out at the sight of couches embroidered in golden thread, but we were separated and each led into our individual door to the rooms waiting beyond.

It was immediately obvious that Prince Andric had planned long and hard to prepare for our coming. The room to which I was shown was dressed in Zalen's blue and gold. Thick dark blue goose-down blankets were piled on the bed with a multitude of pillows embroidered in gold thread. A small day couch sat below one of the wide windows which was surprisingly lined with glass, a luxury I didn't expect. Huge shutters were drawn to each side, ready to be pulled across the windows in case of an attack. Even though we were high up, I was surprised to see the markings of arrows etched in the wood.

Though I was inside a stone castle, it wasn't dark and damp like the few others I had been to. Light from the stones and mortar seemed to permeate everything, giving a warm, bright cast to the surroundings. I walked over to an outside wall and put a hand on it; I wasn't surprised to feel that heat also soaked through, warming the room better than any fire.

A pitcher of clean, warm water and scented soap sat on a small, elegant side table with a towel of soft cotton. I was cleaning what I could of the trail grim from my face and arms when a tap sounded at the door. "Crown Princess Kirit?"

I sighed at the title. "Please come in," I said.

A small maid dressed in green entered and curtsied. She kept her eyes on to the floor instead of meeting my gaze. "I beg your pardon, Crown Princess. I have come to lead you to the royal baths."

Her timid voice made me frown. Was she afraid of me? "Thank you very much," I told her as amiably as possible. "I really appreciate the chance to freshen up. It was quite the journey."

She glanced up at me in surprise, then averted her eyes again. "Yes, Crown Princess."

"I'd really appreciate it if you'd call me Kit," I said in an encouraging tone.

This time she met my gaze, her brown eyes wide with surprise. "Kit?"

I nodded. "It's easier to hear than Crown Princess Kirit; that sounds so stuffy, you know?"

Uncertain as to what she should say, the maid nodded.

"What's your name?" I asked.

"Lady's Maid K-Kimber," she said. She tucked a strand of curly brown hair back under the green laced kerchief across her head, and I realized she wasn't much younger than me.

"Pleased to meet you, Maid Kimber," I said. I looked around for clothing to take with me to change into.

She curtsied again. "Thank you, Princess Kit." She noticed my look and said, "Fresh apparel will be provided at the baths."

I nodded, relieved. "Then I'm ready to follow you."

She led the way through a tiny side door in my room that I hadn't noticed. It led discreetly past the main gathering chamber and joined with several other passageways that must come from the other rooms to meet at a stairway. I followed Kimber down the wide, sunlit stairs until I was certain we were below the first floor. The stairway ended at a wooden doorway painted dark green with golden scroll work on the sides and an outline in black and gold of what looked like Falen's description of an Antoran mountain lion.

Kimber opened the door and stood to one side to let me pass. She gave a small smile before she closed the door to leave me in privacy. I listened for her footsteps back up the stairs, but there were none. She must have orders to wait in case I needed anything.

I didn't like being waited on, and had often gotten around such things back home. Father allowed it, passing it off as one of my little quirks, but I know it bothered my tutors to no end. That was one of the reasons I took to healing. It got me out of the palace and working with real people and real life cares instead of with those concerned more about how you held your fingers while drinking tea or if you curtsied low enough to appease a visiting royal.

Mother insisted that it would help me win over a suitable suitor if I displayed proper royal etiquette, and so I did my best to please her; but when my not too dainty soup spoon habits or fumbling over the wrong form of address for a traveling official brought on too much scolding or discouragement on my tutors' part, I slipped away to the training grounds or healer houses.

I was alone in the room. Though underground, light from the walls still illuminated the area in a dim, peaceful glow. I was tempted to touch their warmth again, then I saw steam rising from a low set pool of water in the middle of the room. The promise of a warm bath made me strip down quickly and slide in. I gasped when the hot water met my chafed skin, but ducked beneath it with a grin. I could stand a little heat to get clean.

I had never been so dirty before that water felt like the best thing in the world. I splashed like a child in a puddle, and held my breath under the water for as long as I could. I then floated around for a bit until I remembered that Kimber waited outside the door. I found a container of lemongrass scented soap next to a small scrub brush. I washed quickly but thoroughly until my skin turned red from scrubbing; I wasn't leaving any trail dirt to remind me of what we had been through.

A thick cotton towel hung near a smaller room on the opposite side of the pool. Inside, I found a convenient closet. A beautifully cut mirror hung above a shelf which held a gold gilded comb, two soft brushes, and a gown made of a beautiful deep blue fabric. I pulled on the small clothes set to the side, dried my hair the best that I could with the towel, then pulled the gown over my head.

It fell to just above the floor in soft, velvety folds, a perfect fit over my shoulders and snug down to the waist. It was simple but elegant, a dress suitable for dining with royal guests, dancing in a ballroom, or strolling in the gardens at night. I laughed at the thought of a garden as I pulled on the soft slippers that were a shade darker than the dress and felt like heaven to my sore feet. Even if they did have a garden here, it would be dormant in the winter and probably wasn't one in which they would allow hostages, or whatever we were, to wander freely.

I stared at the dress in the mirror, puzzled. It wasn't what I expected in terms of attire; the elegance of my room wasn't what I had anticipated either, for that matter. For a country in such a dire situation, they put us up well. I wondered what Andric meant by it all, and how far out of their way the

Antorans had gone in order to make us comfortable during our stay.

I brushed my hair out quickly. The top layer of my hair had lightened from all the time I spent in the sun during the summers. Rory used to joke that I was becoming as fair-headed as the Faynans across the ocean to the east of Denbria. It was said that their hair shone like spun gold.

I gave an unladylike snort and quickly twisted my hair into a simple braid. The strands underneath were as dark brown as Rory's hair, which made an interesting contrast as I entwined it. Finished, I took one last look in the mirror to make sure I looked presentable, then turned and left the room.

Kimber gave a genuine smile when she saw me. "Oh, Princess Kit, you look beautiful."

I grinned. "I'll bet you say that to all the princesses." Her eyes widened and I smiled at her reassuringly. "I really appreciate your help." I gestured toward my ruined clothes that I had left near the door. "I don't know what to do with those."

"We'll take care of them, don't worry," she said. "If you'd like to rest for a bit, dinner will begin soon."

I followed her slowly up the stairs. Exhaustion stole through my limbs after the warm bath. The big bed with its pile of blankets sounded extremely inviting. I almost fell straight into it before Kimber pointed out the night robe laid discretely to the side.

"That way your dress won't be wrinkled for dinner," she explained with her eyes on the floor.

"Good thinking," I said. I slipped it on while she hung up my dress. "Thank you."

She curtsied and excused herself from the room. I was on the bed before the door closed. It took even less time to fall asleep amid the goose down comforters.

Chapter 9

It felt like only minutes had passed before Kimber tapped me lightly on the shoulder. I was generally a pretty light sleeper, but it felt like dragging myself to the surface of a deep pool in order to wake up. I rose groggily to a sitting position. "Is something wrong?" I asked, rubbing the sleep from my eyes.

She shook her head quickly. "Everything is very right. It's nearly dinnertime and I thought you'd like a few minutes to get ready. Honorable Crown Prince Andric has requested to meet with all the Denbrian Crown Princes and Princesses before the dinner." The way she said the word dinner made it sound like it should be capitalized.

The thought of appearing rumpled and wrinkled in front of the rest of the Crowns made me rise quickly. The room was dimmer than when I fell asleep, and I realized that the light from the marble stones that made up the castle had grown fainter. I dressed with Kimber's help, re-braided my hair, and splashed water on my face. She kept saying I looked wonderful, but I felt dazed after my too-brief sleep.

My vigilant maid led me down a different flight of stairs from those we had ascended, across a hallway, and through set of wide wooden doors carved on the front in a mountain landscape with a sun cresting over the horizon. A waiting room was revealed with light colored furniture and a beautiful red woven carpet. Tapestries displaying hunts in the snowy mountains covered the walls.

Andric waited in the middle of the room. He looked even more tired than I felt; by the dark circles under his eyes, I doubted he had taken even the brief rest I had been granted. He nodded at me, a slight smile on his face. He wore a black suit and a cloak of dark green. His dark brown hair was combed and loose instead of pulled back in the short warrior's tail.

Bayn and Freis sat on either side of Andric. The two wolves looked extremely out of place in the cozy room. I wondered if the wolves were why the other Crowns hung back; well, besides the fact that they pointedly hated him. Kenyen and Danyen glared at the Prince from their position near a corner. Kaerdra and Trevin talked quietly with Nyssa and Brynna near a small fire in the white marble fireplace, while Tisha and Landis waited silently hand in hand on one of the couches. They all wore clean clothing and looked fairly refreshed since the last time I saw them. Chagrined that I was the last one to arrive, I walked up to the couch behind Landis and Tisha and waited for Andric to begin.

"Welcome to Antor," the Prince said with a small, wry smile. Danyen snorted, but Andric continued, "We may do things a bit differently than you're used to, but you are welcome to do whatever you would like here as long as it doesn't put anyone in harm's way." I knew it wasn't in my imagination that he glanced at the twins when he said that. "My Hawkmaster, Ayd, will send any messages to your homes that you would like to convey to your families. I urge you to take the opportunity to let them know that you are alright."

"Yeah, right," Kenyen muttered loudly.

"You'll read them or change them," Nyssa accused. Brynna nodded defiantly beside her.

Andric shook his head, his expression clear as if he had expected the accusations. "I give you my word that I'll not look at or alter your letters. You're free to say in them what you will. I'll be sending letters to each of your parents as well to explain to them why you are here."

Trevin stared at him. "They'll tear you apart, you know."

Andric nodded, unaffected. "I know you must be famished, so please come with me. It wouldn't be polite to keep them waiting much longer."

We exchanged looks at the word 'them', but followed the Prince to another set of doors on the west side of the room. At his slight touch, the doors were pulled open. The sound of talking flooded the room, then abruptly fell silent. Andric tipped his head at us invitingly, and then entered through the door, the two wolves right behind him. I followed Kaerdra and Trevin with the others close behind.

The room we entered was bigger than the ballroom in our palace back home. The ceiling met in the center with six branching marble support beams that arched to each side. The center point glowed like a small moon which lit the majority of the room. Rows upon rows of tables were set below a raised dais with what appeared to be most of the citizens of Antor standing beside them. Animals were mixed among the Antorans. The citizens glanced at us curiously, but they mostly watched their prince.

The expressions on their faces were not the fear and formality I usually saw on countrymen in the presence of their ruler. Instead, I saw familiarity, gratitude, and respect. Andric returned the same expression, but more guarded, as if aware of every move he made. It was strange to see someone just a few years older than me with an entire country resting on his shoulders. I wondered where his father was.

"It's good to be home," Andric said in a voice that carried over the crowd with ease. I heard a few chuckles. He smiled back. "I've brought a few guests to spend our final winter in Antor with us. Please treat them well; they aren't used to our traditions." He said the last word with a slight inflection and more people laughed. He spread his arm to include us.

"Please welcome the Crown Princes and Princesses of Denbria."

To our surprise, applause rang out loud and echoed from both ends of the massive hall. I glanced at Tisha; she met my gaze and shrugged slightly, her expression as puzzled as my own. Apparently, we all had misconceptions about how the winter months in captivity were to be.

The Prince of Antor continued, "They have free range of the castle and our city; please get to know them and make them comfortable here." He turned to us, his voice still raised for all to hear. "And if we are under attack, there's a safe room within the foundation of the castle where you will be protected. We'll just hope we don't have to use it." He said it lightly, and the Antorans laughed, but there was a different tone to the laughter this time, and different expressions on their faces. The experience and knowledge in their gazes made a shiver run up my spine.

Andric gestured for us to follow him to the table on the dais. We walked slowly past the Antorans and up the two steps to the higher table. Covered platters waited, and the scent that wafted from them made my stomach growl. Landis stifled a laugh.

"Eat, welcome you," Andric said. But the crowd below waited, and Andric remained standing as if he had expected it. He glanced toward the door and I saw him exchange a nod with a tall, stately man dressed in dark green. "Our journey came at an inconvenient time, forcing us to put off the Winter Festival for these other important matters," Andric said in a voice that carried across the room. He looked around and every eye was on him, an air of expectancy hanging thick above the tables. He smiled a true smile, "So we shall have the Festival tomorrow!"

Cheers and shouts of jubilation met his words. The Antorans took their seats and began to help themselves to the waiting food. We sat at Andric's gesture, and soon only excited murmurs and the sounds of eating filled the air. A pork roast with buttered potatoes and small green peppers sat nearest to me, next to a bowl of sweet white corn and sugared yams floating in an orange sauce. A leafy green salad with carrots cut into a variety of shapes and lightly braised with a sweet vinegar dressing gave a perfect counterbalance to yellow fruits shaped into flowers and glazed with honey and maple syrup.

The food was delicious, and the variety of honeyed drinks brought a rainbow of flavors, both new and familiar. My favorite was iced goat's milk with a touch of cinnamon and a hot powder that cleared my throat. The spice was slightly different from what we were used to, but it made everything taste exotic. I didn't know if it was our long, hard journey or the fight for our lives that made our appetites so great, but we did our share to clear the food from the platters.

As dinner wound down, I had a hard time keeping my eyes open. A jester stood in the middle of the banquet hall juggling a variety of eating utensils to the enjoyment of the cheering audience. Everyone seemed in very good spirits now that bellies were full and with the promise of the festivities tomorrow. But as I looked around, I saw a few sad faces, expressions valiantly positive despite the sorrow that showed through their eyes. It seemed that this was truly their last winter here in Antor, and they were giving their best to the present because the future was uncertain.

Mothers played with their children, laughing at jokes and tickling their young ones, while fathers looked on with tender smiles. They didn't have the attitudes of countrymen eating in the castle for the first time. This seemed to be a common affair in Antor, which made it very different from the royal traditions in the rest of Denbria. Citizens were invited to dine in the presence of the royal families very seldom, and only then upon special occasion where favor had been granted. Here, though, the Antorans laughed and joked with Crown Prince Andric in familiarity. He didn't look offended at being addressed, and they were always very respectful. With the smiles shared, it seemed like the Antorans and their prince held each other in mutual regard.

After the feast began to die down, Andric excused himself and apologized to his people for retiring early. He reassured them it was so that he could be rested for the celebration tomorrow. He also asked them to excuse the other Crowns when they felt ready to retire because they, too, had undergone a hard journey.

Kenyen and Danyen left shortly after he did, and I followed a few minutes later. The urgency of writing a letter to Father pressed on my mind, and I knew I couldn't sleep until I had something ready to send out at first morning light. The least I could do was reassure my family that I was safe and that the Antorans were treating us well.

I made my way down the candlelit hallway. Starlight filtered down the marble stones and gave enough light to see by; stewards had also put out candles as much for the ambiance as the light. I couldn't remember which stairway we had come from, so I took the second one and turned to the left at the top of the stairs like before. I walked quietly down the hallway. Nothing looked familiar. I wished I had accepted the offer of one of the maids to guide me back to my room.

I sighed and turned to go back down the hall when a familiar voice stopped me. "Did you see them?"

I looked up the hall. Faint light spilled from the partly closed door at the end. "They're finally here. I can't believe it worked," Andric said.

I walked back up the hallway, my slippers soft on the carpeted floor. Long tapestries and elegantly framed hand-painted pictures depicted forest scenes on one side of the hall and views of the ocean on the other. In one picture, a ship caught the final rays of the setting sun in its sails; next to it, a seagull perched by a wizened old man on a pier, both of them gazing down into the choppy water below. Across the hall, a young man and a great black bear walked through the trees; the young man rested his hand on the black bear's back. In the frame next to it, a beautiful young woman with long brown hair sat on a grassy knoll; a small gray fox waited beside her with its head on her knee.

Another voice, one I hadn't heard before, stole my attention from the beautiful artwork. "All I see are ghosts. They're all there is now."

Andric's voice grew softer. "I know, Father. Try to get some rest."

I reached the door and stepped just far enough to the right to see into the room.

Andric sat on the corner of a large bed under a double set of bay windows opened wide to the night sky. Winter-chilled, salty sea air, as familiar to me as my own room at home facing the Zalen seafront, drifted in on the evening breeze. Moonlight from the windows made a rectangle on the bed, revealing a man with dark brown hair streaked in gray and a salt and pepper stubble beard on his face. He sat propped by pillows on the bed and stared at Andric as if his son was a stranger.

"I can't sleep," the man said, turning his head to stare out the window. "I'm waiting up for my Maritha." My heart slowed when I recognized the name of his wife who had passed away six years ago.

I couldn't see Andric's face, but his voice was patient with the tone of someone who had repeated the same thing many times. "She's not coming back tonight, Father. It'd be better if you slept now."

His father was torn, his eyes searching the night. "She said she'd be back soon. The captains must be taking their time."

"Maybe the ice stopped them," the son replied quietly. "The ships should be in port soon." Andric rose and closed the windows, latching the great shutters over them. It took a few minutes for my eyes to adjust to the suddenly darkened room. A fire flickered in the corner. Andric went to it and added more logs, causing a shower of sparks to dance and drift through the air. The light from the fire made the marble stones closest to it glow with warm yellow light. "Sleep, Father. Don't worry about Mother; she's safe."

I turned to leave, and saw Andric's head jerk around. I froze in the darkness. His eyes narrowed. It was then that I saw Bayn blink silently from the base of the bed. He stared right at me, his golden eyes reflecting the firelight.

I turned and ran down the hall, my heart pounding. I took the stairs two at a time, turned to my right, and hurried back up the next flight. Counting the doors, I pulled open my own and closed it tightly behind me. I sank onto the bed with my head in my hands. I had no right to be there, and shouldn't have overheard the things he said to his father. Those things were private, and I shouldn't have eavesdropped. I tried to tell myself that I really hadn't meant to, but I couldn't get past the thought that I had also stayed when I realized who was in the room.

I was so ashamed that I could barely write the letter to my family. A beautiful black quill that showed a purple hue when I turned it in the moonlight perched next to the bed on a small nightstand; a fresh sheet of smooth, pressed paper lay waiting as if someone knew I would want to write home before I went to sleep.

I took a deep breath to clear my head, then put the quill to the paper.

> Dear Mother, Father, and Rory,
>
> I want to let you know first that I am safe, and so are the other Crown Princes and Princesses. We have not been mistreated, and everyone is unharmed. We've been given our own rooms in the Antoran castle, and are being treated very hospitably. Prince Andric said we are here to learn how important it is to work together so that our own countries don't go through the same thing Antor is. I'll let you know when I find out more about it, because it's all still a bit confusing to me. I love you very much. Please give Rory my love; I'm anxious to hear how he is doing. Prince Andric said that he is letting us write as often as we'd like, so I'll write you again soon. I miss you.
>
> Love,
> Kit

I finally pulled on my sleeping robe and hung up the beautiful blue dress. My feet felt as heavy as stone and my legs ached from all of the unaccustomed riding. I collapsed on the bed and fell asleep when my head touched the pillow.

Chapter 10

The next morning, shouts of command followed by thuds and grunts resounded through my room. I opened my eyes and saw early sunlight streaming from the window. The air was chilly, but when my bare feet touched the floor, I was surprised to find that it was warm. The white marble lit the room in a pleasant morning glow.

Before I could go to the window and find the source of the sounds, a knock sounded at my door. I slid my feet into slippers that someone had put at the foot of my bed while I slept, pulled on my robe, and hurried to open the door. Kaerdra, Tisha, and Brynna waited for me, each dressed in their own robes with matching slippers. I wondered if the thoughtfulness of the clothing touched them as much as it did me.

"Did you see them?" Brynna asked. She didn't wait for an answer and pushed past me to the window.

"What do you suppose they're doing?" Kaerdra echoed, following her.

Tisha smiled at me. "Good morning."

I smiled back and motioned for her to come in. "Good morning to you, too. Did you sleep well?"

She nodded. "Very well, until the fighting woke me up this morning."

"Fighting?" I went to the window and looked out.

The rear view of most castles or palaces revealed beautiful gardens and orchards designed for ladies' enjoyment and generally were tended by the queen and her women. It turned out to be one of the many other differences in Antor that required some getting used to.

Instead of gardens, a huge training field spread out below us. Most of the snow had been swept clear, revealing hard-packed earth underneath. Hundreds of citizens, at least half of the Antorans that had gathered at the castle for the banquet the night before, spread out below singly and in groups. They each held weapons, mostly wooden swords, axes, and staffs weighted with iron, though some soldiers and citizens in a small group in the middle wielded real weaponry. These were given a wide berth by the rest and wore complete suits of armor.

"What's going on?" Danyen demanded from the doorway.

Surprised, I looked back to see the twins watching us from the door I had accidentally left open. I motioned that it was fine for them to come in. In any other setting, a Crown Prince entering the bedchamber of a Crown Princess would have been entirely unsuitable, but since everything else in our world had turned upside down, I figured there was no harm in stretching normal decorum a bit more.

Kenyen must have felt the same way, because he pushed past his wide-eyed brother to join us at the window. Danyen sighed and followed.

"It looks like they're training," I mused out loud.

"For a hostile takeover?" Kenyen asked, bristling.

I frowned, but couldn't answer him. So many Antorans gathered in the practice ground with weapons made me nervous also. It took me a minute to remember Andric's comments at dinner. "Andric said there was a safe room under the castle in case of an attack. It looks like they've had to defend it before."

Landis appeared beside Tisha. "I noticed that, too," he said quietly. He gave Tisha a good morning hug. "There're arrow marks in some of the shutters. None of the first floor windows have glass, probably because it's too expensive to keep replacing."

Kenyen shrugged, unconvinced. "I think it's a dangerous thing to have enemies this prepared."

"Who says they're enemies?" I asked before I could stop myself.

This time, several of them glared at me. Brynna snorted, "We've been kidnapped and are being held hostage. Of course they're enemies." She shook her head, her tone implying absolute stupidity. "What is your country going to do when you're queen?"

I could feel my face turn red. I ducked away to see Nyssa walk through the doorway. Trevin followed close behind to complete the gathering in my room. For a second, I stood back and just watched them stare at the commotion below. My cheeks burned from Brynna's comment.

"They sure listen well to that thief," Danyen mumbled with grudging admiration.

I went to the next window and looked down to see the Antoran Prince in the middle of the group armed with real swords. He shouted commands which were echoed by Captain Jashe and Falen, his second. Jashe and Falen walked between the long lines correcting stances and adjusting sword holds. After each swing, thrust, or parry, the Antorans held their stance for Andric's next command. A slight shiver ran down my spine at the sight of hundreds of citizen soldiers trained to fight under their Crown Prince's command.

I watched for several minutes and calmed my nerves by telling myself that if there was a possible chance of attack, at least we knew their country wasn't helpless. A cluster of children off to one side swung short sticks with cross handles in time to the Prince's command. I fought back a smile when Jashe leaned over and helped a boy less than a quarter his size straighten his hold on the makeshift blade.

The others finally gave up and drifted back to their rooms. I continued to watch the training warriors. Women swung swords next to their husbands, fathers corrected sons, and daughters trained beside brothers. It made sense to me, countrymen and women training beside hardened soldiers to prepare for whatever the future would hold.

It was obvious by the steady hands, quick responses, and firm stances that these Antorans had trained for a very long time. Most of them hefted the iron shrouded wooden training swords with ease. White puffs rose in the cold air from their mouths as they grunted in response to each of Andric's commands. A few animals watched the training group from the sidelines. Andric's wolves waited near the head in a small pack.

The swords the middle group wielded were smaller than the ones used by most Denbrian armies; they were more like the one that Captain Rurisk had made for me. The design made sense, shorter and thinner than the average broadsword for better manipulation. A broadsword's weight carried it through heavy armor to reach the attacker's flesh, but from what I had seen of the Breizans, they wore little armor and attacked with a ferocity that would quell the heart of the strongest warrior. These swords were better able to make multiple wounds and allow for escape instead of the brief, heavy-handed combat for which the broadsword was designed.

I fought the urge to go down there, reminding myself that it would definitely be out of place for a stranger to be seen watching their training, let alone the designated ruler of a country that possibly had something to do with their demise.

When I finally left the window, I dressed quickly so that I could see the letter I had written last night sent off as soon as possible. I longed for word of Rory's condition. I had to know if he was getting better. Father would let me know; of that I was certain.

A new dress of light blue and gold hung in the wardrobe where the dark blue one had been. I quickly slipped it on and combed my hair with the soft brush on the small end table, then braided it again. The bowl held fresh, cool water with an unfamiliar, subtle scent that felt pleasant and refreshing to my skin. I left the room with my letter clutched tightly in one hand.

I was pacing the room with anxiety by the time the others finally made it to the small waiting chamber where we had met Andric the day before. I didn't really want to rely on the others' company, but I also dreaded seeing Andric again after my imposition last night. I didn't know how he would react, but I didn't want to leave him a chance to confront me about it until I could get the situation straightened out in my own head.

The Antorans had finished their training and most were already eating breakfast when we entered the banquet hall. Andric rose when he saw us, and the rest of the Antorans followed. I fought back a blush at both the Antorans' show of respect and Andric's gaze as we made our way to the table on the dais. I made sure that Kaerdra and Trevin sat between me and Andric with Landis and Tisha on the other side. When we sat down, Andric and his citizens also sat and continued their breakfast. The Crowns ignored Prince Andric and he seemed satisfied to eat in silence.

The morning meal was a heartily cooked grain with dark sugar and the same sweet pumpkin milk that we had been served on our journey to Antor. It was satisfying and filling, though I heard Kenyen comment to his brother about the lack of options. I glanced sideways to see if Andric had noticed, but he watched his people, a pensive look on his face.

Though he must have been hungry after the morning's training, the Prince's food was mostly untouched. The dark shadows under his eyes had lessened somewhat, but he still looked tired and troubled. With a pang, I remembered the sword wound down the back of his shoulder. I vowed to ask Jesson if I saw him to make sure he was tending to Andric's wound. If he strained his left shoulder too much he would tear through the stitches and the Antoran Crown Prince didn't seem like one to hold back, as attested to by his actions on the practice field.

He looked my way and I stared down at my plate. I scraped the remaining oats from the bowl and finished the pumpkin milk before I allowed myself to look back up. I was surprised to see that Andric had already left; I didn't remember him excusing himself, but most of the other Antorans had left as well.

We met back in my room. The steward who came to get us didn't seem surprised to find us all together. He bowed when I opened the door at his polite knock. "His Honorable Crown Prince Andric has asked that I escort you to the hawkery to meet Hawkmaster Ayd so you will know who is sending the letters to your families."

"So we'll know who's reading our letters," Nyssa said in a vexed voice to Brynna.

The steward looked up, his glance indignant at Nyssa's not so quietly spoke words. "Crown Prince Andric has reassured you that your letters will be treated with the utmost respect and privacy, and so they shall. Any implication to the contrary will be viewed as doubt of the royal word; such implications are not healthy to those being protected under the Prince's roof."

Surprised and chagrined, Nyssa mumbled an apology and glanced furtively at Brynna. The other Princess shrugged, her cheeks red. None of us were used to being rebuked by a servant, but his firm gaze and quick defense of his prince left no room for argument.

We followed the steward in silence down the stairs, across a hall, and out a side door to a small path that had been cleared of snow. The path led around the castle and through the training grounds we had watched earlier.

We were led through a door in a short wall that followed one side of the training ground, through the small, snow-covered yard beyond, and ended at a gray-bricked building.

The steward held the door open for us to pass, his expression still showing his displeasure at Nyssa's comment. I was the last in the door, and thank him quietly for showing us the way. He mumbled something about us hopefully able to find our way back through the snow by ourselves and left. I glanced at the others and was relieved to find that they had missed the comment. It only bothered me slightly, but they were accustomed to being respected and I didn't want them to have something else to complain about.

The inside of the gray building seemed dim after the bright sunlight bouncing off of the snow. The scent of birds and hay tickled my nose. It was quiet, and only the occasional brief murmur or rustle of a bird preening its feathers broke the silence. The birds were bigger than I expected. They perched on posts made of stout branches that had been trimmed smooth and lopped clean of twigs and leaves.

Each bird had its own spot, designated by a tassel of leather on which was strung what looked like a small whistle. The difference between the hawks here and the ones in our countries was that here they weren't bound by jesses or hoods. They perched freely, and a few wide windows stayed open around the room so that they could depart if they wished.

The birds were mostly shades of brown, though toward the back I saw a few big black ones that I thought were eagles. They ignored us for the most part. A few turned bright, piercing eyes our direction, then looking away. But I could still feel their attention on us despite the indifference.

"Welcome."

The sudden voice behind us made us all jump. A boy close to our age smiled sheepishly. "Sorry," he apologized with a slight bow, "I didn't mean to startle you."

"And you are?" Trevin asked without bothering to return his bow.

"Hawkmaster Ayd," the boy replied.

We all stared. I definitely wasn't the only one surprised to see how young the Antoran Hawkmaster was. Usually, a Hawkmaster was the oldest hawker at the castle or palace. It was a revered position appointed by the king because the Hawkmaster was the one entrusted with royal mail, the contents of which could make or break a kingdom.

Hawkmaster Ayd smiled amiably. "Crown Prince Andric said you would be curious about who sends out your mail." I wondered if he read something on the other Crowns' faces because his eyes creased with laughter. "You don't have to worry about your letters being read."

"Why is that?" Kenyen asked, his gaze suspicious.

Ayd grinned. "Because my hawks don't know how to read."

I groaned along with several of the others at the bad joke and had to fight back a smile when Kenyen rolled his eyes. Ayd shrugged. "Hard audience." He winked at Nyssa and her cheeks turned red. Despite his station, it was obvious she was taken by Ayd's sandy blond hair and bright blue eyes that sparkled with laughter in the sparse lighting.

I couldn't blame her. It was hard enough to find a suitable suitor within the lower royal lines of the kingdom to not give in to wistful thinking now and then. We Crowns were within the same age group due to the fact that our great-great-grandfathers along the royal genealogy were the four sons of King Denbrow, two sets of twins born within two years of each other. The King had split the kingdom into four quarters when the youngest set of twins turned twenty, telling them to find suitable queens immediately who could rule beside them and bear healthy children.

The new kings were obedient to their father's wishes and married within months of each other, bearing their first child within a year of marriage. Prince Dareth divided his country between his twin son and daughter, creating Zalen and Faer. Prince Veren left his country to his son, Tyneth, who then divided it between his three daughters before he died, naming the largest country after his father in tribute. Nichas, with the southern lands, was unable to have children. He ended up leaving the lands to his wife's two brothers, who then divided it for their two older sons. The King of Antor, King Toren, kept to himself behind the northern mountains and established the mines.

The oldest child of each became the Crown Prince or Princess, heir to the throne. Because our parents were so close in age, and the founding roots were not yet so distant, the first generation from each family was generally born within a few years of each other. In our situation, Tisha was the youngest at sixteen, with me only a few months older than her. Kaerdra was next, reminding everyone that she and Trevin were just shy of seventeen.

Kenyen and Danyen were seventeen, born only a month before Landis. Nyssa and Brynna were the oldest among us at eighteen. Rory had been the oldest of the group. He had turned nineteen a month ago, though there had been little to celebrate as he struggle to take a bite of his favorite meal of maple sweetened ham and sweet potatoes that Mother had made for him by her own hands.

I wondered if that was one of the reasons the others resented me so much. Rory had been their leader, the oldest and most adventurous of the group. He had arranged for all of the Crowns to go on a camping and hunting expedition each year. I was never allowed to go, though Rory always told me about it when he got back so that I wouldn't feel left out. It sounded like the 'hunts' were mostly full of swimming in sun-warmed lakes, the girls sunbathing on the beach, and the boys trying to top each other's stories about their parents, battles, and dangerous hunts for creatures that had long-since been trapped out for the safety of the citizens.

Once in a while we heard about the rare dragon or nightbeast being spotted; hunting expeditions were sent out but it was usually a false alarm. The creatures that had kept our land from being populated by humans long before King Denbrow reached its shores had been killed-off in organized forays when Denbrow and his followers escaped from the Fayn prisons and fled across the ocean. I never knew what they had done to be thrown into the prisons in the first place, but their stories of courage and bravery when they first reached Denbria wiped out most speculation. Denbrow had been given the crown after risking his life to save two of his companions from a nightbeast.

The door opened in the hawk house, bringing my attention back to the present. Bright light filtered into the room. Tiny motes of dust from the layers of straw on the ground danced and sparkled in the air.

Kenyen and Danyen walked out, followed by Nyssa and Brynna who whispered to each other in annoyed tones. Tisha and Landis wandered through the hawks. I remembered from Rory's stories that Landis' father had a big aviary in Faer where they raised a variety of birds. Ayd and I watched him point out traits of the different hawk species to Tisha. The Crown Princess of Maesh actually looked as interested in learning as Landis was of teaching her. It seemed like a great relationship.

I noticed Ayd watching me. I thought back quickly to see if he had asked me a question; unable to find one, I blushed. "Sorry," I said in embarrassment. "I didn't hear you."

The Hawkmaster shook his head. "No offense taken, my Lady. I noticed after I spoke that your attention was elsewhere." He indicated the letter I still held with a respectful nod. "I was just wondering if you wanted me to send that out with the first flight."

I glanced guiltily down at the letter. There was no doubt my family was worried and anxious to hear from me, and I was busy gawking at hawks. "Yes, please. My father's likely to tear down the whole mountain if he doesn't hear from me soon."

Ayd nodded and took the letter from me. I noticed that several of the birds closest to us already had letters fastened to the light harnesses on their backs. Back home, letters were usually delivered by carrier pigeon and tied into tubes on their feet, but it was obvious such a contraption would hinder a hawk whose sustenance depended on its ability to catch prey with its sharp talons.

These hawks had been rigged with very lightweight soft leather harnesses that looped across their chest and crisscrossed past the back and around the wings securely enough to keep it snug, but without hindering any movement. It was a cleverly devised contraption, one of which Ayd seemed quite proud as he secured my letter to the back of one of the huge brown hawks.

"Crown Prince Andric already sent out a batch of letters early this morning to all of the royal families in Denbria," he explained affably. "He knew there would be some controversy from the Crown Princes and Princesses when they learned that his letter reached their parents first, but he wanted to assure them of their children's safety immediately." Ayd frowned from where he fastened the buckle on the pouch as though he realized I was one of the Crowns he referred to. "I mean, your parents." He turned to study me, his gaze frank. "You know, you don't act like them."

I didn't know what to say. I didn't want to act as snobbish as Brynna or highhanded as Nyssa, but I also doubted that I carried the same respect their very bearing demanded. Could I lead without that kind of respect? I couldn't help it when my answer sounded a bit sullen. "I know. I'm not really one of them, just sort of a stand-in."

Ayd's brows creased and I saw another question on his lips, but Landis and Tisha came back, interrupting him. The Hawkmaster turned smoothly to answer Landis' question about a rare crested hawk from the plains below Tyn.

"They're neat, don't you think?" Tisha asked me. Her tone was anxious as though she hoped I was enjoying myself as much as she was, and also hoped that having a good time wasn't a bad thing given the circumstances.

I nodded honestly. "I think they're amazing. I like how they don't have to be tied or bound at all."

Tisha's eyes widened as though she had just noticed. "Is it magic?" she whispered. She peeked over her shoulder to make sure Ayd was far enough away so that he couldn't hear us. The Hawkmaster and Landis stood in front of a tiny hawk who stared back at them insolently as though disgruntled that they had disturbed its sleep.

I shook my head quickly. The sooner the rumors about Antor could be cleared up, the better for everyone involved, especially if the Antorans were serious about heading south in the spring. "The animals aren't enchanted or forced to obey; they have a bond with their human, and they can communicate and understand each other."

"Oh," Tisha said. Her eyes grew even wider. I wondered if I had said the wrong thing, but she turned and looked back at Landis. The boys were still talking about the little hawk that now stood quietly on Ayd's gloved hand. "I don't really understand, but I think Landis does. I think he wishes he could talk to the animals, too. He said it would make hawking so much easier."

I couldn't help but stare. I never thought about anyone wanting that kind of a bond with an animal. I was still coming to terms with the whole situation. From the way Andric described it, I didn't know if I would want to share my thoughts with animals, or how it would be to have their thoughts in my head.

A bell tolled loud enough to echo around the room and startle the resting birds. Several of them squawked or clicked their beaks and flapped their wings. Ayd smoothed a few feathers on the back of a beautiful silver and black one, his blue eyes bright. "It's time for the picnic!"

"A picnic?" Landis and I repeated in unison.

"In the snow?" Tisha asked at the same time.

"It's one of the highlights of the Winter Festival! They'll bring blankets and light bonfires, so everyone'll be warm," Ayd said. He opened the door for us to exit the hawk house.

"There'll be horse racing, mock fights, and then storytelling at dinner when we eat the feast." He sobered a bit when he paused to shut the door firmly behind him. "I don't think we'll have many feasts after this one, or much to feast about. After the Spring Festival, it'll be time to leave." He shook his head, then gave us a smile that looked a bit forced. "Well, the least we can do is enjoy the celebration at hand, right?"

I nodded in agreement and he grinned again. We followed in his wake through the snow. When I turned to close the gate, one of Andric's wolves, the small, dark gray male, paced up to me along the inside of the wall. He gave a slight wag of his tail and sniffed my hand. Snow stuck to his nose and I brushed it off. The wolf gave my cold fingers an amiable lick and then trotted off along the wall again.

"Kit, come on!" Tisha shouted.

I looked up to see that they were already at the castle door. The brisk mountain air nipped at my face as I ran to catch up to them. I had a scarf inside, and the warmer cloak that Prince Andric had given all of us on the journey. I made a mental note to grab them before taking off to the picnic.

Ayd held the door open for me and bowed when I neared. "Princess Kit?" He said it as a question.

I nodded. "I prefer it."

He smiled and I wondered briefly who could get mad at the good-humored Hawkmaster. Brynna and Nyssa managed, and the twins, but they were mad at everything. He closed the heavy door behind us and took off down a different hallway. I followed Landis and Tisha up a set of stairs, careful to make the right turns this time.

Chapter 11

The horses stomped in excitement, as eager as the riders for the races in the snow. An obstacle course had been laid out in an oval that raced along the wall, then veered off through the huge, jagged, snow-covered boulders that filled the back half of the castle grounds. Antorans sat on blankets in choice spots all along the track, eating picnic food and playing games while they waited for the races to start.

A snowball sailed through the air and I ducked; it whizzed by inches from my ear. I looked around to see who had thrown it. A little boy peeked out at me from behind his mother's skirts.

"I am so sorry," she apologized, her expression a mixture of horror and embarrassment that her son had just thrown a snowball at a member of foreign royalty. "I didn't realize where he was throwing, I-"

"It's alright," I replied with a grin to save her from continuing. "I used to snowball fight with my brother all the time back home."

"You did?" the little boy asked. His mother gave me a grateful smile.

I nodded and scooped up some snow in my gloved hands.

The sound as I packed it together made me smile with the memories it brought. "Rory had a really good aim." I winked at the little boy. "But I think he let me win a lot of the time. He's a great big brother."

"Why isn't he here with you?" the boy asked.

My smile faltered. The mother must have seen my change in expression, because she thanked me for talking to her son, gave a low curtsey, then led him away to look at the horses. I dropped the snowball and scuffed the snow with the toe of my shoe.

I fought back sorrow that would damper the celebrations; I kept reminding myself that this picnic was for Antor, not to appease my aching heart. I couldn't do anything to help Rory from here, and I wouldn't have word from home for at least two more days if Ayd hadn't exaggerated the amazing speed of his hawks.

"Searching for something?" a voice asked.

I looked up to see one of Andric's stewards watching me. He was dressed in the Antoran colors of black and green, and his robes bore the steward emblem of a white fist over his heart. His eyes were kind and his smile held the kind of warmth that beckoned my trust. I was surprised at how many who worked at the castle bore the same expression; Andric had a good group of people to help him.

I shook my head and thanked him for his concern. "Just waiting for the races," I told him, forcing a nonchalant smile to my face.

He nodded. "Horsemaster Drade is racing Sorn; if you're a betting person, I'd place my bets on him."

I heard an echo of Father's voice and shook my head. "My father taught me that gambling was just throwing away money better spent on something worthwhile."

The steward nodded appreciatively. "He sounds like a wise man." He gave a dramatic sigh. "On the other hand, my father enjoys a good bet. He taught me that the best way to make a small fortune gamboling was to bring a large fortune to bet with." He laughed. "He also taught me that to lose is a great way to ensure that you never become to prideful."

I couldn't help but laugh at the chagrined expression on his face. "Your way sounds more fun than mine."

He nodded with a grin that brought laugh lines to the corners of his eyes. "Would you like to see the horses? They should have them out of the stables by now."

I thought of Trae and nodded. It would be good to see how he was doing. The steward guided me through the crowds who gave way when they saw us. Everyone finished off the last of the roasted pork and fresh rolls in good cheer. Hot chocolate and spiced pumpkin milk steamed in huge bowls on big tables set out in the snow. Children with red noses and big grins ladled out cups of the sweet drinks. One of them offered a cup to me and I couldn't turn down the little boy's big green eyes.

"Thank you," I said. I took a sip of chocolate and the hot liquid warmed me from the inside out. "It's delicious."

He giggled and ran back to his friends to coax other picnickers into having another serving.

The horses milled about expectantly by the starting line. It was funny to see how their enthusiasm surpassed even that of their riders. Drade's herd was easy to pick out because they didn't have any bridles and weren't tied to posts to wait. A few more bridleless horses waited by their bonded owners, but none showed the same enthusiasm as Drade's thick-coated, shaggy herd. Several already bore riders and paced up and down the set track, flattening down the snow for the start of the race.

Trae stood near the starting line. He looked depressed, his head low and ears twitching as he watched the other horses prepare to run. He recognized my scent before I reached him and lifted his head. His nostrils flared and he whickered a welcome.

"Looks like you have a friend," the steward said with a perceptive smile. "I will leave you to catch up." He patted

Trae's shoulder as if they were familiar comrades, then gave me a low bow.

"Thank you very much," I replied, more grateful for his company than I could express. He gave a nod as if he guessed as much and walked away. A young boy held out a cup of pumpkin milk and he accepted it with a dramatic flourish that made the children at the table laugh.

I turned back to Trae. He walked to meet me and his limp made me ashamed. I rubbed his head in apology.

"How are you doing, boy? It's my fault you can't race, and I feel so bad about it." Trae nuzzled my cheek as if he knew what I was saying.

"It's not your fault at all," replied a familiar voice behind me.

I turned to find Drade, the horse Tisha and I had ridden, Pantim, at his side. "It's good to see you again," the Horsemaster said with a welcoming smile. "And I mean it about Trae's injury. He wasn't the only horse to get hurt out there; that's the price of battle." His smile saddened as we both thought of the horse that he was forced to put down.

I pushed aside the thought and rubbed Pantim's nose in greeting. The horse whickered and bobbed his head. I reached up to smooth his fetlock across his forehead when something jolted from my fingertips up my arm and into my mind. I saw the racing path from a horse's point of view, hooves pounding the ground, churning the snow underfoot. A steaming breath was whisked away; the thrill of the run filled my veins.

"Are you alright?" Drade's voice broke through the thought.

I stared at him, then back at Pantim. The horse watched me with knowing eyes; he gave a quiet nicker.

"Do you want to ride him in the race?" Drade invited, his gaze curious.

Pantim bobbed his head and pawed the snow with an eager hoof. It was easy to see that he understood exactly what the Horsemaster said.

"I-I wouldn't want to take him from someone else," I fumbled, still dazed.

Drade shook his head, a warm smile on his face. "My horses choose who they want on their backs, not the other way around. Pantim's usually one of the first to decide on a rider, and he's just wandered around. I think he was waiting for you."

I looked back at Trae. "I'd hate to leave Trae by himself."

"Trae doesn't mind, do you?" he asked, rubbing Trae's whiskery nose. The horse nuzzled his hand. "He'll be fine, but Pantim won't give you a break until you agree." The older man's eyes twinkled mischievously.

Pantim reiterated the thought by nudging my chest with his nose hard enough to knock me off balance. I had to laugh. "Alright, alright, I'll race with you," I finally agreed. Pantim snorted and led the way toward the starting line. Drade walked beside us. Sorn already waited for him patiently by the others.

The number of riders surprised me. It looked like every family had someone riding in the race. There was no prize, that had been announced at the beginning; although, when good-natured protests rang out, Andric promised he would find something suitable to give the winner. Everyone laughed at that, which made me wonder what kind of a suitable prize they expected.

With a start, I saw Prince Andric sitting on a dark brown horse near the right side of the starting line. I hadn't expected the Crown Prince of Antor to ride with us, but given his relationship with the Antoran citizens, I shouldn't have been surprised. I still felt embarrassed about my eavesdropping and didn't know how to face him. He glanced down the row of horses toward us. I ducked behind Pantim and pretended to check his hooves for rocks, then swung up on the horse's back a few seconds before the whistle blew.

My body remembered Pantim's gait. I gripped with my knees, and let my body sway with the horse's rhythm. It was very different to ride the horse at a full-out gallop, and turned out to be easier than the bone-jarring trot through the mountains.

It was immediately evident that Pantim loved to run. He wasn't built for it like the horses my father and the other kings bred on the plains, but he threw himself into the gallop across the snow. He held his head low and pushed hard. His breath came out in short clouds of steam in the crisp air. His hooves easily maneuvered the snow-covered rocks and branches, and I was grateful for his sure footing. I couldn't help laughing at the simple joy of racing, the feel of the air rushing past my face, stealing the breath from my mouth, the thunder of the hooves which pounded in my bones.

We didn't win the race, but we weren't far behind, either. Drade and Sorn won, which wasn't a surprise to anyone, followed closely by a young girl on a big black horse, and Andric on his dark brown one. We waited for the others before dismounting, walking the horses to cool them down. I kept my distance from the Prince and instead joked with Drade along with several other riders he had beaten.

After the other riders had finished, Andric held up his hands. The crowd grew immediately silent. Trevin, Kaerdra, and the other Crowns stood near the wall trying to look impassive about the proceedings, but it was obvious by their attention that they were also interested in what the Prince would say. Though I had received several glares from them after the rest, Kaerdra and Brynna especially, I knew several of the boys had secretly longed to participate. I wondered what Rory would say about me racing with my captors.

"I've thought long and hard about an appropriate prize for the winner," he said. His dark eyes danced. "And who would have guessed it would have been Drade?"

A laugh went up from the crowd and several people slapped Drade on the back. He chuckled good-humoredly with them, but his eyes stayed on his prince, his expression a mixture of chagrin and curiosity.

"Allow me to retrieve his reward," Andric continued. He disappeared into the nearby stables and left the Antorans to speculate. When he returned carrying a little pink pig wearing a big red bow in his arms, I burst out laughing. The audience laughed even louder.

The Horsemaster accepted his prize with an affable grin that grew wider when his little daughter ran up and held out her hands, her face lit up like a tiny sun. He sighed and put the little pig in her hands, much to the enjoyment of the onlookers.

"Great, now he'll have to be a pet," Drade grumbled with a long-suffering smile.

His wife, a blond-haired, rotund woman smiled back. "We'll just add it to the menagerie."

Andric laughed and patted him on the back. "Well won, Horsemaster. Although, I don't know how fair it is for the rest of us to race against the one bonded to the other horses."

Several others shouted in good-natured agreement. "That's alright," Andric said loudly, winking at Drade. "If it was a wolf race, we would have had a different ending."

Amid laughter and cheers, the crowd made its way toward the castle to warm up in the banquet hall. Fires had been stoked to roaring in all of the fireplaces, and with the sun-warmed bricks, the hall was toasty and comfortable. The tables had been moved to the sides to leave the middle floor wide open. A string band was already there, and at Andric's cue, they struck up a merry tune.

Tisha, Landis, and I made our way to one of the waiting tables. Soon, the other Crowns joined us. "Enjoying yourself a little much here, don't you think?" Kaerdra asked brusquely.

I fought back the urge to drop my eyes and met her gaze honestly. "I've grown up racing horses. We're stuck here until Spring, so I don't see the need to withhold from participating in a little familiar activity while we wait."

Landis' eyebrows rose. "You've gained a bit of bite being here," he pointed out.

A blush rose to my cheeks and I shook my head, but he cut me off. "A good ruler acts not according to the dictates of others, but in line with the premonitions of his or her own heart. You don't have to defend yourself to Kaerdra."

The Princess of Cren glared at him while the others stared. Appreciation swelled in my heart and I gave him a smile of gratitude. He smiled back and turned to Tisha who grinned at me from his side. "Would you like to dance?"

The Maesh Princess' cheeks blushed red. "I don't know the steps to this song."

Landis smiled encouragingly. "Me neither; we'll improvise."

She smiled and accepted his hand. With a laugh, the Prince pulled her to her feet; they hurried to join the circle that was spinning in time to the catchy tune.

Trevin glanced at me furtively. I grinned, for the moment happy and content. "Don't worry," I reassured him, "I'm bushed after that race. Your toes are safe."

It was true. Racing with Pantim had taken more out of me than I thought. I wondered if it had more to do with the brief, strange contact I had experienced. I could still picture the galloping hooves churning up the snow from the horse's point of view. It confused me, but I didn't want to consider the implications.

"I can't believe they're enjoying themselves," Kenyen grumbled next to me.

Danyen elbowed his brother. "Oh, lighten up." He rose and bowed to Kaerdra. "Would you care for a dance, my lady?" She gave a small smile and accepted his hand, and without looking in my direction, she joined the others on the floor.

Trevin glanced at me and then quickly turned to Brynna. "Care to join me?"

To my relief, Kenyen sighed and asked Nyssa to dance as well. I was happy to not be stuck with his sulking while the others spun around the dance floor.

I sat back against the table and watched the others attempt to learn the complicated steps. Trevin and Brynna picked it up quickly, while Landis turned out to be a very accomplished dancer. He coaxed Tisha through the steps until she was confident enough to join the circle. The other two couples spun to the side of the main group, making up their own dance instead of learning the foreign one.

A servant brought over a cup of red punch, and I sipped at its fresh, crisp taste. Before I had a chance to finish the glass, though, a fair-haired young man in his twenties stopped in front of me. His cheeks were bright red and his hands shook slightly with nerves. He clenched them into fists in the hopes that I wouldn't notice and gave a low bow, his eyes on the floor. "Would you like to dance?" he asked in a nervous, hopeful voice.

115

I didn't hesitate; I took his hand and smiled at the surprise on his face. "Yes, thank you!"

I had never been one to turn down a good dance, as bad as I was at it. Thankfully for both parties involved, it turned out that my feet were better suited to the quick steps of the Antoran melodies than the long, graceful strides and twists of the regular Denbrian dances.

I turned from one partner to another throughout the evening, resting only long enough to grab some refreshments before being asked for the next dance. It was a strange, refreshing feeling to have young men, and some older ones, asking for dances in advance instead of me lingering around the outside of the dance circle hoping no one noticed that I stood out. Each person was a stranger when we started, but we laughed like friends by the end of the evening.

I let my guard down and forgot to worry about impressions and propriety. I realized afterwards it was those fears that had made me a bad dancer; too much concentration and worry messed up my steps more than my own clumsiness. I talked and joked lightly, and the men I danced with responded in like terms, as if we realized we were dancing just to dance, and were able to lose ourselves in the enjoyment of the evening.

I began to feel guilty as the dancing wound down. I wondered how close my letter was to Zalen, and how my parents would react when they got it. I wondered how they would feel if they knew I danced with the same people who had kidnapped us. I tried to console myself with the thought that they would be happier I was dancing than if I was held hostage in some prison, but it didn't help much. The other Crowns retreated back to their chambers as the evening waned. Though they kept to themselves and I felt their stares on me as I danced with common Antorans, I no longer cared

116

what they thought and had the most enjoyment I had ever experienced at a ball.

Finally, when my feet felt like they were ready to fall off and the punch could no longer chase the weariness from my limbs, I bid my last partner goodnight and left the hall filled with light, cheer, and more friends than I had ever had in Zalen.

Chapter 12

Starlight filtered down amid the stones and lit the walkways in twilight. I walked slowly up the stairs and along the hallway, enjoying the hush after the cacophony of the crowd. I had almost reached my door when I made out the form of a lone figure wandering slowly in the darkness with one hand trailing along the wall.

I almost ducked into my room anyway, passing the figure off as a stray partier, but something about the way he walked caught my attention. There was an air of loss about him, a searching cast to the way he peered down the hallway.

"Are you alright, sir?"

He paused and turned, uncertainty in his step. He merely looked at me.

I couldn't see his face in the shadows. I walked closer. "Are you lost?"

He nodded. "Yes, I think so."

My eyes widened at the voice of Prince Andric's father. I hesitated for the briefest second, then continued up the hallway toward him. "King Fayne, Sir?"

He nodded. "Yes, may I help you?"

I fought back a smile at the sudden concern in his voice. "Actually, I was wondering if I could show you to your rooms."

"Well." He paused and looked around, his brow creased with confusion. He wore a dark green robe and soft, black slippers. "This definitely is not my rooms. I seem to have misplaced them," he concluded with a nod.

I crossed the remaining space between and gave him a warm smile. "I might know where they're hiding. Allow me to lead the way, if you please."

He looked down at my offered arm, and his tired brown eyes, a few shades lighter than Andric's, lit up for the briefest second. "Thank you, my lady. It's been a while since I've had the pleasure of walking with a young woman. My wife's been away for so long, I fear her ships have been delayed."

I nodded and led the way back down the hall. "It must be the ice," I said, remembering Andric's words from the night before.

The old King nodded in agreement. "It's been a cold winter, and I fear it will get colder before the spring comes."

My stomach clenched at the statement and I changed the subject. "It's a beautiful castle you have here. I've never seen stones like these."

King Fayne nodded with a reminiscent smile. "My ancestors mined them out of the mountains; that's how they found the Elder diamonds. Building this castle out of white marble was the smartest move they made. It's beautiful, keeps us warm in the winter, and," he gave me a conspiratorial wink, "It's great for defense." He smiled as if we both knew what he meant and patted my arm. "It'll keep those beastly Breizans from getting to those we hold most dear."

The name sent a shiver up my spine. I led him down the stairs and along the hall. The brief glimpse I caught of the banquet hall showed that most of the revelers had retired for the night, leaving only the castle servants to tidy up for the coming morning. I thought of how long I had danced and wondered how soon morning would be. It couldn't be that far away.

We turned up another flight of stairs, the one I had accidentally gone up the night before. "Did you see the races today?" I asked him.

"Hmm?" he glanced over at me as if he had forgotten I was there. "Oh, um, no. Those are games for ghosts, now. I find myself better if I keep to my rooms." His brow creased again. "Which makes me wonder how I got into this predicament."

I smiled at him. "My mother sleepwalks sometimes. She finds herself in the oddest places." I fought back a laugh at a sudden memory. "One night, I wasn't tired and went for a moonlit walk in the gardens only to find her pruning her beloved roses in her sleep!"

King Fayne chuckled, a cheerful, hearty sound out of place with his slightly confused, lost gaze. "I'll bet those roses were lovely."

I sighed. "They would have been if she hadn't pruned the bushes into the shape of a rabbit in her sleep. And it was one of her favorite species of rose. It took her a long time to coax anything to grow from it again after that annihilation."

He laughed out loud. "I'll bet she kept her sleepwalking to a minimum after that."

"She did, actually!" My throat tightened unexpectedly at the thought of her.

"Where are you from, little ghost?" the King asked amiably as I opened the door to his rooms.

"Zalen, Sir, south past the mountains."

He continued to hold my arm, so I led him into the room and to his bed. He sat against the pillows and pulled the thick blankets up to his chest. The expression on his face was childlike and trusting. "That's a long way from here. What brings you to Antor?"

"Your son," I replied quietly, remembering how enthusiastic the Prince had been when he had explained the kidnapping to his father the night before.

The King frowned thoughtfully. "I don't recall having a son."

The words sent a pang through my heart. "Andric is a wonderful person. He cares so much about your country, and seems to care more about your people than he does for himself."

"Sounds like he'd make a fine ruler someday. I'll have to meet him."

"Yes, Sir," I replied. I tried not to sound as sad as his words made me.

I turned to go, but he called out, "What's your name, little ghost?"

"Kit, Sir," I replied. I turned back to him. There was something pleading about his voice, as if he didn't want to be alone. I went back and sat on the chair that waited beside the bed. I could picture my mother in the same place in Rory's room. I tried to see myself sitting at my father's bedside, his own memory faded and expression confused. I shook my head to chase away the thought. "My real name is Kirit, but my family's called me Kit since I was little."

He thought about it and then nodded. "I like Kit. It suits you."

I smiled, hoping it was a compliment. I was about to ask him something else when a voice near the bed startled me.

"How are you doing, Sir?" The tone of the question, though, was directed toward me. I looked up to find Andric watching me, his dark eyes guarded.

"Well, very well." He tipped his head to indicate me. "I found myself quite lost, and this little Kit helped me get back to my rooms." He winked at Andric, though there was no sign of recognition in his eyes. "She even let me hold her arm."

Andric gave a short, careful nod. "That was very kind of her. I'm glad that you're safe."

The old King nodded, looking tired. "I'm waiting for my sweet Maritha, though Kit feels her delay might be due to the ice." He yawned. "In which case, she might have to wait until spring for the floes to break."

"I'm sure she's safe, wherever she is," Andric said quietly. I stood and took a few steps away so Andric could reach the bed. He helped his father settled in so that he was lying down with the blankets tucked around him.

King Fayne closed his eyes. Andric stepped back and tipped his head at me, indicating that we should leave the room. As I reached the door, the King said faintly, "Good night, little ghosts." He then mumbled softer to himself, "I must get someone to look at the ghost problem in this castle."

Andric shut the door quietly. I noticed then that the wolves, all five of them, had followed Andric to the King's room and waited by the door. They watched me now, their gazes steady.

The dark gray wolf I had met earlier in the snow along the wall touched my hand in greeting. In that split second, I saw the hallway through the wolf's eyes, the glowing light of the laced bricks, the shadows lighter than what I was used to; scents I didn't detect in my own body were identified and cataloged by his brain as swiftly as his nose sorted through them. The sound of a tiny mouse scrabbling up a beam inside the floor seemed loud to my ears.

"Kit. . . Kit?" My hand dropped and I was brought back to my own senses to find the Prince staring at me.

"Are you alright?" he asked in concern, his eyes searching mine.

I shook my head, then stumbled when the movement threw off my equilibrium. Andric caught me, his arms steady. "You need to sit down somewhere." He glanced around quickly, then led me to a smaller chamber a few rooms down, his arm around my waist in case I stumbled again. I could hear the wolves following us, and wondered if the gray one was as confused as I was. I risked a peek and saw that all of them were watching me.

Andric helped me into a soft armchair that sat in a pool of moonlight spilling through the window. "Is that better?"

I nodded. "Yes, thank you." His eyes were stormy when I looked up at him. He met my gaze for a moment, then turned away.

The Prince paced once around the room, then stopped by the window and stared out. After a moment of silence in which I nervously toyed with the hem of my dress, he turned back to me. "Thank you for helping my father."

"I would do it for anyone," I said. Another wave of dizziness swept through me and I put a hand to my head to stop the spinning.

Andric was immediately at my side. He knelt down so that he could look into my face. "Are you sure you're alright?" he asked.

I blushed, embarrassed, and turned away. "I'm fine," I said. "Just dizzy, that's all. Must be from all the excitement today."

Andric watched me for another minute, then rose and took the seat across from mine. I looked up to see him shake his head. "I didn't mean for the journey to be so stressful for all of you. It wasn't fair of me to put you through it." His eyebrows were pulled down, the anger directed at himself. "If anything happens to the Crown Princes and Princesses of Denbria because of my selfish wants, I will never forgive myself."

"Your selfish wants?" I replied in surprise. "I haven't seen you do a single selfish thing since we left Eskand."

He glanced at me, his expression guarded.

I stumbled over my words in an attempt to explain myself. "Y-you say you do this all for yourself, but you're really doing it for us. I've seen the looks your people share, and I know the truth of what you say about Antor's demise. You're trying to hold a lost country together, and you're doing it all by yourself." I couldn't help glancing toward the room where his father slept.

Andric closed his eyes and rubbed his forehead. It was the most unguarded action I had seen him do since the night I stitched up his sword wound. He sighed and spoke with his eyes still closed. "You make my actions sound so noble, but they're not. I try to do my best, but it's not good enough. We'll still have to walk away from Antor come spring, and my people will be scattered all over Denbria in search of a new beginning. Nothing I do now can change that."

I frowned. "From what I've heard, this started way before you became the leader of Antor. This isn't your fault, and you're left holding the bag."

A slight smile drew up one corner of his mouth. "You have a funny way of putting things."

Chagrined, I shot back with the first thing I could think of, "Well, your country has a funny way of celebrating."

His smile grew bigger. "Is that your comeback? You're going to have to work on that." He laughed at my reddening cheeks, then frowned thoughtfully. "You do dance well, though."

His comment caught me off guard, and my heart gave a strange sideways thump. I couldn't think of a response.

At my silence, his expression changed. He put his elbows on his knees and leaned forward; his eyes bored into mine. "You're different from anyone else I've ever met." His tone made it sound like that wasn't such a bad thing. "You," he paused and dropped his gaze to the floor as if he expected the right words to be written there. Exasperated, he finally looked back up at me. "You don't take people for who they are, or look for what they are hiding, you take them for who they could be, who they want to be."

It was my turned to be confused. I didn't know if it was a bad thing or a good thing, and if it was bad, how I could change it when I didn't even know how I did it.

Andric must have read my expression because he gave a little smile and spread out his hand, palm up, as if offering me a token. "Take the dancing, for example. You danced with many Antorans tonight who never dreamed they would ever have the opportunity to dance with a princess, and you changed their lives because of it. And I know it didn't cross your mind once that you made my people feel as if you held them in the same regard as you hold the other Crowns who didn't venture to dance with anyone but themselves once the entire night, even to the point of turning down offers."

I gasped, surprised that the other princesses would refuse after the courage it took for a young man to even ask.

Andric smiled, nodding as if I had proven his point. "The Antorans you danced with will remember tonight for the rest of their lives. I doubt you ever judged them as common countrymen, miners without even a mine to work. You treated them like equals."

I finally forced myself to speak. "It's something I never learned in Zalen, the propriety of rank. My mother tried to drill it into me, afraid that someone would take advantage of who I was." I sighed and shook my head. "It never made sense to me to judge someone by where they'd been born in life, or what circumstance forced them to do."

Andric nodded again. His brown hair hung loose around his face; I wondered when he had taken it out of his usual warrior's tail. "That's what I mean. Those of us who have been born to lead, trained so from birth, were never given the luxury of taking people at face value; but you go beyond that. I've seen it in the way you treat the other Crown Princes and Princesses, the way you treat those of my people who are bonded with animals, and the way you've treated me." His voice fell soft at the last part, and he turned to stare out the window at the dark winter night.

I didn't know what to say. I frowned as I puzzled it out. I looked up and saw that he was watching me again. Embarrassed, I tried to change the subject. "How's your back? I'll bet you haven't let Jesson look at it."

It was Andric's turn to look chagrined. "He's been so busy with the wounded soldiers that I haven't wanted to bother him. But it feels fine, thanks to your stitching."

"Let me see." I said it as more of a command than an offer.

Andric grimaced ruefully. "Give you an inch, huh?" But he obeyed and turned in his chair so that his back was to the moonlight streaming through the window.

When he lifted up his shirt, I was surprised to see how well the wound was healing. The stitches held true, and though the wound still looked sore, there was no telltale angry redness surrounding it to indicate infection. I touched it gently and was relieved to feel that it wasn't hot.

He lowered his shirt and grinned at me. "See, I'm a fast healer."

I sat back in my chair. The small, dark gray wolf I had touched earlier came to sit at Andric's side. The Prince rested a hand casually on the wolf's head, his thoughts elsewhere. Mine wandered tiredly through the experiences of the last few days until Andric's expression sharpened and he turned to look at me.

"Tyd says he thinks he touched your mind, like he does with me."

I looked at the wolf, reluctant to admit what had happened. The wolf met my gaze. I felt very tired, and longed for the comfort of my bed. Still, I nodded unwillingly. "Something like that."

He sat up straight, heedless of how it must tug at his shoulder. He had raced today without any sign of pain. He was stronger than me in so many ways that I would never be able to meet for my own country; it made me feel inadequate, especially under his searching gaze.

"Animals seldom bond to more than one person," he said slowly, his face troubled.

I shook my head quickly. "It wasn't a bond, or anything like that. It was more like a brief passing hello, nothing concrete. I felt the same thing with Pantim today before the race."

The Prince's eyes widened. "You touched minds with a horse, too? No one's ever been able to touch minds with more than one species, and definitely not casually, as you describe." He looked over at the other wolves in the room who lounged in various places along the cool floor. "Would you mind trying it again?"

I was more than reluctant now that the strangeness of the action was pointed out. I didn't like feeling odd and under scrutiny for something I shouldn't be able to do. It made me extremely self-conscious. "Maybe it was just a fluke."

"Then we have nothing to lose by testing it. Do you mind?" His tone was encouraging.

I couldn't say no to the eager expression on his face. "Fine, I'll try it."

Freis came and stood in front of me. Her tail waved slowly from side to side as if she, too, was trying to encourage me. I held out my hand, hesitated briefly, then set it on top of her head.

Immediately, I could see the room from the white wolf's point of view. The moonlight that streamed in through the window illuminated it sharper than I saw with my own eyes; the lines in the marble stood out as bright streaks, like I had seen with Tyd.

The scents were strong, filling the room with a pattern of smell that seemed almost as tangible as the light. Andric's scent was one of the outdoors, of the mountains, the salt of the nearby ocean, and of the stone of the castle as if it permeated his very being.

I was surprised to smell myself, also, and to have my scent categorized in the wolf's mind as one of the plains, grassy, light, and with a slight touch of the plants I had often used for healing; I could also smell sunlight as the wolf classified it, warm, golden, and full of life. It made me miss the warm summer, and I was amazed that all of the time I had spent outdoors in our country had actually branded itself on me the same way it had lightened my hair and tanned my skin. It was a part of me.

I could smell the horses we had ridden, and not just categorized as horses, but by each individual horse from which the scent came. They didn't have names in the wolf's mind, but they had shapes, outlines, and traits. It seemed that Pantim was known for stomping testily at the wolves if they got too close to his mare, while the dark horse Andric had ridden loved to run, and didn't care if they joined him.

I found that the wolves could also smell emotion, a fact which surprised me. Freis smelled my uncertainty, weariness, and a sharp loneliness that made me sad to have it revealed; Andric, on the other hand, had a sense of calm, of confidence, but also contained a small hint of uncertainty that I never would have guessed was there.

Freis changed her thoughts so that she showed me a memory from long ago. She was a scared, young wolf, muzzled and caged in a wire kennel with a blanket thrown over it that smelled of dirt and men. She had been captured from her country, a land of mountains with peaks so high they were lost in the clouds, and trees wider than a man was tall. They had cornered her in a ravine, and shot her with arrows that pricked like pins and made her fall asleep. When she awoke, she was in the cage tied down against the rocking of the ocean.

By the time they reached solid ground, she was sick and disoriented. The men who threw her food were scary and foreign, though I recognized Falen's scent among them, set apart now through better memories. She had been taken to what she now recognized as a small sitting room in the castle, and left to rest there until the stones under her paws started to turn light with the day.

When the blanket was removed, I looked into the face of a very young Prince Andric. His dark eyes were lit with curiosity, and his hair was shorter and wavy. It fell into his eyes and he brushed it away impatiently as he knelt to open the cage door.

"Be careful," King Fayne's voice cautioned from a corner of the room.

Andric nodded. Freis' attention turned to the dark gray wolf at his side. The wolf stared at her with the same curiosity in his eyes that was on the Prince's face. There was no hostility there. Freis could tell by their scent that she had nothing to fear from them. The young boy reached a hand through the cage. She hesitated, then touched it with her nose. Colors, never a part of her visual spectrum before that moment, filled her vision. She blinked. "You're safe here," she heard Andric's voice in her mind, and knew immediately that she could trust him.

Freis ducked from under my hand, bringing me abruptly to the present. A wave of dizziness swept through me and I almost fell off my chair. Strong arms were suddenly there to support me.

"She thought it would be too much," Andric said quietly, leaning me back. "Looks like she was right."

I tried to open my eyes, but I was so tired that they felt like weights instead of mere eyelids. My head spun even with my eyes closed. I heard footsteps leave the room. A cold nose touched my hand, the head resting on me knee. It took a great effort, and a bit of courage, for me to move my hand so that it rested on the wolf's head again. This time, no thoughts swept through me.

The footsteps returned quickly, almost at a run this time. I heard water poured, then a cool glass was put against my lips. "Drink," Andric urged. I was touched by the concern in his voice and obeyed.

Fresh water flowed soothingly down my throat, reviving my senses. I sat back and opened my eyes. The spinning lessened.

I heard the Prince sigh in relief and looked over to see him standing in front of me, the glass held so tight in one hand that his knuckles were white. He offered me the cup again and gave a small, forced smile when I accepted it. He sat back down in his chair, his arms on his knees and his eyes on my face. "Maybe that wasn't such a good idea," he said quietly, his voice strained.

I shook my head, then put a hand to it and closed my eyes. "It's alright. We had to know." I was more concerned with the fact that it was real than with the side-effects. "What does it mean?" I hated how small my voice sounded.

I heard Andric shift in his chair. "I don't know. I've never heard of anyone who can communicate with animals like that without a bond. No one else I've met has been able to touch minds with someone else's animal."

I opened my eyes again, more worried this time. "Is it a bad thing?"

Andric's brow creased, but he shook his head. "No, definitely not a bad thing. In fact, the possibilities could be amazing."

"How do you mean?"

"We don't know what limits you have, but if the dizziness that comes with it is just a side effect that you can get over with time, then you could communicate with anyone's bonded animal."

The thought worried me. If just the rumor that Antorans were able to talk to animals caused such suspicion and fear in the rest of the Denbrian countries, what would happen if anyone found out about me?

Andric seemed to guess my thoughts. "Don't worry," he said quietly. "I won't tell anyone. It'll be up to you if you choose to let anyone else know." He glanced down at Freis' head resting on my knee. "Of course, the animals you talk to might tell their humans, so be careful."

I nodded and smoothed the hair on the white wolf's forehead. She closed her eyes under my fingers. Tiredness made it hard to think of the walk down the hall and stairs, then up the other flight of stairs to my room, but I knew I couldn't stay. I didn't belong in the King's wing anyway, and wouldn't want anyone to question Andric's actions.

"I'd better get to bed," I finally forced myself to say. I rose slowly to my feet. Freis moved to stand at my side. I wavered slightly, and saw Andric reach for my arm to steady me. "I'm fine," I told him with a tired smile. I made my way carefully to the door, then turned back.

Andric was standing by the chair I had just vacated. His face was silhouetted against the window, so I couldn't make out his expression. "You know," I said to him honestly, "I didn't expect to find a friend here."

I turned and left the room. The white wolf stood in the doorway and watched me make my slow way back down the long hall.

Chapter 13

I slept late and was the last one to breakfast the next morning. Andric had arranged for the Crown Princes and Princesses to have a private breakfast in a small, sunlit room on the second floor overlooking the practice grounds. The grounds were empty, and I realized I had slept through the morning practice. By the time Kimber showed me to the dining room, the others had already started eating. Bayn and Freis rose and greeted me with slowly waving tails, sniffing my hands in welcome. I felt the other Crowns' curious gazes on me as I made my way to the last empty chair.

"Welcome," Andric said to me with a formal bow. The other Princes rose and bowed as well, but with less formality. I hoped the traditions would be discarded soon, if only so their little slights wouldn't be quite as noticeable.

Andric sat after the rest of us and smiled at me. "I was just explaining to the others the arrangements we've made for your comfort here." His food sat untouched before him. "You're free to do whatever you'd like while you are here. The only thing I ask is that you take at least one ride through the city a day to see the state of things." Kenyen and Danyen rolled their eyes at each other. Andric must have caught the look, too, because he spoke a bit sharper, "You will have the opportunity to do anything you would like for entertainment. Everything in my castle is at your disposal, the dance hall, instruments, horses, hawks, painting, sculpting, the forge, needlework and materials, writing implements, and the library. I have also arranged for any activities you might desire to do, so horse racing and some of my best warriors are available to practice with." His eyes tightened just a bit. "All I ask is that you work with the animals under their handler's supervision, and that you try not to wound any of my warriors when you duel."

Danyen turned to Trevin and said in a voice loud enough to carry, "Well that defeats the purpose of practicing."

Andric's jaw clenched as he fought back a reply that probably wasn't fit for a princess' ears. I hastily turned to Kaerdra who sat on my left side. "Would you like to paint with me after breakfast?" The Crenan Princess was renowned for her artistry, and I hoped it would be enough to give me a break.

She hesitated, studying me; then, finding no reason to doubt my offer, she nodded. "I would enjoy that. It's been a while since I've had the pleasure to do something befitting a princess."

Andric ignored the obvious jibe. I was thrilled when the other girls offered to come as well. Perhaps it wouldn't be such a bad morning. I knew I didn't imagine the look of relief on Andric's face when Landis tactfully asked if they could have a tour of the forge. Andric winked at me when nobody else was looking, and I smiled despite the blush that colored my cheeks.

After breakfast, Kimber showed us up two more flights of stairs, down a long hallway, and into an eastern-facing parlor that was lit up like gold from the rising sun streaming through the wide glass windows. Easels already spread with canvas were waiting beside little jars of paint; several of the jars held colors I had never seen before. Kaerdra and Brynna were the most eager to begin, and picked positions closest to the windows. The rest of us took what was left and began to paint goofy pictures of each other.

By the time we were done, Kaerdra had painted two beautiful masterpieces of the sun rising over the stone and brick town, Brynna had artfully created a very good likeness of her own palace back home, and Tisha had painted one of Ayd's hawks. Nyssa and I exchanged rueful smiles about our own attempts, which looked like children's finger paintings next to the others.

When they saw my effort to paint Trae, which ended up with his head so big he looked like he would tip over at any moment, they tried to be civil and polite. But Nyssa's endeavor to paint a ship on the ocean, which would have looked better if a fish spit up on her paper, had us all holding our sides and laughing.

Everyone was smiling and joking by the time we made our way downstairs. We changed into riding clothes, and then met the boys in the small dining room for a quick lunch. Andric wasn't present, and I found myself watching the door for a sign of either him or the wolves while we made plans to ride out that afternoon to fulfill the Prince's request.

It was nice to see how the morning's activities had lightened everyone's mood. We ate a pleasant lunch of bread, rich, creamy butter, light cheeses, pieces of beef and turkey breast, and an assortment of dried fruit topped off with cold milk. We munched eagerly and I listened to them chat while we ate.

The Princes, it turned out, had also had a good time at the forge. Landis started to describe the sword he had asked the smith to make, and the others chimed in about the weapons they were having created as well. The Smith told them he would shape the swords for each them, but they would have to do any detail work on their own.

Trevin spoke in a low, gravelly voice that I assumed was a decent representation of the Smithy by the grins on the other boys faces, "The final touches are what make a sword your own. Learning every nuance of your sword during the forging process is as vital as the hours upon hours spent practicing with it. It'll be an extension of yourself if you let it, but you must know every inch as well as you know your own hands in order to trust it fully."

The others laughed, even Kenyen. I was surprised to see him in a rare good humor. He turned to Nyssa. "So, how'd the painting go?" That started the girls off laughing again.

Then an idea occurred to me and I blurted it out without thinking. "How about we switch activities tomorrow?" The laughter stopped and everyone turned to stare at me. I could feel my face turning red, but didn't let them cow me into taking back the suggestion.

"I'm not very good at painting," Landis said finally, breaking the silence.

Brynna scowled. "Me, in a dirty forge? Never."

"What, afraid your sword won't be any good?" Trevin teased. I stared and he winked mischievously at me. My astonishment grew when he continued, "It's sad you Princesses are only good for the women stuff."

Brynna bristled, Nyssa beside her. "I can make a sword better than you."

"Yeah," Nyssa chimed in. "Then we'll have a duel."

Trevin's eyes widened and he exchanged a worried glance with the other boys. "I don't think we need a duel."

"Yeah," Danyen protested. "That's going a little too far."

"Afraid our swords'll be better than yours?" Kaerdra asked, the challenge in her voice unmistakable.

Kenyen stood up and shook his head. "This is silly. We won't fight you. It wouldn't be proper."

Brynna snorted. "Since when are you worried about proper?" She sighed dramatically. "It didn't stop you last year in the garden."

Kenyen's mouth fell open with the rest of ours. "Nothing happened!" he protested, looking at us.

Nyssa shrugged. "I don't believe you. You're going to have to prove it."

Kenyen sputtered. "I. . . uh. . . Who's going to train you?"

"Kit," the three girls said together. They turned and looked at me expectantly. I glanced at Tisha who stood to one side and she gave me a small shrug.

I immediately began to regret my suggestion to swap activities. I looked back to see the boys watching me as well. Their looks of apprehension would have made me laugh under different circumstances, but now they made me nervous. I had really gone too far this time. "Alright," I finally breathed.

"Yeah," the three girls cheered; Tisha nodded her head once as if she had known I would do it.

"Fine then," Kenyen said with a worried frown. "We'll give you a month."

"That will be fine, since we've nothing better to do," Kaerdra replied dryly.

A tap at the door followed by a steward's entrance into the room broke the growing tension. "If you please," he said with bow. "The horses are ready."

Landis groaned. "Not more horses."

I followed him out of the room with a small chuckle. I wasn't the only one still sore after the long journey.

I was the only one who had raced yesterday, and surprisingly, I felt pretty good despite a few aches. With Trae recovering, I was surprised to see that Drade had given me the dark brown horse Prince Andric usually rode. Tereg sniffed me thoroughly and then accepted me without any problems. I swung up and realized that I was getting more comfortable in the saddle.

"Stinky, smelly horses," Nyssa muttered behind me.

"I always smell like a stable after riding one of these things," Kaerdra agreed. Her horse, a light brown one with extra-long, shaggy hair, crow-hopped to one side and almost dumped her off. She shrieked and clutched frantically at his mane.

Landis urged his horse up to where Tisha and I sat on Pantim and Tereg. "You'd think the animals could understand them," he said quietly with a wink.

Tisha and I laughed when Nyssa's mount shook itself and she had to grab at her saddle to stay on.

My heart rose when Falen rode through the gate of the courtyard toward us. His hand was still wrapped from the battle, and I suddenly felt guilty. I hadn't thought once how the other soldiers were doing after the Breizan attack. They had defended us with their lives and they deserved better. I promised to ask him how they were before the day was out.

The Captain bowed low to our group without dismounting. "We have several options for today's ride. We can view the older housing district, take a trip to the mines, or go to the house where Prince Andric is working to refinish a roof before the next snowfall."

"Which one is the closest?" Nyssa asked, shifting uncomfortably in her saddle.

Danyen gave a snort. "Who taught the Prince how to refinish a roof?"

Falen turned an unruffled gaze on the Prince of Tyn. "King Fayne wished for his heir to be sympathetic to his people's needs, so Prince Andric was trained since he was young in hands-on tasks like roofing or fencing to judging the proper punishment of a citizen who has committed murder. After the passing of the noble Queen, the Prince carried on with his father's wishes and trained in every form of labor required of his people."

"What happened to the King?" Trevin mused out loud.

Falen threw me a quick glance, but he didn't reply to Trevin's question. He turned his horse instead and started toward the gate.

"Where are we going?" Kenyen demanded, a bit agitated at the Captain's refusal to answer the question.

"You doubt the good Prince's ability, so you'll have the chance to join him if you'd like," Falen said over his shoulder.

The rest of us fell in behind him at the mercy of our reinless horses.

***

The house they worked on was small and cozy, and in between two even smaller houses. As we drew near, I smiled at the sight of the Antoran Prince working beside his countrymen. Andric climbed down from the unfinished roof to meet us. He wore a short-sleeved shirt and rugged pants, and had put his cloak aside despite the cold winter air. There was sweat on his brow and his cheeks were flushed. He smiled at us in welcome.

"There was a fire here while we were gone," Andric explained, indicating the house behind him.

"It seems that the trip was hard on more than just us," Kenyen commented darkly.

Andric nodded, ignoring the other Prince's scowling countenance. "A spark from the fire somehow made it to the roof; luckily, they were able to stop it before it spread to the other houses, but the house has been uninhabitable without repairs. We're rebuilding the roof and repairing the fireplace so this doesn't happen again."

Now that he was closer, I could see that the Antoran Prince's face was smudge with soot, and he had ashes in his dark brown hair. My heart gave a little jump and I frowned at myself.

"Is something the matter, Princess Kit?" Andric asked.

I looked into his perceptive dark eyes and shook my head quickly. "No, I was just imagining losing everything to a fire in the middle of winter. That would be hard." I tried my best to make my tone sincere.

"It would be hard," he agreed. A covert glance showed that he didn't believe my little fib, but he brushed it off. "The Kasan family has been living with friends and family for the past few weeks, but they deserve to have their own place back." His expression grew troubled. "We're running low on building supplies, so we'll have to hope that we don't run into any more fires this winter."

Falen spoke from the position he had taken beside the Prince. "And if fires happen, accommodations will be made available. We have very giving citizens."

Andric nodded. "Very much so." He turned back to the house. "We're currently swinging the rest of the lumber to the roof, then we'll cover it with straw for insulation, tying it to the wood for support and to keep everything in place."

"What's that?" Landis asked. He pointed to a large wooden contraption that looked somewhat like the depictions of dragons I had seen in the books in Father's library. It had two main front support beams and a long back beam that went to the ground where it met the planks that were attached to the front two. Two boulders the size of small cows rested on the back to weigh it down against the weight of the wooden beams that were being levered up to the roof by a system of pulleys managed by three well-muscled men. The entire contraption pivoted on a large base that squeaked as it swung around toward the house.

"My father and his men designed it long ago to make building a lot easier. It saves time and backs," he concluded with a hint of a proud smile.

"It's neat," Kenyen said begrudgingly, he dismounted and walked closer to get a better look. He began to question the three men who worked the contraption, and Danyen walked over to join them.

The rest of us followed Andric to the side of the house where piles of wood and straw lay ready to be hoisted. He looked up at the roof and then back at us, and I could tell he was a little unsure of what to do. He opened his mouth when a shout behind us made everyone turn. We jumped out of the way just in time to dodge a pile of wood that came loose from the pulley system.

"What happened?" Andric asked. Danyen and Kenyen both mumbled apologies from where they stood at the ropes.

"Rookies," Falen said with a shake of his head. He, Andric, and several other people began to pile the wood back together to be lifted again.

I jumped in beside them, eager to be of assistance. Several of the Antorans threw me questioning glances, but I just smiled at them. It felt good to be outside working again, even if it was in the freezing snow in the middle of winter doing manual labor that I wasn't used to. I could tell by the look on Andric's face that he wanted to protest, but he knew by the expression on mine I wasn't going to listen.

By the end of the day, I was on the roof helping to tie down the cords of straw as they were settled into place. It was one of the lighter jobs that Andric had maneuvered me into doing, and for which my tired muscles were secretly grateful. Danyen and Kenyen had finally gotten the hang of the pulley system after only two more spills; they now guided the straw over to where Andric and Trevin waited on the roof with several other Antorans. Landis was working with Falen to bundle the straw, and Tisha labored stoically alongside him despite his protests.

Even Nyssa, Brynna, and Kaerdra finally gave in. They were in the little houses on either side helping to clean the sparse furniture and possessions that had been saved from the fire. Once in a while, Kaerdra came out with Jesson's wife, Isea, and gave everyone water. I hadn't seen Jesson anywhere and wondered if he was still tending to the wounded soldiers. Isea's little ferret ran up and down the building with an ease that I think everyone envied by the end of the day.

Various other animals provided assistance in unique ways. Two crows carried us long strands of twine that men below cut when we ran out. A squirrel chattered constantly as he made his way across and under the almost completed roof; he then conveyed to his human, a tall, red-headed fellow with mismatched eyes, any weak spots he found in the insulating straw. A little white mink went in with the cleaning crew while we worked on top and I wondered what he could do until he came out covered in soot; it occurred to me that he would be very handy in helping to clean the hard to reach places. My favorite animal to watch was a big black bear that helped scrape bark off of the new beams of wood with his strong claws before they were put into place.

Andric's wolves were always around. Though they couldn't assist much with the house, they did provide entertainment when the small dark gray male and the black male got into a play quarrel and spent an hour chasing each other all over the grounds. Men debated which one would win, though the chase ended when both wolves tumbled full speed into Bayn. He only had to show his sharp white teeth to sober the younger wolves up immediately. I caught a gleam of humor in the wolf's eyes as he chided his pack for their frivolousness, reminding me greatly of a proud father tending to reckless children.

By the time the roof was finished, our hands and faces were numb and it was dark enough to require torches, but no one wanted to leave until the Kasan family was moved back into their house. By that time, the saved furniture was ready, and other furniture had been donated by various families to replace what couldn't be saved. The beds were put in place on the freshly scrubbed stone floor, a small dresser, table, and three chairs were set up, and pots were arranged by the newly mortared fireplace.

An accomplished pride shone on the faces of all the Crowns as we surveyed our work. None of us had ever done anything like this before, and I knew we would all put it in our letters home. The thought of home made me anxious to hear from Father and see how everyone was responding to our absence. I longed for word of Rory, and hoped he didn't blame himself because he would have been the one here in Antor if he hadn't gotten sick.

I wondered how it would be if I hadn't been the one in Eskand. Somehow, though we had only been in Antor three days, it felt like things had changed so much. I could see it not only in myself, but in the other Crowns as well.

I shook my head and chided myself for being foolish. I was tired and I doubted much change could really happen in the time we had been gone from Eskand. I couldn't believe that it had only been eight days since we met under the tree by the Eskand castle wall. But even though I tried to tell myself it was only my imagination, I felt different from the girl who stood alone by the shadows that night.

The Kasans gave everyone warm hugs of gratitude. Several of the Crowns returned the hugs awkwardly, and it made me smile to see their walls come grudgingly down. It would have been hard to ignore the smiles of excitement and shrieks of joy that made up the three children's reaction to their new home. Mrs. Kasan couldn't say thank you enough, and her husband regarded the Princes with such obvious awe and appreciation they each gave him formal bows of respect.

We rode back to the castle with grumbling stomachs, and I realized only after we left the house that we had worked through dinner. I wondered if it went on without us at the castle, and if the Antorans wondered where everyone was. Then I realized that the prominent people I had seen at the first dinners had all helped at various times with the house. It amazed me how much the citizens really did work to help each other. I wondered if the same camaraderie existed in Zalen. It opened my eyes to see the inner workings of a kingdom in a way I had never realized existed. I promised myself to take a closer look at my own city when I got home.

Falen rode next to me on the way back to the castle, and I asked him how the soldiers were that had been injured by the Breizans.

"They're recovering," he said with a smile at my concern.

"And the two on the stretchers?"

"Much better." He winked at me. "Nothing a lot of love and pampering from their wives couldn't help."

I laughed. "Please give Jesson my well wishes and offer my services if he needs any help."

Falen nodded. "As you wish, Princess."

He left us at the courtyard and bid us a good night.

Chapter 14

After a brief, delicious dinner of cold turkey, potatoes, and spiced pumpkin milk that chased the chill from our bones, everyone retired to their rooms. I was the last one out of the dining room and was making my way slowly up the stairs when I heard hear my name called. Surprised, I turned to see Andric standing at the base of the stairs.

He had been quiet all through dinner, and I passed it off as exhaustion because he had worked far longer on the house; but now, by the preoccupied look on his face, I realized he had just been biding his time. I made my way back down the stairs and sat on the second to last step facing him.

"Tired?" he asked with a kind smile.

I nodded. "Yes, but happy. It was a good day."

Relief flooded his face, chasing away shadows I hadn't realized were there until they vanished. "Really? You had a good time?"

I smiled up at him. "Is it so hard to believe? I had a great time painting, though I'm so unaccomplished at it they need to make a new word for what I do, like plunking, only worse." I grimaced at the thought of my picture of Trae, and saw an answering grin on Andric's face. "You saw my picture?" I asked in horror.

He nodded. "It was pretty bad." He laughed and danced out of the way to avoid my slap. "Well, almost as bad as mine on a good day," he put in to appease me. At my expression, he turned serious again.

"What?" I asked.

He slid down the wall so that he sat at the base of the stairs and looked up at me. "What else did you like about the day?"

146

"Why do you want to know so badly?" I asked curiously. We were already here and couldn't leave until spring. What did it matter to him if we enjoyed ourselves?

He shrugged and studied the wall across from him. "I don't know. I guess I feel guilty and want to make sure that the stay isn't too miserable for all of you."

I stared at him a moment, realizing this was truly important to him. I thought the day over. "Well, I really did have a good time painting with the other girls, although I didn't think I would." His look asked me to explain, so I continued, "They don't know what to do with me, really. I don't fit in, but I think they're alright with that now. I think they realize that it's alright if I'm not like them, and I hope they can see I'm not trying to fill Rory's place."

I swallowed and continued quickly, "It sounds like the boys also had a good time at the forge designing swords. I made the mistake of suggesting that we swap activities tomorrow to give everyone a challenge."

Andric stared at me. "You did?"

I nodded, chagrined. "Yeah, and they actually accepted."

His eyes grew wider. "They did?"

I had to laugh. "Yeah; can you imagine the Princesses in the forge designing weapons? I feel bad for your sword smith."

Andric laughed too, a pleasant sound. "Hensas will be beside himself when you girls walk in. I should probably warn him."

"It gets worse," I admitted. I couldn't meet his gaze.

"What?" he pressed in a cautious tone.

I took a deep breath and rushed forward, "Somehow, Nyssa and the other girls challenged the boys to a duel when the weapons are done and we've had a chance to train." I swallowed. "And they talked me into training them, though I don't know the least bit about teaching."

He was quiet for so long that I stole a glance at him. His brow was lowered, but he had a small smile on his face.

"What are you thinking?" I asked carefully.

He looked up at me. "I was just thinking that you'd make a good trainer. The skills you showed when we were attacked by the Breizans were first class." His dark eyes sparkled in the moonlight that drifted from the high slit windows.

He was teasing me, but was serious at the same time. He truly thought that I could train the girls. "I still don't think it's a good idea." I sighed. "But I gave my word so now I'm stuck. I can't figure out how they got me involved."

Andric laughed. "Princesses are pretty wily. They learn a lot more than just sewing."

I laughed with him, then sobered, realizing the fact that they had weaseled me into agreeing was proof I didn't know much about the wily side of being a princess. I turned back to our conversation. "My favorite part was helping with the house. I've never done anything like that before."

Andric nodded thoughtfully. "I didn't know if I should stop you for fear that you'd hurt yourself." At my look, he chuckled. "But I realized you wouldn't really give me a choice in the matter. I was happy to see everyone else get involved, even though the twins almost killed us a few times with that pulley."

I nodded. "The best part was when the Kasans got to move back in. Did you see how happy they were?"

Andric nodded. "They needed that. It broke my heart when I found out they'd had a fire while we were gone." His brow creased. "They lost a son in the last attack with the Breizans we had a few months ago. It was a hard battle, and more were lost than in any other attack. With fewer supplies and some families already gone to make their own way, it's getting harder to defend our small country."

He took a deep breath and held it for a few seconds before letting it out slowly. I could see how much this ate at him. Loathing crossed his face, hatred for his inability to do anything to save his people.

"You didn't do this to them," I whispered.

He turned and stared up at me, his expression hard.

"This isn't your fault," I continued. "You're holding together the shattered remains of a country that someone else handed to you."

"Someone else?" he repeated, his tone sharp. "That someone else was my father and my grandfather. They were able to keep this kingdom alive and prospering, well supplied through the diamonds that were mined."

"Diamonds that are no longer there, which is something you are not able to fix. The same thing would happen to us if all of our ships were lost at sea, and to Tyn and Veren if the plains caught fire. It would happen to Maesh if their herds became sick, or to Cren if the trade stopped. Things happen and there's no way to prevent them."

Andric was quiet, and I could tell by the look on his face that he didn't believe me. I knew I wasn't going to win the argument. "Fine," I relented. "You believe what you want, but your people look up to you and respect you in a way I haven't seen in any other country. You must be doing something right."

I rose to my feet. "Good night, Andric. It was a good day, and I look forward to another one."

"Good night, Kit," he said quietly. He looked at me, but I could tell that his thoughts were elsewhere. I made my way slowly up the stairs to my room. When I undressed and climb into bed, it was a long while before I could sleep.

***

I wasn't the only one who was sore in the morning; muscles I didn't even know existed ached when I bathed and eased into a dark green dress assisted by the ever attentive Kimber. She already had a bottle of one of Jesson's ointments waiting, and the scent of mint, wintergreen, and lavender filled the air as I rubbed it into my sore muscles. The oils started working immediately, and though I smelled like a sweets shop, I felt much better by the time I made my way to the breakfast room.

I wasn't the last one there this time, and I wasn't the only one that smelled of Jesson's healing oils. We grinned at each other sheepishly over our bodies' protests at the simple act of dishing up food. I think we all were becoming conscious of what a sheltered life we really lived.

We watched the Antorans practice below; their unison grunts and calls of command made an interesting clamor around the quiet table. Instead of bristling with contrived thoughts of ambush or attack, the boys watched the training Antorans as much as I did, talking quietly about different forms and movements they recognized. I realized we were missing a valuable opportunity to teach, and a way for me to see how to train; I made a mental note to have the girls down there the next morning without telling the boys.

As planned, we were guided to the forge by Andric who met us at the door at the end of our breakfast. A steward took the guys to the painting room, and I knew it wasn't my imagination that put the small smirk on his face. I saw answering embarrassment on the boys' faces and a slight heightening of color in their cheeks when they passed Prince Andric, but I had to give them credit for accepting what they said they were going to do instead of shirking due to its feminine nature.

The forge was nestled close to the castle wall past the hawkery and stables. Already, we could hear the ringing of an anvil through the crisp morning air. When we entered the wide front doors that were open to the rising sun, the scent of a roaring wood fire, hot iron, sweat, and an amazing amount of heat met us.

We blinked as our eyes adjusted to the suddenly dim interior countered by the hot raging fire in a fireplace that took up most of the far wall with various bricked ovens. I was surprised to see at least eight people working at the forge. Most were engrossed in their activities and didn't look up when we entered.

Only one large man that I guessed to be the sword smith came forward to greet us, though I don't know if I would call it a greeting. He wore a large leather apron that went down below his knees and thick gloves wrapped with leather that were scorched in various places and colored black with use. He scowled at us as if annoyed that we were interrupting his work with our presence.

Andric gave him a respectful nod. "Good morning, Smith Hensas. I appreciate the time you've allotted for the Crown Princesses. I know that their knowledge of sword making is limited, and so would appreciate it if you would fill them in on your methods."

The sword smith nodded, but it was clear he wasn't happy with the request.

Andric gave him a small smile. "Only the methods you want them to know. I promise that they won't be taking your secrets home with them." The Prince turned and left. We bunched together, feeling out of place in the dark workshop.

Smith Hensas stared at us for a moment with his massive arms crossed on his chest. At our timid glances back, he finally cracked a smile in a face that seemed little used to such an expression.

"Who ever heard of princesses in a forge?" he asked more to himself than to us. He shook his head and his shaggy black hair flung sweat in all directions. "Fine then. If this is the way it's going to be, then you might as well learn something while you're at it." He turned and motioned with a massive hand for us to follow.

Despite the chilly morning we had just left outside, sweat broke out on our faces as we drew near to the fire. A boy about ten years old pumped a giant bellows to heat up the forge. He was covered in soot from head to toe, but grinned at us shyly when we drew near. Another man heated a long bar of metal in the fire, the tongs in his gloved hands glowing red where they held the iron. The constant ringing came from a tall, skinny man who worked on a silver hilt, rounding a groove out of it so that the user's hand could fit comfortably and be protected from other blades.

"As you can see," Smith Hensas explained, leading us to a quieter corner, "It takes more than a sword smith to make a sword. I could spend all of my time taking a sword from a misshapen chunk of iron into a beautiful, deadly weapon, but I've found that giving the grunt work to the grunts saves a lot of time." He winked and chuckled when several of the men within hearing protested. "Aw, stuff it," the Smith shouted in a good-natured roar, obviously accustomed to being heard over the roaring fire and ringing anvils. "Given the big picture, everyone's just a grunt. The goal is to be good at grunting." The other men laughed and turned back to their work.

"Sorry about that, ladies," he apologized as if just remembering we were there. He turned and pointed out the men. "The two by the fire are the strikers. They forge the blade when I have it prepared. The bear-like man next to the bear is our grinder." I looked where he indicated and realized that the big black mass in the corner was indeed the bear we had seen at the roofing the night before. He snored next to a man even bigger than Smith Hensas who sat at a big stone grinder. Another boy worked next to him pedaling a small wheeled contraption that in turn spun the grinder.

"Maes, our cutler, crafts the hilts according to the wielder's grip size and what the weapon will be used for. We then send measurements to Saren, the tanner, to create scabbards so that they're ready the same time as the swords." We must have looked surprised because he laughed, "What, you thought we simply pounded a piece of metal into a sword and we're done?" He chuckled. "We'd all be out of a job if that was the case."

There was a hint of pride in his voice when he continued, "Our setup surprised even some of your young Princes. I think they'll be writing home some notes on how to improve their forges. Although," he said with a shake of his head. "It won't help if they don't have a good smith, and I've got all the best here."

The ringing ceased when Maes stopped to inspect his work. I forced myself to speak up in the silence. "This place is amazing. Thank you for letting us come."

He grinned. "I hope you're still saying that by the time we're done. Forging is a lot of work; it takes time, patience, and someone who's not afraid to get down and dirty." He looked us over pointedly and I could tell that he doubted our ability to get dirty. I think I actually heard Brynna shiver at the thought of it.

"Alright," Smith Hensas said as he lead us over to a flat board propped up on two big barrels that served as a table. "The first step is to decide what you want. Most of the blades we fashion here are smaller than the average blade you'd find south of the mountains because they are used by both men and women, and because iron is getting a bit scarce in these here parts." He opened a rolled sheet of paper that had been wrapped in oilskin to keep it from the harsh forge climate. Spreading it out on the table, he indicated a series of drawings.

We all leaned in, and I know I wasn't the only one surprised to see the skill with which the variety of swords had been sketched. They ranged from short swords no bigger than daggers with crossed handles, to a sketch of a huge axe better suited to defend against the long extinct dragons than to be of much use in battle. A box had been drawn around a sword in the middle of the page; I recognized it as the type the Antorans used in practice every morning.

"Your Princes were a bit, shall we say, flamboyant with their picks. They're used to having the finest weapons already available to choose from." He gave an exasperated shake of his head. "It took me some time to convince them that the months it would take to create such a weapon would defeat the purpose of having one available." He smiled wryly. "They eventually decided on some more conservative blades with the promise that they could do their own scroll work under Maes' supervision." He shrugged. "I never saw much use for such details on a sword besides maybe a good blood groove, but that's also used to give strength to longer weapons."

He walked away to leave us to our decisions and I turned back to the page. The swords that had been sketched were practical, not something normally commissioned by a prince or princess. That struck a good chord with me and I chose a sturdy short sword much like the ones the Antorans had been using. The only difference was a lighter handle that I thought would fit my grip better.

The other girls chose similarly, though I could tell they were put out by the lack of options. Smith Hensas appeased them by allowing them to help design their hilts under Maes' direction. He also said that Tanner Saren would let them choose their design for the scabbards. "It'll take a few days to finish making the blades; we forge the iron together with a type of metal that we were fortunate to find in our mountains. It's stronger than iron, and when we forge the softer iron in the middle and this ore on the outside, it holds an edge much longer and is more supple." He frowned sternly, "Which is an Antoran secret."

We promised not to tell, though it was obvious he didn't believe us.

"Then Bagan will do the grinding, which takes another couple of days, especially with the number of swords we'll be working. The days you ladies are here you'll be with Maes to make sure the hilts fit your hands. They'll then have to be fitted to the blade. Our goal is to come out with well-balanced, sharp swords that you can wield easily."

"What do you do?" Nyssa asked a bit haughtily, still nettled that she had been denied an intricate, but useless, lady's sword. At her question, several of the men around the forge guffawed.

Smith Hensas silenced them with a single look. His tone indicated that it was a foolish question. "I do the initial shaping and mixing of the metals, an art I've practiced since I was a six year old apprentice at my father's knee. It takes time and skill to mold the softer iron in the middle of the blade for flexibility, and edge the sword with the stronger ore to give it strength. If done incorrectly, even the strongest looking sword will give under a direct blow, and its edge will hold only until the first strike."

He looked around at his men. "Without me, these oafs'd have nothing to do." They laughed and he grinned good-naturedly.

He brought us over to the fire to watch one of the men take a heated sword out of the forge and carefully rub red clay along the main body of the blade, leaving the edge bare. He then thrust the blade into a tub of cool water. Steam swirled up and the metal sizzled as it cooled.

"What does the clay do?" I ask curiously.

The man turned to look at me; he had a thick black beard trimmed close to his jaw and dark smudges under his eyes. "The clay prevents the body of the blade from chilling too quickly; it lets the metal cool evenly and makes it that much stronger." His voice had a thick, strange accent. I wondered if he came from across the ocean. I was glad the others had the courtesy not to ask.

A servant came to the door and announced that lunch was ready. I was surprised at how quickly time had passed, and saw the others' raised eyebrows as well. Apparently I wasn't the only one who had enjoyed our time at the forge.

We thanked Smith Hensas, promised to return soon to help with our swords, and crossed the threshold into the bright day. We blinked at the sudden light. Clouds had formed while we were inside, and tiny flakes drifted down. "Looks like another storm," the servant said quietly. I thought he was talking to himself until I noticed the small dog that trotted at his side. The animal sniffed the wind and wagged his tail as if in agreement.

Chapter 15

Andric met us at lunch this time. He gave me a smile and I wondered if he felt better after our talk last night. The boys came in laughing and covered in different colors of paint. Kenyen blamed it on Landis, but Landis, Trevin, and Danyen pointed their fingers at Kenyen. They were eager to hear about our experience at the forge; we kept the details to a minimum, unwilling to give away any hints about the swords we were having made.

"Was Smith Hensas good to you?" Andric asked.

"Very," I said. "He taught us all the basics."

"Yeah," Kaerdra cut in. "We might know even more than you guys."

"I doubt that," Trevin told his sister. "You forget that we were at the forge, too."

"Yes," Nyssa said, "But do you think a sword smith is more likely to share his secrets with princes who might use them in their own countries against his people, or with princesses who probably won't remember."

Trevin's eyebrows rose. "Did he?"

Brynna nodded. "But we promised not to tell, and a princess knows how to keep a secret."

"She does?" Kenyen put in skeptically.

They bantered over lunch and avoided Kaerdra's suggestion that we compare paintings, for which I was grateful. Thankfully, the steward had taken the initiative to hide our creations from less than sensitive minds; though I doubted anyone would think a princess had painted mine or Nyssa's.

"The Kasans have invited you over for dinner in their home," Andric said as lunch drew to a close. He said the invitation carefully, but everyone took the news eagerly. I think we were all anxious to see how their new roof was holding up under the few snowflakes that had fallen. Though we did the work to the best of our ability, we still doubted that a family could live comfortably under a roof we had helped build. It would be good to see it for ourselves.

"Are you coming?" Landis asked. He directed the question at Andric.

The Antoran Prince studied him carefully. "I figured you might want to go by yourselves, after what you accomplished."

This time, Kaerdra was the one to speak. "You have as much right as we do to go; plus, you're their prince and should be there to make sure everyone is doing well."

Andric nodded, his face carefully expressionless. "Alright, I'll be there."

A tap on the door caught our attention. The atmosphere changed immediately when Ayd came in with sealed letters in his hand.

Andric didn't wait for anyone to speak. He rose smoothly and excused himself, saying that he had things to attend to.

I broke the seal and opened the letter Ayd handed me. A small pit had formed in my stomach. Glancing around, I saw that the others weren't as enthusiastic as they had initially been upon seeing the letters. I think we all felt a little guilty about having a good time in Antor, like we should be angry and intractable instead of painting, making swords, and helping to improve Antoran houses.

I went over to the window to read my letter. Father's concise handwriting filled the entire page.

> My dearest Kit,
>
> I can't tell you how worried I was when I found you gone. I didn't have the patience to wait for King Trand to organize his army and I

left before the others. By the time we found the trail, you must have been gone over a few hours. I pushed Megrath almost to death trying to catch up before you entered the foothills.

Your message in the snow calmed us down. You probably guessed that by this point, we were getting very irrational. We knew that if we didn't get to you before you reached the pass, you'd be stuck, so we pushed even harder, foundering two of Trand's horses.

When we saw you in the foothills, we thought we would make it in time, but then we saw the Breizans closing in. I would never have believed it if I hadn't seen them with my own eyes. We tried to reach you before the avalanche, but we were too far away. We thought we'd lost you all."

The words were a bit harder to read, and there were a few splotches on the paper. It made my heart ache to know that I had caused Father so much pain. I forced myself to read on.

I didn't know what to tell your mother and Rory, but I didn't have to say anything. Prince Andric's letter reached home before me, and your mother was furious and worried sick at the same time. She had the palace upside down before I got there, and I thought she was going to kill me by the look on her face. When I read what Prince Andric wrote, I was furious. I doubt his intentions, and even though you seem to believe them, I beg that you be careful.

I skimmed the rest of the letter anxiously. Mother had written quite a bit below Father, and I could tell how worried she was by her sharp letters and briefly ended sentences. She always wrote so elegantly that her writing portrayed more than her words.

Father wrote how troubled he was, stressing again and again how careful I needed to be and to not trust anyone. He said that carrier pigeons were coming in from all of the other countries faster than he could keep up with them. Apparently, the other Kings and Queens were looking to him, the oldest ruler, to guide their actions. He said he was hard put to convince them that trying to storm the mountain while the pass was closed would be of no avail, and the ocean would be gridlocked with ice for months, impassable by ship.

He said that I needed to look after the others, that their constitutions were such that they weren't used to this kind of situation and might not handle it well. He warned me that they might be as irrational as their parents, and to be prepared for anything. He trusted that I would be able to take care of myself, a statement that made me feel warm inside. But despite all that he wrote, it was the things that he didn't say that became more and more obvious.

Father didn't answer any of my questions about Zalen's involvement in Antor's situation, and he didn't answer my pleas for an update of how Rory was doing. The last one scared me more than anything. My eyes started to burn and I blinked to keep back the tears when I realized that no news meant he was probably getting worse, otherwise they would have told me.

"Well that's just great," Kenyen growled. He slammed the letter he and Danyen had been reading onto the table.

Trevin, who was frowning at the letter Kaerdra held, asked, "What?"

"There's nothing they can do. We're stuck here until the pass clears." He pointed at me. "At least, that's what your father tells them."

I bristled, already upset. "You doubt my father's intentions? He's the smartest of them all and they know it."

"He's the oldest," Tisha replied calmly from her chair by the table. "It's right that they would go to him for advice." She looked over at me. "When did you have time to leave a note?"

Some of the others nodded. "My father mentioned it, too," Landis said.

I shrugged and blushed under their stares. "The second day. I wrote with a soot-covered stick on a rock by our camp to let them know we were alright. I knew they'd be worried."

Kaerdra gave a small smile. "That was brave. Father said knowing we weren't hurt really helped them calm down."

Brynna scowled. "But they're right. We need to be more careful. We can't trust that prince."

Danyen nodded in agreement. "He's still a thief."

I stared at them, amazed at their sudden change in thought. "But we know his intentions. He's not keeping us in the dungeon or feeding us moldy bread and rice. He made us rooms in his castle and has seen to it that we are comfortable and as happy as possible."

Trevin rose from the table and shook his head. "Who knows what his real intentions are. We're still stuck here because of him, and our parents are the ones we need to listen to, not you. I'm not trusting the thief prince and I advise you all to do the same."

"He took a sword for your sister, Trevin," I reminded him darkly. "He risked his life to save ours, and said that he wished it hadn't turned out like this."

"Tricks," Nyssa said with a grimace. "He's crafty, like my mother says."

"Your mother doesn't even know him," I pointed out.

"Neither do you," Kenyen said. He closed the distance between us, talking in a careful, even tone. "Because Rory is my friend and I respect him, I recommend you steer clear of Prince Andric. If Rory was here, he'd have this situation under control and not be the friend of the person who kidnapped us and brought us here for who knows what reason."

"He told you his reasons," I argued. We stood face to face now, and I knew I should back down but I couldn't. "You're just too stubborn to see it."

He shook his head. "No, I'm too smart to be fooled by his excuse that he brought us here to teach us how to work together in ruling our countries." He said the last bit in a poor impression of Prince Andric's careful, even tones.

"Why does everyone have to have a secondary motive?" I forced myself not to crumple the letter I held.

Kaerdra rose from the table. "People aren't as perfect as you think they are, Kit. Everyone has other intentions than what they show. You have to learn that if you're going to be a good ruler."

I grimaced and felt tears begin to burn in my eyes. "Why does everyone assume that I want to be a ruler at all? Rory is the Crown Prince, and he will rule our country, not me." Angry at myself for the outburst, I stormed from the room. Tears spilled down my cheeks as I ran down the hall, heedless of the stares of servants.

I didn't pay attention to where I ran, I just wanted to get away from everyone and find a place where I could make sense of the swirl of thoughts clouding my mind. I went to where I would have gone at home, the highest point of the castle.

It wasn't hard to find stairs leading up. A castle built for defense like this one usually had many routes to the roof; the stairs I followed were wide and unadorned to prevent weapons from catching on unnecessary decorations. I pushed open the door at the top. A light skiff of snow dusted the roof, fallen either earlier today or last night and not yet brushed off by the servants.

A swirl of biting winter wind stole my breath, but I stepped onto the roof and made my way to the parapet. It wasn't until I looked out over the short, rocky hills at the base of the towering mountains that I realized I was still clutching the letter. I took a deep breath and forced my hand to open. Father said I was always so level-headed. I was angry at myself for losing my temper; I was also angry at the other Crowns for their stubbornness and the ease with which their parents' opinion of what was happening here swayed them against Andric. Just moments before, they had almost been friends.

Most of all, I was angry at the fact that my parents hadn't answered my questions, making me doubt their actions. I had been so sure that Zalen would have had nothing to do with the state Antor was in, but now I wasn't sure and that shook me. And they didn't once mention Rory. The fear that filled my chest made it hard to breathe.

I was surprised when I heard the door open behind me, but one glance told me I shouldn't have been. Our palace had eyes in all places; of course this one would be the same way. I turned back to study the mountains again hoping my face was somewhat more collected than the emotions that filled me.

"I take it I shouldn't go to the Kasans' tonight." Andric's voice was light, but forced. His feet crunched on the snow as he walked to stand beside me. He put his elbows on the parapet and stared out at the jagged black mountains.

The spark of anger rose in me again, but I forced it back down. I wasn't used to being so volatile, and I struggled to check my emotions. "You should do whatever you want. This is your country, not theirs, and you know why you're doing what you do."

Andric turned to look at me. I pretended not to notice and instead concentrated on a particularly rugged outcropping of rock that looked like the claws of some ancient creature stretching toward the sky.

When I didn't turn, I heard him breathe out forcibly as if he had been holding his breath as he contemplated what I hoped was my emotionless profile. "You really do care, don't you?"

Something in his tone made me turn. His brow was creased and his left fist was clenched on the parapet. "I shouldn't have brought you here, any of you. This was a bad idea."

In a move that surprised me even as I did it, I reached for his fist and opened it, emptying the snow he clenched onto the ground. "It wasn't a bad idea, just one no one understands. I'm trying, but even I am having a hard time of it." He didn't answer. I felt a thin line across the back of his hand and turned it over to get a better look. A white scar ran from the base of his wrist to the beginning of his middle finger. "How did you get this?"

"Breizan attack on the castle," he replied, his words soft.

I shook my head. "I don't know what I'd do if that happened while we were here."

"You did marvelously at the pass. Someone would have gotten hurt if it wasn't for you."

I frowned. "You and some of your soldiers did get hurt."

He nodded. "You know what I mean. You did well and shouldn't worry so much about how things are going to be in the future."

My eyes filled with tears again. "They didn't tell me how Rory's doing."

Andric hesitated a moment, then said, "I know you worry about him every day you're apart."

I dropped his hand and traced random shapes in the snow. "I worry so much, and their not telling me isn't protecting me. It's so much worse not knowing."

He let out his breath again slowly. "You know what they're doing, don't you?"

"No."

He set his hand in the snow, watching the way the soft white powder formed around it. "They're treating you like a daughter, not a Crown."

I shook my head. "I don't get the difference."

"Do you think they would give Rory an update if you were in the same situation he is?" He asked the question quietly because we both knew the answer. Of course they would.

Andric gave me a moment of silence for the implications to sink in. A Crown would need to know about her sibling's failing health; a sister would be protected against her brother's illness. My parents were treating me as their daughter, not a Crown Princess. It made me feel better to know that my parents still thought of Rory as the Crown of Zalen. A weight lessened in my chest. "You should come to the Kasans' house," I said. My tone must still have been a bit more defiant than usual because a slight smile tugged at his lips.

"You trying to prove something?" he asked.

"Just that the Crowns need to realize it means more to the Kasans that you're there than it does to them that you're not. Their parents are trying to turn them against you. Changing plans would just make them more suspicious and destroy all you've accomplished."

"You think I've accomplished something?" This time, Andric was the one staring out at the mountains and carefully avoiding my gaze.

I nodded. "Just wait. This will all be worth it in the end."

Chapter 16

Before we left for the Kasans' house, I wrote a letter back to my parents. I told them how much I missed them, and reassured them that things were still alright here. I then asked Father pointedly what involvement Zalen had had in Antor's present condition, and if he knew what the other countries had done as well. I told him honestly that the information would help me be better able to handle the situation here. I also begged both he and Mother for word of Rory, letting them know that it was harder not to hear anything at all.

I gave the letter to Ayd on my way to the stables to help Drade ready the horses for the ride. Trae whinnied when he saw me and trotted over to bump his head against my chest. I laughed and rubbed his ears.

"His leg's getting better," Drade reassured me. He chuckled. "He's jealous that you're using a different horse."

"Don't worry, Trae," I told the animal. "As soon as you're better, we'll go riding." As I ran my hand through his thick, tangled mane, an image of racing headlong through a long, winding valley full of huge, twisted black boulders came to my mind. I glanced up at Drade, worried that he knew his horse was talking to me.

He gave me another friendly smile, his eyes sharp. "It's a beautiful valley, one of our favorites. When he's healed, we'll have to go there."

I nodded with a knot in my stomach. "Drade, I. . . ."

"I know," he cut me off. "Don't worry. I won't say anything."

I thanked him gratefully and left, my heart pounding. If anyone else knew? I shuddered away from the thought and made my way to where the others waited.

Andric wasn't there, but I took comfort in the fact that his horse, Tereg, was gone as well. Drade had saddled a blond mare for me to ride, and she stepped gracefully through the snow as though she was the princess. She didn't send me any images when I ran my hands through her soft fur, but I could feel her contentment and let myself absorb as much of it as I could.

The celebration at the Kasans' house was noisy and full of cheer. So many Antorans showed up that their neighbors opened their houses as well. They served simple but well-seasoned food, and there was plenty of spiced pumpkin milk and hot chocolate to keep the chill off us as we danced in the snow to lively tunes.

The Crowns grumbled at Prince Andric's appearance, but they got over it quickly enough when they realized their attitude wouldn't chase him away. He simply treated them with perfect respect and though he didn't converse with them for more than a few minutes at a time, the conversations were civil.

Everyone was exhausted but happy by the time we went home that night. The festivities had chased away most of the solemnity brought on by our parents' letters insomuch that the boys actually invited the Prince to ride home with us instead of later like he had planned in order to give the Crowns their space. Andric rode near the head of the group, and though he didn't speak to anyone, he threw me a slight smile when they weren't looking.

***

The next few days passed uneventfully while I waited for my next letter to arrive from Zalen. Both the Antorans and Crowns were surprised when I had the girls join me at the morning practices. Andric, though, was as smooth about it as he was with everything else. He handed us a couple of practice swords that were lying nearby, and some of the Antorans graciously fell to the back to give us a spot near the front of the lines.

When the boys saw we were accepted so easily, they came out as well. I teased them about fearing we would become better than they were, but I think they could tell how worried I was about the upcoming duel and took it in good humor. They might have laughed a bit loud when Tisha asked if Andric had anything lighter than the wooden swords, and scoffed when Brynna kept tripping over the long dress she had chosen to wear that morning, but everyone took the jesting good-naturedly and some of the Antorans even took time afterward to help the girls with their stances and grips.

When the birds finally came back with responses to our last letters, I accepted mine from Ayd with a nervous pit in my stomach. We had just finished morning practice and took the letters to our rooms to read as we changed for the day's activities.

I scanned the letter and saw that Father had indeed answered my questions about Zalen's involvement with Antor, but that didn't matter to me. I turned the letter over and saw that both he and Mother had written briefly about Rory.

"Rory's condition is slowly getting worse. We didn't want to worry you because there's really nothing you can do from there," Mother wrote, "Don't worry, honey, everything is going to be alright. Rory will write you when he gets feeling better."

A lump formed in my throat. I just had to know. Without thinking past an immediate course of action, I left my room and ran down the stairs. The steward opened the door and I dashed out across the snow to the hawkery. I was glad to see Ayd there. He stared at me as I caught my breath and wondered how to phrase my request.

"May I. . . May I talk to the bird that brought my letter from Zalen?" I asked him. I was aware of how the words sounded when they left my mouth.

His brow lowered slightly. "I think the real question is, *can* you talk to the bird," he replied pointedly.

At my nod, his eyes widened a bit. "I have to touch the bird, I think." I wasn't sure of my own abilities. Andric had pretty much implied that it shouldn't even work, and I wasn't positive it would.

Ayd looked over his shoulder and a beautiful brown and black hawk flew over to land on the perch closest to us. The bird cocked its head and regarded me speculatively with golden eyes. "Go ahead," Ayd said with quiet curiosity. "His name is Rush."

I reached my hand out toward the bird, then hesitated.

"Don't worry, Princess, your secret is safe with me," the Hawkmaster reassured me. I smiled at him gratefully and he grinned, gave a short bow, and left us in privacy.

The hawk clicked his beak and waited for me to move. I shook off my sudden nerves and set a hand gently on his back. The feathers felt soft under my fingers, and it was a minute before anything came to my mind.

Ayd must have told Rush why I was here, or at least why he guessed I was here, for the hawk's first vision was of our palace as seen from above. The image was amazingly bright and clear, the colors and lines sharper than I had ever seen them. I could make out the minute textures of the palace walls even from so far above. He dove and it grew closer at a surprising pace. At the last minute, the hawk banked and soared up to a third story window which I recognized with a quickening heartbeat as Rory's.

The window was closed, but when the hawk rapped on it with his beak it opened immediately as though someone inside had been waiting close by. The shutters parted to reveal my father. He looked tired but hopeful as he swung the glass inward to allow the bird entrance. A small bowl of water was waiting on the table next to the window, and my father pushed it closer so the bird could drink while he untied the letter I had sent.

The bird took a quick drink and glanced sideways so he could see my mother sitting next to Rory's bed. Her hair was undone; she wore a robe and looked as though she had spent several nights without sleep. My heart gave a painful thump at the sight of them both, but it wasn't my parents I was anxious to see.

As though Rush knew all along that I would come to him for this memory, he turned to stare directly at Rory's bed against the far wall. My heart slowed. The hawk's keen eyes took in the shallow rise and fall of the blanket pulled up to Rory's chest. A sheen of sweat stood out across his pale forehead, tangling his dark brown hair. His mouth opened and he moaned softly, weakly, as a shudder wracked his entire body. Mother rose and bathed his forehead with a damp washcloth; tears slid slowly down her cheeks.

I dropped my hand and the memory vanished swiftly. Rush gave a soft sound that I thought was meant to be reassuring. I smoothed the feathers I had ruffled though I couldn't see his back through my tears. He nuzzled my hand with his beak. I whispered thank you, then turned and ran out of the building.

I was wrong. It was worse knowing, so much worse to see my brother wasting away to nothing with my parents standing by helpless to do anything against the sickness that destroyed him. I stumbled through the door a steward kindly opened and ran to the stairs before he could ask any questions. Trying not to think, I ran down the hallway and up the next flight of stairs. I reached the roof sooner than I expected and opened the door to the biting cold that I embraced as a welcome distraction from the pain that tore at my heart.

Barely minutes passed before the door opened behind me. I wasn't surprised when I turned to see Andric there. He looked concerned, worried, as if the reports he had been given didn't prepare him for my tears. He took one step toward me and I buried my face against his chest. "Kit," he said quietly; his arms hesitated, then closed around me.

"He's dying, Andric. Rory is dying and I'm not there with him," I sobbed. "He's supposed to be the Crown, not me. He loves the people, he cares so much, and he always knows what to do." The tears came faster now and were absorbed by Andric's soft shirt. "He can't die, Andric. He's my brother. He's supposed to get better."

"I wish you could be there," Andric replied softly, his voice full of guilt.

I shook my head against his chest. "It wouldn't matter. I can't stop the sickness, no one can. They've tried everything." Another sob forced its way past the knot in my throat. "I just don't want him to leave me. I can't do this alone. He's the one who was meant for all of this."

Andric spoke quietly into my hair. "Write to him, Kit. Tell him how much he means to you. You know that your parents will read it to him. It will mean a lot to him to hear from you, and you'll be able to tell him what he means to you." He breathed softly, stirring my hair. A hitch caught his voice as he continued as if experience echoed in his words, "Everyone deserves that, and now might be the time he needs it."

Andric's words made sense to me, and as he said them I felt a pressing need in my chest to do just that. I nodded and he stepped back and waited quietly for me to wipe the tears from my cheeks. "You're right," I said in a tremulous voice. "I'll write him right now. Do you think Ayd could send the letter immediately?"

Andric nodded. "I'll see to it." He studied me a second, his eyes unreadable. "Will you be alright?"

I nodded even though I wasn't sure myself.

His eyes tightened in concern. "I'll meet you back here."

I nodded again and left the roof, intent on my room.

Tisha saw me in the hallway and took in my tear-stained cheeks and red eyes. "Are you alright?" she asked quickly. She gave me a hug without waiting for my answer. "It's not so bad here," she said. "I think our parents don't understand because they aren't here."

"I know," I tried to reassure her, sniffing back more tears before they could betray me. "Things will be alright."

She smiled and walked me to my room. "Are you going to sew with us tomorrow?"

I shook my head. "I've never been good at stitching. I think I'll head to the forge to see how the swords are coming along."

"Alright," Tisha replied with a grin. "Please check on mine. I think Smithy Hensas is going to be upset I haven't been by in the past couple of days."

"I'll let him know you asked me to check up," I said as I opened my door.

"Thanks, Kit." She paused. "And remember that you always have someone to talk if you ever need it."

"Thanks," I told her with a rush of gratitude.

She smiled and continued down the hall.

I shouldn't have been surprised to see a quill and fine paper already waiting on my nightstand. Andric's servants were quick and efficient. I smiled slightly to see that Kimber had also left a small plate with two pastries saved from breakfast. I took a bite to calm myself, than picked up the quill and dipped it in the waiting ink bottle.

The words came as quickly as I could write them. Before I knew it, I had already filled the first sheet and part of a second. There were a few splotches, and the writing wasn't as elegant as my penmanship tutor would have liked, but I was satisfied with the final product inasmuch as I could read it through the tears that spilled down to stain the pages.

Kimber waited at the door when I opened it, ready to take the letter to Ayd so that it could be sent right away. She didn't question my tears, and only asked discretely if she could get me anything when she returned from the hawkery. I thanked her and declined, grateful that I didn't have to give the letter to Ayd and explain myself.

I made my way back to the roof and my heart lifted when I opened the door to see Andric waiting for me with an armful of blankets. His breath fogged in the air and his cheeks were touched with red. I wondered how long he had waited. I was grateful when he didn't ask any questions. Instead, he wrapped a blanket around me and led me to the parapets overlooking the hawkery. A few minutes later, the hawkery door opened and Ayd brought a bird outside already harnessed with my letter strapped to his back.

"Won't Rush be tired?" I asked when I recognized him.

Andric shook his head. "Ayd said the bird requested to be sent personally when he found out where the letter was going. Rush wouldn't ask if he couldn't handle the assignment."

We both watched in silence as Ayd checked the harness one last time and then held out his arm. Rush spread his massive wings and rose gracefully into the air. He flew as high as the castle rooftop where we waited, circled once in the air above us, then winged his way south toward the black mountains. We watched as the bird turned into a small speck and then disappeared in the distance.

"He'll be there within two days," Andric said. "Rory will be glad to hear from you."

"I wish I could fly with him," I replied. My heart quaked at the thought of the letter arriving too late. Fresh tears came to my eyes.

"I know, and I regret that more than you can imagine," Andric said.

The sorrow in his voice made me turn. The Prince wouldn't meet my gaze. "If anything happens to your brother while you're gone, I hold myself personally responsible."

I shook my head. "If anything happens to him, it would happen whether I'm there or not. There's nothing I can do about it." The truth brought a sob to my chest. I fought back the emotions, took a blanket from Andric, and spread it across the snow by one of the walls. I sank down onto it, exhausted from the sorrow that pounded behind my eyes. I pulled the other blanket close around my shoulders and wiped my cheeks on the corner. "He's been there all my life, Andric. I don't know how to think of a world without him. I feel so alone." The sob finally broke free, and I buried my head in my hands as my body shook.

Another blanket settled gently across my shoulders and I felt Andric kneel on the blanket beside me. He lifted his arm and I ducked under it so that I cried against his already wet chest. The tears were cold on my cheeks as the setting sun stole the remaining warmth from the air.

"You're not alone," Andric said after a few minutes, his voice thick with emotion.

I turned my head and saw that he, too, had tears in his eyes. "You're crying," I forced out past my tight throat.

He nodded, his dark eyes glittering as tears slid slowly down his cheeks. "I've been alone since my mother died, and I've never had anyone to even talk to until you came here." He wiped the tears from one of my cheeks with his fingers. "You will never be alone, I promise."

"How do you do it?" I asked, my voice barely more than a whisper. "How do you let someone go and move on as though there isn't a dark void in your life where they used to be?"

Andric's expression darkened. "My life is one dark void," he said quietly. "When Mother got sick, Father used to tell me to hope for the best and prepare for the worst. But he didn't take his own advice." Andric's jaw tightened. "When Mother left, Father left as well. He lost himself in his mind. He forgot me, he forgot our people, and he eventually forgot himself."

A sob escaped his lips and he turned his head away. "He forgot his own son who was hurting just as badly as he was. He left me alone to rule a country even though I was only twelve and barely able to find myself after losing my mother."

"What did you do?" I asked. Fresh tears filled my eyes for his pain instead of mine.

He was quiet for so long I thought he wasn't going to answer. He finally took a deep breath. "I threw myself into ruling, pushing my pain and sorrow away to deal with later, telling myself that there were other people who needed my time more than I did." He turned back to look at me, his eyes clouded. "I've never talked to anyone about it until now. I was always afraid that if I did, I would lose the control I've gained over the pain. There are too many people counting on me to let that happen."

"I couldn't do it," I said. "It's bad enough that I'm close to losing my brother. I don't think I could handle my mother and father being gone." I saw their worn, haggard faces as they had been in Rush's memory. They looked so different from the proud, confident parents that ruled side by side over Zalen. I wondered how they would cope if they did lose Rory. More tears slid down my cheeks at the thought that I wouldn't be there to help them through it.

I leaned against Andric's chest and felt his tears fall in my hair as he held me. "It'll be alright," he whispered quietly. "You'll get through this. I'm here for you. We'll do it together."

I nodded, though the tears refused to stop. My sobs eventually slowed and I fell into an exhausted sleep against him. A long while passed before his breath slowed and he slept as well, holding me close against the cold.

At nightfall, we were awakened by Andric's head steward, the same kind steward I had met at the outdoor picnic. The elderly man had brought our cloaks with him. There was no judgment on his face when he handed them to us and gathered the blankets we left.

"Handmaiden Kimber has hot chocolate and a bowl of warm soup waiting for you in your room," the steward said with a bow. He turned to Andric, a kind twinkle in his eyes. "The same for you, my Lord."

"Thank you, Trayd," Andric said gratefully. He turned to me. "Are you alright?"

I nodded and gave him a small smile. "Better, thank you."

He nodded and led the way off the roof, the discreet steward following behind.

Chapter 17

Andric changed the big dinner gatherings to once a week, which gave us time to relax in the evenings and cut down on the heavy use of Antor's supplies. I spent my time between the forge helping Cutler Maes fashioned our hilts; at the stable visiting Trae who was almost completely healed from his sword wound, and on the roof with Andric during the few moments that he could steal away from his duties as ruling Crown Prince.

Andric was always exhausted after long days of working with his counsel. Some days he was more closed off than others, and I could tell that he had been making hard decisions. With this being their last winter in Antor, there were a lot of issues to be resolved; I didn't know how I would handle the same situation.

The Antorans tried valiantly to be brave and put on a good front, but we saw the dwindling supplies and the more simple fare served at the group dinners. The Antorans needed help; they just didn't have anything that they could trade to the other countries in return. It made me frustrated, and I voiced my opinions on more than one occasion to Andric about how it was wrong that the other countries had let Antor fall to such ruin.

"It's our fault for relying on only one commodity; we didn't plan on the diamonds running out, and that the other kingdoms would stoop to stealing them instead of trading. We should have prepared better so that we were self-reliant." He looked out across the snowcapped land; dark lava rocks created a stark contrast to the white landscape. He shook his head and his wavy brown hair fell unruly across his forehead. He had told me once that he didn't wear a crown to remind his people that their king still lived. I thought it a noble and selfless gesture, but he waved it aside the way he did with many of his noble acts.

He pushed his hair back and frowned in frustration. "I just keep thinking that we didn't look hard enough. There's got to be more that Antor has to offer." Bayn paced the roof, then paused to look over the edge before lying down at Andric's feet. Freis, who had curled up near my legs to keep me warm, rose to move closer to her mate.

The wind whipped my hair around, free for once of its usual braid. I seldom had time to do much with my long hair, and had threatened more than once to chop it off so that it was easier to deal with, but Mother had forbidden me to do so, saying that princesses were to look elegant for their suitors. I compromised by stubbornly refusing to wear it in more than a braid. With everything we did here, it was easier to keep it out of the way.

But I had just finished a late afternoon practice with the girls to prepare for the duel they refused to give up. They were getting better and by the time we were done, I had to swim in the baths to freshen up for dinner with the Antorans. I left my hair down to dry in the brisk winter breeze, something nursemaid Morren would have had a fit over back home.

"Why don't you wear your hair down more often?" Andric asked, cocking his head to watch me braid it with well-practiced fingers.

"It gets in the way," I said. I sighed as a lock flew free, forcing me to start over.

"I like it down," Andric said. He caught my hand to stop me.

A jolt of lightning ran through me at his touch and my heart jumped.

Our relationship felt as though we were two long lost friends who had been looking for each other our whole lives and just didn't know it until we met. We laughed and joked and let down our walls in ways we never could around the others, but it was also a careful relationship. We were both aware of the precariousness of our situation, and of the fact that Crowns were not allowed to marry each other and leave a country heirless, as one of ours would be in either situation. So we were good friends, someone to talk to in confidence.

But I couldn't help admiring the way Andric treated his castle servants with respect, and how they treated him because of it. He was kind to everyone, even if he kept very careful walls up no matter who he dealt with. Trayd, the head steward, seemed to be the closest thing he had to a true friend, and he asked the older man for advice if a situation required a serious decision that would affect many people. The fact that Andric had no one his age that he trusted made me sad.

There were very few times when the Prince revealed how much the burdens he carried affected him. The time we cried together on the roof had been one of those, and I had only seen it twice after that. Once, when I found a hidden patch of beautiful blue snow roses and had wrapped them to take up to King Fayne's room, I found the King asleep and Andric sitting in a big armchair next to the fire, tears on his cheeks and his jaw tight as he stared into the flames. I turned and quietly left him to his thoughts, knowing the interruption wouldn't be pleasant for him.

The other time was on the roof not too long ago, just after he had been confronted at one of the dinners with the Antorans. The family that appeared at the doors bore hard countenances and grim expressions. They had demanded in front of everyone why Andric didn't lead the townspeople through the mountains to pillage the other countries just as their own diamonds had been stolen.

Andric reminded them that the majority of Antorans had agreed that stealing wasn't the way to live; though they had succumbed to it for a while, it wasn't a dependable source of the supplies needed to keep Antor running. They had decided instead to go out with their honor. They would more likely be welcome in the southern countries if they didn't precede it by further theft.

The family had been furious when they left, and a few of the Antorans at the tables left as well. I saw the sadness in the Prince's eyes when the doors shut behind them, but he calmly apologized to the gathering for the interruption and invited them to continue their dinner. I wandered the halls that sleepless night and made my way to our normal lookout. I found him there, his fists clenched and skin chilled with the bite of winter he didn't feel.

He refused to talk about it, but when I turned to go, he asked if I would wait with him for a bit. We watched in silence as the eastern mountains edged in faint gray that soon blushed to smoky red, chasing the darkness away with the first rays of the morning sun. I shivered and Andric had given me his cloak; I could still remember the way his scent stayed with me when I finally made my way downstairs to catch a few hours of sleep before the others were up.

"I'll leave it down then, just for you," I forced myself to say, my voice skipping only slightly as I undid the braid.

Andric stared at me for a moment in silence.

I smiled and said with false lightness, "But it'll drive me nuts all day and I'll blame it on you."

Andric nodded and smiled. "Fair enough; I take your blame. It's worth seeing the way the gold shines in your hair."

He turned and led the way to the door and down the stairs, unaware of the way I tripped over my own feet. I was glad that he didn't know my true feelings, but at the same time it hurt to see his ignorance, because sometimes it felt like rejection. I knew we couldn't get involved, but it would help to know that this was as hard for him as it was for me.

***

At dinner, I thought about my family. Over the past few weeks I found myself getting homesick at strange times, sparked by a familiar scent, the cast of certain shadows, or the sweet rolls at dinner that tasted just like the kind Cook Mumphrey made. Those thoughts usually turned to Rory and wondering how he was doing.

After the first time, I didn't feel the urge to see him through Rush's memories. It was hard enough to hear how Rory's health went up and down between each letter. Mother told me that after she read him my letter, he seemed to get noticeably better. I took that as encouragement and started to write him every day. But after the first improvement, he went downhill again. I found it harder after every letter to keep positive, but I forced myself to write about the activities we were doing, even though Mother expressed her concern when I mentioned the duel I was helping to train the girls for.

Father asked questions about the animals, and I tried to explain the relationship between the animals and Antorans the best that I could, knowing that it might also help me later on. I could tell when I was done that he still didn't understand, but he tried and that was something at least.

The other Crowns spent most of their time at the castle. The girls did crafts and I participated in those I wouldn't mess up too horribly, we all practiced our swordsmanship, and the boys entertained themselves by dueling and racing. Though the twins were still angry about being in Antor, they finally accepted the fact that they really didn't have a choice at this point. There was still a lot of grumbling and complaining between Nyssa and Brynna, but they enjoyed the dances that took place once week after the dinner with the citizens.

Both girls whispered about which of the boys would ask them to dance. Brynna liked Danyen, which wouldn't be a horrible thing if Danyen didn't mind going to Eskand and leaving Kenyen to rule Tyn. Nyssa and Kaerdra danced with whoever asked, as long as it was a Crown. Landis and Tisha spent as much time as they could together. They seemed happy no matter what they did, and minded our confinement in Antor the least because it was an excuse for them to spend all of their free time together.

Dinner was just winding down one evening when the doors to the banquet hall opened and a woman came in. Those eating grew silent with shock when they saw the fox that she carried was wrapped in bloody rags. The woman shook as she made her way toward the table where we sat with Andric. He rose and hurried around the table toward her, his wolves flanking either side.

"He's up there somewhere, Honorable Prince," the woman said in a quavering voice when she reached Andric.

Everyone had risen to their feet, and several citizens came forward to comfort the distraught woman.

"Who's up there?" Andric asked, his eyes on the bleeding fox. The animal shuddered, its eyes half-open and glossy.

"My husband. He was hunting and didn't come back last night. Sleek made his way home in this condition, though I don't even know how he made it at all." She hugged the fox, tears rolling down her cheeks. "They must have been attacked."

"I'll lead a search party for your husband," Andric told her. "But the fox is in no condition to go back up the mountain. He needs care right away."

Two servants exited discreetly out of one of the side doors and I knew they would be back with Jesson.

"We've got to find him," the woman said. "Sleek wouldn't leave him unless it was the only way to get help."

Andric nodded, visibly troubled. Then it seemed he and I had the same thought. He lifted his eyes to mine questioningly. I hesitated and glanced at the other Crowns, but it no longer mattered when someone's life hung in the balance. I nodded.

Andric smiled gratefully. "Mrs. Voise, I have someone who can talk to Sleek and find out where your husband is. Is that alright with you?"

Her eyes widened and she nodded quickly. "Oh yes, please hurry."

"Crown Princess Kit?"

Silence followed my name, and as I walked over to them, I could feel every eye on me. I imagined how horrified the Crowns would be, and I tried not to care. I chased the thoughts away and cleared my mind, then set a hand on the fox's blood-soaked back.

Pain coursed through my body. I gasped in surprise and took my hand away; my back tingled where it had been filled with pain moments before. I could hear whispers spreading around the banquet hall and tried to shut them out.

Andric caught my arm. "Are you alright?" he asked quietly.

I nodded, shut my eyes, and touched the fox again. This time, he seemed to understand what I was doing. Instead of projecting his pain, Sleek forced it to go into the background. It was still there coursing through both of us, but it was clouded by the images in his mind.

The fox showed me a man that I guessed to be Mrs. Voise's husband. The image came with a myriad of scents, sounds, and an overall feeling of belonging. It was the same feeling I got from Andric's wolves when they showed me either him or other members of their pack.

The image turned to a memory of the man trudging through the snow as the fox walked lightly by his side. The sun was setting and shadows colored the air in gray and black. Sleek saw as much with his nose as his eyes, and took the lead through the twisted trees and large boulders. He and the man touched minds often, searching for large game that would be settling down at this time of the evening.

It wasn't until the animals were almost on them that Sleek scented the mountain lions. The big black and gold streaked creatures the size of small bears had outdistanced them and climbed into the trees to wait for them to catch up. Sleek cried out a warning to Bown Voise, but one of the lions sprang out of the trees above them and landed on Bown.

The man yelled, twisted out of his backpack, and rolled away, leaving the huge mountain lion to worry the cloth to shreds. A second mountain lion pounced, knocking Bown against a tree. Sleek jumped between them and nipped at the lion in an effort to drive it back. The animal swiped out a paw faster than the fox could dodge. Sleek yelped as the claws caught him across the back and one side, slamming him against a boulder.

He heard Bown yell and forced himself to his feet again. The man had his back to the tree and was now fending off both lions with a knife. His head bled from where it had struck the trunk; he held one hand against his side and grimaced in pain. Sleek could smell the dark blood oozing from the hidden wound.

"Run, Sleek," Bown growled.

Sleek refused, turning instead to dart around the boulder in an effort to find an escape for Bown. He found small opening where two boulders rested against each other and would just fit the man, though if he didn't have his knife he would be easy prey.

Sleek sent the image to Bown and the man understood. He made his way backwards slowly through the trees, the knife darting out to keep the spitting, hissing mountain lions at bay. Sleek darted to each side of Bown, heedless of the blood that poured from the lacerations along his body. If a lion got too close, he flew at it nipping and tearing with his sharp teeth, then dodged back before another lucky swipe could catch him.

Finally, Bown fell back into the opening between the boulders. The back of it was closed by a rise in the earth, and he still had his knife to fend the creatures off from the front. Sleek ran past the opening, chasing the mountain lions back as far as they would go. They stopped by the trees and hissed, ears flat against their skulls and bright white teeth bared like brilliant daggers.

Suddenly, both lions looked over their shoulders. They shifted their paws uncertainly, looked back at Sleek, and then vanished into the rapidly growing darkness. I could feel Sleek's split second of relief before the wind shifted and brought him the scent that had chased off their attackers.

The smell of carnage and hate was unmistakable. Terror filled Sleek as he sent the image to Bown. He heard the man's sharp intake of breath. "Breizans," he breathed.

I jerked my hand back from the fox; my body trembled. I could see the animals they wore, faces frozen in angry snarls and stained with the blood of the prey the men ate.

"What is it?" Mrs. Voise asked, clutching Sleek to her. "Can you find him?"

The fox met my eyes, his own bright with pain and fear. Andric took a step closer to me, and I realized that most of the people in the banquet hall had gathered tightly around us, waiting for my answer. No one spoke.

"Yes," I said, forcing my voice to remain firm. "But we've got to go now."

"Oh, thank goodness! You're an angel," Mrs. Voise replied. Fresh tears streamed down her face. She pulled me close and hugged me as tight as she could with Sleek between us. The fox reached up and grabbed one of my hands gently between his needle sharp teeth. The image of Bown crouched between the boulders came to my mind again with urgency in the fox's thoughts.

"I know," I promised. "I'll find him."

Sleek let my hand go and his eyes closed with a shudder of pain.

"Where's the animal?" Jesson's familiar voice rang out. The crowd gave way and he hurried up to us. The healer gathered Sleek up in his arms and spoke quietly to Mrs. Voise. He nodded once to Andric and me, then disappeared through the onlookers.

"I'm coming with you," Mrs. Voise told me, her voice determined.

I nodded, knowing that if I was in her situation, I would be going as well.

"Right," Andric said. He turned to address the Antorans. His voice carried easily over the crowd with the tone of one accustomed to giving orders in crisis situations. "We leave in fifteen minutes. Anyone coming along meet us at the southern gates and bring your weapons. There might be more than mountain lions waiting for us."

I hadn't said anything about the Breizans, but somehow he had guessed. Andric came with me to our hallway; the rest of the Crowns followed. I heard them speaking quietly among themselves, but I didn't want to hear what they said. Andric turned and faced them. "This'll be dangerous. Anyone who doesn't want to come, please don't feel forced. In fact, I'd prefer it if you stayed here."

He looked directly at me, but I shook my head. "I'm the only one who knows where he is."

"You could tell Bayn and Freis. They'll find it."

This time, Tisha and Kaerdra's mouths fell open and Kenyen and Danyen exchanged glances, but I ignored them. "No. I told Sleek I would find him, and I keep my word. You'd do the same."

Andric opened his mouth to argue, then realized we had an audience. He closed it again, nodded without a word, and walked back down the hall.

"You talk to them?" Nyssa asked breathlessly.

"Not now," I cut her off. Did no one else comprehend what danger Bown was in? Then I realized that they didn't. No one but Andric knew. At her hurt expression, I put a hand on Nyssa's shoulder. "I'm sorry. It's just that Mr. Voise doesn't have much time. There are Breizans up there, and he's surrounded. It'll be chance if we find him before they do."

"Breizans!" Kaerdra said in horror. Tisha turned white.

Trevin spoke firmly to his sister. "You should stay. You don't want to get in the middle of another Breizan attack."

"You, too," Landis put in, grabbing Tisha up in a hug as if she was already in danger. "If you go, I'll be too worried about you and won't be able to protect anyone else."

Tisha nodded, and when he released her, she grabbed Kaerdra's hand.

"Nyssa, Brynna?" I asked. Both girls shook their heads, and I was relieved. After spending a month training them, I knew their weaknesses in battle, and neither acted well under pressure. I couldn't think of a situation more pressured than an attack by a Breizan horde.

I ran to my room, pulled on thick riding pants and a woolen shirt, then fastened the cloak Andric had given me around my neck. I was already sweating and slightly dizzy from the contact with Sleek, but I ignored it and pulled on my boots. I hurried to the stable thinking that I would be early, but I was surprised to see at least twenty-five Antoran men and women ready to ride out. Andric addressed them, and I couldn't help but wonder how he had managed to put on his black and green riding gear, organize the departure, and be composed enough to prepare his people for a harsh ride.

I felt anxious eyes on me as I made my way to Andric's side. He nodded in welcome, but his eyes were tight with worry. Knowing perhaps more than the others what to expect, I couldn't leave this ride up to chance. I dropped to one knee in the snow and, putting a hand on both Bayn and Freis, showed them the images the fox had given me. If something did happen on our journey, I wanted to be sure they found Bown as quickly as possible.

When I stood up, I could feel Andric watching me and knew he guessed my intentions. He opened his mouth, I assumed to tell me to stay, when Drade appeared. "Princess Kit," he said, motioning me to one side. I followed him to his horse Sorn. "I need to stay," he said quietly.

At my look, he frowned with anxiety. "Sleek's not doing well and Jesson needs my assistance. Sorn will protect you on this trip and bring you back safely."

The horse whickered quietly and took the corner of my cloak in his teeth.

"Thank you," I told the Horsemaster. I ran a hand through Sorn's shaggy hair. "We'll be careful, I promise."

Drade shook his head. "Don't promise what you can't guarantee. Fighting Breizans is no joke, but Sorn is experienced and can handle himself. It'll be dangerous, but he's the best protection you can get."

A shiver ran down my spine, but I thanked him again and swung onto Sorn's back. Without guidance, the horse made his way to where Andric had mounted Tereg. The other Crown Princes were already on their horses and accepted swords that Smithy Hensas handed out. He stopped next to Sorn, his eyes apologetic.

"Your sword isn't ready yet, Princess, but I've got one that should do you well." He handed me a plain but strong short sword about the size of the one he was making for me. "It's held up under worse circumstances, and should defend you well with the skills you've shown at practice."

"Thank you, Master Smith," I told him, touched. I strapped the sheath's belt around my waist and my heart started to pound with the impact of what we were about to do. The ghost of an eerie wail echoed in my head. I clenched my jaw and pushed it away.

"You'll be alright," the Smithy said. He reached up a beefy hand to pat my shoulder. His eyes were reassuring, but his brow creased with worry. "We'll see you back here soon."

"Fall in," Andric commanded. His voice rang through the crisp evening air.

The sound of horse hooves on snow, creaking leather, and the chink of metal on metal answered his command. At the Prince's motion, I took up position just behind he and Jashe. The Captain nodded to me in welcome, his expression calm. The sight of him reassured me, though my anxiety made Sorn jittery. He sidestepped and pawed at the ground. I forced my whirlwind of thoughts to slow and smoothed the fur on his neck.

192

Chapter 18

Andric and Jashe led the way, following the directions I gave them. Bayn, Freis, and the other wolves ranged out ahead and picked up the scent of Sleek's blood on the snow. The group was quiet, anxious, and expectant. Andric had warned them about the Breizans, for which I was grateful; we all knew what lay ahead.

Snow started to fall until we were peering into the night. We had to trust our horses' sure feet to keep us on the right path as we galloped. I kept my hands wrapped in my cloak, gripping Sorn's muscular sides with my legs as Andric had once shown me.

We slowed the horses from their mile-eating lope well after midnight. Bayn waited for us in the scattered moonlight, his ears pricked and teeth bared. I could see the bloodstained snow that he followed, and hoped that Drade and Jesson had been able to bind Sleek's wounds. I recognized the pattern of the trees and the rising slope from the images the fox had given me. The mountain lions had attacked them not far from here.

The horses breathed hard, but their ears turned at every sound and they inhaled the air loudly as they searched for what had stopped the wolves. Andric motioned for us to ride carefully. He led Tereg ahead at a cautious pace, and the rest of us followed, starting at every sound and straining our senses for any sign of Breizans.

"They're too smart to let us see them even if they are here," an older man whispered behind me.

"Shhh," his neighbor hissed.

Fear prickled along my spine. It was easier to think of the savage men as mindless beasts than it was to accept them as coldly calculating creatures waiting for us to ride into a trap.

My heart started to pound so loud I worried Andric could hear it. Sorn snorted softly; his head turned from side to side as he peered into the shadows. I ran a hand down his neck and tried to project calm thoughts.

We made our way through ghostly white boulders and trees that twisted as though writhing in pain. The only sound was the crunch of the horses' hooves in the snow. Their breath fogged white in the moonlit air as they picked their way along the snow-covered path after Andric's pack. Our nerves strained with every broken twig. Finally, we came to a place where the snow was scattered; huge paw prints and the footprints of a single human marred the haunting, moonlit landscape.

Andric slid from his horse and I followed despite the look of caution he threw me. Mrs. Voise dismounted as well and caught my hand, her eyes wide and lips tight with the fear of what we might find. Falen fell back to protect us, his eyes on the ever changing shadows in the lightly falling snow. We followed Andric, Captain Jashe, and two more Antorans as they trailed the path Bown had left.

I knew I wasn't the only one who saw the other tracks. Freis walked beside me, and when I sat a hand on her head I could smell decay, pain, and fear. Her hackles were raised and she kept her eyes constantly on the darkness around us.

When we reached the boulders that leaned against each other, trepidation slowed our steps. Andric bent down and peered into the darkness between them. "Bown?"

A moan answered.

Mrs. Voise dropped my hand and ran forward, crying his name. She fell to her knees in the snow at the base of the rocks and reached in for her husband. "Oh Bown, Bown, never leave me again. I don't know what I'd do without you."

"Mylena?" His voice was weak at first, unbelieving. "Is it really you?"

Andric crouched near the opening while Jashe gently guided her back enough so they could lift the man out. Bown yelled in pain and clutched his side when they eased him from between the rocks. Falen threw down his cloak. They eased Mr. Voise onto it so that he sat against the rocks.

"Mylena, it is you," Bown said, his voice filled with relief and pain as she threw her arms around his neck and threatened to never let go. Bown's eyes shone with disbelief when he lifted them to stare at all of us, coming to rest on his prince. "Prince Andric?"

"Sleek found your wife and she bought him to us." He gestured to me. "He showed Princess Kit where you were and she led us here." Andric rose and looked around. "But we're in danger. We need to get moving."

Bown nodded. "Something chased the lions off, and they aren't friendly."

The rest of us exchanged glances. 'Aren't friendly' was the mildest description of Breizans I had ever heard.

"Is Sleek alright?" Bown asked his wife as she wrapped his side in clean rags.

"He was pretty bad when he found me. I don't know how he made it home," she told him honestly. "But Healer Jesson and Horsemaster Drade are looking after him. He's in the best hands possible."

"Right." Bown failed to disguise the worry on his face that overshadowed the pain from his wounds. He lifted an arm to Jashe. "We'd better get out of here."

Jashe was helping him to his feet when the howl of a wolf sounded behind us. Andric unsheathed his sword and shouted, "Everyone to defensive positions!"

Immediately, the atmosphere changed from one of reunion to fear and tension. Jashe settled Mr. Voise back against the boulder and handed him an extra sword. The rest of us took up positions around the fallen man. Andric stood at my left with Trevin at my right; Kenyen and Danyen waited anxiously next to Trevin, and Landis stood at the other end near several Antorans. I saw their exchange of worried looks and adrenaline rushed through my veins.

Before we got completely set, the wolves howled again. The horses started to whinny and stomp where they waited down the hill. A shrieked sounded, and my blood turned cold with the memory. My mind froze at the sight of long, stringy hair, bared human teeth, and bodies covered in bloodstained animal carcasses. An Antoran stepped forward and slashed the first attacker across the throat hard enough to throw the Breizan backwards. Then we were engulfed.

I let go of the present and let my body fight the way it was trained. The sword Smithy Hensas had given me was a good one and held true during the onslaught of jagged, blood-stained blades. I closed off my fear and let my arms block the swings and thrusts meant to end my life.

Freis appeared at my side, sent there by Andric who fought desperately against three Breizans. He had been backed against a tree with low branches that impeded his swing. Out of nowhere, Tyd, the small gray male wolf, leaped from the darkness with a snarl of rage. Distracted, the Breizans turned. Andric and Bayn finished them quickly.

The Antoran next to me cried out, then fell to the snow clutching a spear that stuck through his chest. I sliced at the now unarmed Breizan and caught him across the stomach. His entrails spilled onto the snow. The scent made me want to vomit. I fell back to the wounded Antoran to see if there was anything I could do, but his eyes had already glazed over and stared blankly at the snow that fell through the trees around us.

Two more Breizans rushed at me before I could think. Landis sliced one of them across the shoulder and he fell, tripping his companion. I chopped down with my sword like an axe and cut off his head before he could rise back up. Landis and I stared at each other for a split second and horror reflected in both of our faces before another attack tore us apart.

I found myself back at Trevin's side. The Prince held his sword in his left hand, and a deep cut ran down the right. I moved to his right side to protect his weakness. The blocks and parries came naturally to me though my brain was fogged with fear. Horses let out horrified screams and the Breizans sounded their wordless shrieks that sent mind-numbing shudders up my spine. I could hear the growls of the wolves and the hiss of a bobcat that had come with one of the Antorans.

It all blurred into one big mess of blood, shadows, snow, and tangled bodies. I forced myself to keep a grip on my sword despite the blood that covered its hilt, though I couldn't remember how the blood had gotten there. Snowflakes landed on the fallen bodies as if they were a natural part of the landscape instead of recent losses in a life and death battle.

The stark contrast between the still forms and the demented, hideous creatures that attacked us made me want to laugh and cry at the same time. I was torn between the adrenaline of battle and the urge to curl up in a corner and wish it would all go away.

By time the Breizans stopped attacking, there wasn't an inch of white snow in sight except the flakes that landed on our bloodstained faces, hair, and arms with a normalcy that felt severely out of place amid the wreckage. Surprisingly few Antorans had been injured considering the number of Breizans that lay dead around us. Besides the man killed by the spear, one other man and one woman bore potentially fatal wounds.

The rest of us who had more minor injuries helped the others down to the horses. Sorrow filled me to find that two of the horses had been killed and two more injured enough to have to be put down. The two dead horses had bite marks on them as if they had been mauled by wild animals. Ice ran through my veins at the realization that it was the Breizans, not wild animals, who had done it.

I made my way slowly back up to the boulders to where Mylena waited with her husband. Bown was pale, but he nodded at me when I neared them. I was about to ask him how he was doing when a blur of motion caught the corner of my eye. I turned in time to see a black and gold creature leap from a tree at Mrs. Voise.

Without time to think, I ran forward and unsheathed my sword. Time slowed. I heard Bown yell, followed by echoes from below as I shoved Mylena out of the way and turned with my sword raised. The weight of the mountain lion crashed into me. My head hit one of the boulders and stars exploded in front of my eyes. The hilt of the sword I gripped was jammed against the rock. I heard the mountain lion yowl and felt it slide down the blade, the weight of its body thrusting it deeper than I could have managed.

It tried to free itself, and a claw caught me across the cheekbone like a blade of fire. The lion's movements slowed, and its weight crushed me down. Men and women yelled. I could hear Andric's voice above them calling my name. Sharp pain ran from the back of my head and I could barely breathe past the suffocating mass of the lion. I tried to answer, but dark spots danced in my vision and grew larger until I fell into the hole they created.

***

The ground was softer than I expected, and a lot warmer. The scent of lavender touched my nose. I moved my fingers and felt soft sheets beneath them. My head pounded, centering from the back of my skull. Bandages had been placed around my forehead. I opened my eyes slowly.

I was in my room at the Antoran castle. Moonlight filtered down the white stones, giving the room a dim glow. The snow must have stopped if the moon no longer hid behind snow-laden clouds. I reined in my dazed mind and forced my gaze back to the room.

A person sat hunched over in a chair pulled next to the bed. Andric. He held his head in his hands and leaned his forehead on the bed; his dark brown hair hid his face from me. I couldn't tell if he was asleep.

"Andric?" I whispered.

A dark head rose beside him and Bayn's golden eyes glittered in the faint light. On my other side, Freis stood up and whined.

Andric lifted his head, his gaze confused and exhausted. Then his eyes focused and he stared at me as if he couldn't believe what he saw.

I gave him a small smile.

Andric rose without speaking and sat on the side of my bed so that he faced me. His eyes held mine as if he thought I would disappear. He lifted a hand as though to touch me, then set it back down uncertainly on the bed. "Are you alright?" he finally asked in a tight voice.

"Yes," I said with a nod. The motion brought a wave of nausea from the sharp pain in the back of my head straight to my stomach. I grimaced and fought down the urge to lose whatever was left of my last breakfast.

Andric's eyes widened. "What? Do you hurt?" He looked as though he didn't know whether to stay or run to get Jesson.

I held a hand to my head until the pounding slowed, then gave him a wry smile. "I guess I'm fine unless I move. I need to see if Jesson has any peppermint salve to get rid of this headache before it kills me."

His jaw tightened and I regretted my poor choice of words; then he smiled, relief stark on his face. "Kit, I thought I lost you," he said softly. He gently touched just below my cheekbone where a line of ointment covered the mountain lion's claw mark. Andric moved his hand to the back of my head. I winced when he touched the sore spot. "Sorry," he whispered. He sighed and leaned down to put his forehead against mine. "You're too brave for your own good," he said softly. His breath touched my lips.

I looked up into his dark eyes, so close to my own. They burned into mine, holding me, memorizing me. When I breathed, his scent filled my lungs and my heart skipped sideways in my chest. His forehead felt cool against mine, his skin smooth. "I'll try to be more careful," I said breathlessly.

He gave a shallow nod and his hair tickled my cheeks pleasantly. "You better." He frowned, a worry line forming between his eyes. "I thought I lost you," he repeated. This time, I saw the pain in his gaze.

"It takes more than a little cat to put me down," I replied, though both of us knew how very close to being 'put down' I had really been.

He sighed and moved back. My forehead tingled where we had touched. "What I am going to do with you, Princess Kirit."

"Kit," I said firmly. "Just Kit. You know that."

"Yes," he replied with a hint of regret in his voice. "I do know that."

This time, it was my turn to frown. "What's wrong?"

He gave me a tight, wry smile. "You mean besides the fact that you were almost killed by a mountain lion more than quadruple your size, and that my people were fighting for their lives against a horde of cannibalistic monsters three days ago?"

"Three days ago?" I sat up, then grabbed my head when the room spun and my brain threatened to explode.

"Whoa, now," Andric said, rising quickly. He eased me back down on the pillows. "No sudden movements. Do I have to get Jesson?"

"No," I replied sullenly. I kept my eyes closed to stop the spinning.

Andric's gentle fingers smooth my mussed hair back from my face. Ice and fire trailed his touch and made my heart pound. He stopped and I opened my eyes to find him rubbing his forehead with one hand.

I noticed the dark circles under his eyes. "Have you had any sleep?" I asked.

He shook his head. "How could I?" he asked softly. He took one of my hands in his and studied it. I realized that it was wrapped in a bandage just above the wrist; my wet sword handle now made sense.

Unfortunately, thinking of the sword led immediately to other memories of the battle. Bloody faces, a piercing yowl, and an overwhelming number of flesh-chewing Breizans invaded my mind. Panic made my blood pound in my ears.

"Did everyone get back?" I asked, aware of the sudden urgency in my voice.

He nodded and ran a finger along my hand, soothing me. "Everyone that could, made it. We brought the others home to be buried and mourned. Bown's going to be alright, and I think Sleek will, too." He gave a slight smile.

"What?" I asked.

"Nothing," Andric said. At my persistent stare, his smile grew. "I thought I lost you and here you are worrying about others instead of the fact that you nearly died."

I shrugged. "Wouldn't want the mission to have been a waste now would we?"

He shook his head. "No, we wouldn't."

A yawn overtook me before I could stop it, and the worry returned to Andric's eyes. "You should sleep."

"Apparently I've been sleeping for three days. You'd think I wouldn't be tired," I protested.

"Yes, but I can tell you are. Get some sleep, alright?"

I nodded; each of my limbs felt extremely heavy. But at the thought of sleep, the image of Breizans flashed through my mind again. I trembled.

"What is it?" he asked quickly. He knelt down beside the bed.

"I'm afraid to close my eyes," I admitted. My voice was quieter than I would have wished.

His expression softened and, without warning, he leaned over and kissed my uninjured cheek. "I'll keep you safe, my little warrior." A blush rose to my face, centering around the place where his lips had touched my skin.

He rose and pulled his chair closer. I protested in an effort to hide the way my heart pounded at his nearness, "You need sleep more than I do. I'll be fine."

"I won't have you afraid to fall asleep in my own castle," Andric said.

"And I won't have you dropping out of exhaustion when you have people to lead," I replied. My words slurred slightly from fatigue.

He shook his head. "Your health means much more to me right now."

I could tell I was losing the argument, then thought of a compromise. It would push every boundary we had, but I was so tired I didn't care about propriety anymore. I could barely keep my eyes open, but was afraid of what I saw when they were closed. It was the only way I could think of to sleep without fear of reliving the battle. I moved over gingerly, then said in a voice as worn as I felt, "This bed is big enough for ten people. It's better than you falling asleep in that chair."

He studied me for a minute, his expression unreadable. The shadows below his eyes made them even more unfathomable than usual. He swayed slightly with weariness as he stood, the dim light playing across his face.

"They couldn't get me to leave you," he finally admitted as if searching for anything to say. "I told Jesson to get some rest. He'll be anxious to know you're awake."

"Tell him in the morning," I replied, fighting to keep my eyes open. "I don't need any more people losing sleep on my account, and maybe they'll let you rest if they think you're still here waiting for me to wake up."

He shook his head and my heart fell in a way that hurt. I blinked and felt tears on my cheeks. I couldn't explain them other than my pounding headache, the weariness that spread through every inch of my body, and the fear of what my dreams would bring. I turned my face away and lifted a hand to wipe my cheeks.

Andric caught my hand in his, then the bed dipped as he leaned over and brushed the tears away with the back of his fingers. "Don't cry, little warrior," he said in a soft whisper. He curled my hand in his and settled on top of the blankets, his face turned toward me.

The nearness of him made my breath catch in my throat. My body wanted to curl next to him, to feel the comfort of his warmth and sleep in his arms, but I settled for putting my other hand over his and not questioning the confusing thoughts that cluttered my weary mind. "Good night," I whispered before my heavy eyelids drooped shut.

"Good night," he replied quietly. I could feel him watching me, a comforting presence to chase away the nightmares, but I couldn't force my eyes to open. "Good night, Kit," he whispered again as my thoughts drifted away.

***

I crouched down and looked between the two boulders. Instead of Bown, I found Father injured and waiting for rescue. His eyes widened when he saw me, then filled with tears. He held out a hand, and I reached for it. A non-human scream rattled the air. Breizans swarmed from the trees, the snow, and behind the rocks. I pulled out my sword, but it was broken. I fought, but they pulled me away and made me watch as they attacked Father. His screams pierced the air, then turned into my own.

"Kit, Kit, wake up!"

I opened my eyes, my cheeks wet with tears. My throat hurt as if I had been screaming. My head pounded horribly. I blinked and tried to remember where I was.

Andric's face hovered above my own. His dark eyes searched mine. "You're alright. It was a nightmare."

I closed my eyes tightly and felt more tears squeeze free. "It was horrible," I said past my rough throat.

"I could tell," he answered. He pulled me close and wrapped me in his arms. His head settled on top of my chin and I felt safer than I ever had before. I set a hand on his arm and felt the muscles ripple underneath. "You're safe," he whispered into my hair.

I nodded and sleep stole me away again into a blissfully Breizan-free dream.

Chapter 19

When I awoke late the next morning, it was to a full room of smiling faces peering down at me, quite the stark contrast from the moonlit night with Andric. He was the first one I saw, leaning next to Jesson with a smile on his face. The circles under his eyes had lessened, but not by much; I felt a pang of guilt for keeping him up with my nightmares, but his expression was carefully guarded and didn't let on what he thought about the night.

Captain Jashe and Falen were there, along with all of the Crowns. Tisha and Kaerdra had tear stains on their cheeks. Trevin's arm was wrapped and bound in a sling, while Danyen had a bandage around his forehead. I saw Kimber peering anxiously from the doorway, and gave her a smile which she returned immediately. Drade, some of the soldiers from our trip, and even Smithy Hensas watched me with encouraging smiles. My cheeks flushed from the attention.

"How do you feel?" Jesson asked as he checked my pulse.

"I think I'll make it," I told him; chuckles rose around the room in response.

He grinned. "Do you think you can sit up? I need to check those bandages."

I remembered not to nod. Kaerdra surprised me by helping me up while Tisha pushed the pillows behind my back. The room spun and I closed my eyes, but it slowed quickly. I was embarrassed at the concern on everyone's faces when I opened them.

"I'm alright," I said, blushing again.

Andric grinned. "I think we all have things to do," he said to the others.

Smithy Hensas laughed. He stepped forward to ruffle my hair, towering over me. "Your sword's done," he said with a wink. "A little late, but it's perfect. I might be a bit biased, but I think it's the best sword I've ever made."

"Hey!" Kenyen protested behind the Smithy.

I laughed. "I can't wait to see it," I told him sincerely.

He nodded with a beam of pride and turned to leave the room. When no one else followed, he motioned, "Give the Princess a little space. She's had a rough couple of days."

The others hurried to obey his gruff tone; before they left, each came over to tell me how glad they were that I was alright until I was certain I couldn't be more red with embarrassment at all the attention. By the time Trevin closed the door behind him, leaving only Prince Andric, Jesson, and Kimber, I wanted to curl up under the covers and hide.

"They're just glad you're safe," Jesson said, reading my expression accurately.

"I hope they're as concerned for the rest of the Antorans that were injured during the fight," I replied, overwhelmed.

Andric chuckled. "It's not the same, you know. It's not every day a foreign princess risks her life to save an Antoran citizen."

I frowned at him, then winced when Jesson touched the sensitive spot on the back of my head.

Andric's tone changed. "Is it bad?"

Jesson put new bandages on the wound and began to wrap my head again. "No; it's better than it could have been. When I saw all the blood I feared the worst, but it's just a gash. You're lucky you're skull wasn't cracked," he said, addressing me now. "It sounds like you hit that rock pretty hard."

I frowned, remembering. "Was Mylena hurt when I pushed her?" In my fear, I remembered shoving her hard to get her out of the mountain lion's way.

Jesson shook his head. "Mere scrapes; nothing compared to what she would have suffered if the lion had gotten her." He gave me a kind smile. "They want to thank you, you know. Bown is under orders to stay in bed until Jesson clears him, but he's already asked Prince Andric's permission to have a party for you when he's better."

Concern filled me. "But what about the families who lost loved ones in that fight? Wouldn't it be cruel to have a celebration while they're in mourning?"

Jesson finished tying the bandage around my head and turned to get his salve for the cut on my cheek.

Andric answered my question. "Not in Antor. Loved ones are remembered for the joy they brought while here, not the sorrow left behind. We celebrate life and help each other to not get lost in the death of a family member. The celebration will be as much for them as for you." His brows drew together when he said this, as if he feared I would think the Antorans callous for their traditions.

But it made sense to me. I thought of families who had lost loved ones back in Zalen. The tradition was for the family members left behind to wear black and mourn solemnly for a year. I had a clear memory of a young boy about nine years old who had lost his father a few months earlier in a ship accident. He was having fun with his friends in the street when his mother scolded him roundly for playing when he should have been mourning like a grateful son.

How much better would it have been for the boy to rejoice in the memory of his father rather than focus only on the pain of losing him? I'm sure the father would rather his son play a game of ball in the sun with his friends instead of mourning indoors in black.

I nodded. "Then I'd be honored to have a celebration with their families."

Jesson smiled and Andric looked relieved. "It'll be done."

A polite tap at the door announced one of Andric's heralds. "My Prince, your presence is required in the judgment room."

Andric's face clouded. He turned to me apologetically, but I smiled. "Go ahead, your country needs you more than I do."

"Does it?" he asked, his eyes unreadable.

Before I could figure out what he meant, he left the room.

Jesson smoothed the salve on my cheek. "You'll have a slight scar, but it could be worse."

"A lot worse," I agreed distractedly. I hesitated, then said, "Prince Andric's tired."

Jesson nodded, unsurprised. "He works hard, and the people love him for it." He wiped his hands on a clean white rag as he continued, "He started young and put a great effort into it because of that, convinced that the only way the Antorans would take him seriously was if he dedicated himself to them entirely." He gave a slight smile and a wink. "What he didn't realize is that they loved him already. They knew to some degree what happened to his father, and couldn't help but love him when he gave up everything to serve them in the King's stead."

"He's young to be ruling," I mused quietly.

"Very young, but my wife often says he seems older than all of us." Jesson gathered up his supplies. "Thank you."

"For what?" I asked, surprised.

"For being his friend." He gave me a kind smile. "And for not being biased by what you were taught about Antorans before you came here. We're not that bad."

I laughed. "No, not bad at all."

With his help, I rose from the bed and waited on wobbly legs while he summoned Kimber, and then left me in her capable hands. She practically beamed when she saw me up and set about helping me change from the soft beige sleeping gown someone had dressed me in, which I found to my relief had been her.

I sat patiently in a light blue dress while she gently worked a comb through my hair. The bandages were in the way and very inconvenient, but when I offered to just take them off, Kimber turned white in dismay. I then had to convince her I was just kidding. I could tell by her worried expression that she thought the bump on my head had caused more damage than Jesson surmised.

"Your hair is so long," she commented, then caught herself and glanced at me in the mirror as if afraid she had offended me. "It's beautiful, m-my Lady," she rushed on. "Most hair around here is dark, and yours is like spun gold. I didn't mean-"

I cut her off with a warm smile. "It's alright, Kimber. I appreciate your opinion. You can say whatever you'd like, even if you hate it."

Her eyes widened and she shook her head. "But I don't hate it at all. I love your hair and I'm honored you allow me to brush it."

I met her eyes in the mirror. "Kimber, be honest with me."

Her face paled. "I have always been honest with you, my Lady."

I held up a hand to appease her. "I know, and I appreciate it. What I want to know, honestly, is what you would like to do if you weren't attending me."

She opened her mouth, saw how serious I was, and shut it again. She ran the comb a few times down my hair in silence.

"Honestly, Kimber," I prompted.

She swallowed and her eyes darted to the door, then back to my gaze in the mirror. She took a nervous breath, then let it out in a loud rush. "I want to work in the gardens."

At my smile, she dropped her eyes and looked embarrassed. "It's silly, really. It's just that my mother always grew flowers in our window box, and they remind me of her. I thought I might have a green thumb like she did." Her voice caught and she turned away.

I grabbed her hand. "It's not silly at all." I smiled up at her from my seat on the bench. "My mother likes to grow things, too." A lump rose unexpectedly in my throat at the thought of her excitement when Father brought a wagonload of rich dirt from the forests near Veren. "I miss her," I admitted out loud.

Kimber raised her eyes slowly to mine. "I miss my mother, too."

I gripped her hand tightly and blinked back tears at the loss in her voice. "Us girls have to stick together," I said in a conspiratorial whisper.

She grinned and the lines of worry disappeared from her face. "I've seen the way you take care of yourself. You need someone to remind you to take it easy."

Her eyes tightened as if she worried she had stepped over the line, but I laughed and touched my head meaningfully. "I definitely need someone like that." I paused, then smiled. "Tell you what. Help me take better care of myself and I'll see to it that you get a chance to work in the gardens." I glanced at the snow that fell past the window. "If they do garden here."

"There's a small garden," she reassured me. "It's just covered in snow right now, and most of the year." The relief and happiness in her voice cheered me. She ran the comb through my hair again, then asked, "Would you like me to braid it like you usually do?"

I was about to say yes when I remembered my promise to Andric that I would wear it down. "I think it's alright unbraided." I met her eyes in the mirror. "What do you think?"

She hesitated, then another smile lit up her face. "It's beautiful down. You'll be the envy of the entire city."

I grimaced at the dull, persistent ache from the back of my head. "I doubt that, but we can pretend."

We smiled at each other and I felt like a young girl for the first time since arriving at Antor. It was good to feel carefree if only for a moment, and the way Kimber's expression practically glowed when she left the room made even my aching head worthwhile.

I was grateful dinner was to be in the room on the second floor. I didn't think I could deal with many people all at once. Freis met me on the stairs and walked with me to the door. I kept a hand on her head and it steadied me.

At my entrance, the Princes and Princesses rose and I blushed again. The girls rushed over and led me to my seat while the boys all tried to get my chair, leaving the servant whose job it really was to stare at them in amusement.

I caught a smirk on Andric's face from where he waited quietly behind his chair for the others to resume their seats, and it was all I could do to keep from sticking my tongue out at him. He was enjoying it way too much. But when I sat down I had to put a hand to my head to stop the pounding caused by all of the commotion, and I glanced up to see a worried expression on his face. I shot him a reassuring smile and turned to the others.

"You look so much better!" Nyssa exclaimed. Brynna, Kaerdra, and Tisha all nodded in agreement, making me wonder how bad I must have looked when they brought me home.

"I can't believe you killed a mountain lion single-handedly," Trevin said, his eyes wide in awe.

I laughed, then regretted it at the increased ache in my head. "Actually, the lion did most of the work." When they pressed me for details, I explained what happened from my point of view in my best storytelling voice. The girls' eyes widened with horror, while the boys kept asking for all of the grisly details. Andric listened quietly with his face an expressionless mask and his eyes concealing any thoughts he had about my story.

***

It was only later that night when I went to the roof in an effort to clear my persistent headache with the crisp night air that I found out how Andric really felt about everything.

"You should be asleep," he said when I opened the door and found him staring out at the dark mountains.

"So should you," I reminded him, surprised by his guarded tone.

"I wasn't the one who almost got killed."

I frowned and crossed the remaining few feet between us. "Why the sudden hostility? I thought you were worried about me."

In one smooth motion, Andric turned and grabbed my arms firmly. "Hostility? You laugh about the fact that you almost died and you think I'm hostile?"

At the pain in his eyes, I stuttered, "I'm sorry-"

He cut me off, his dark eyes passionate. "Do you understand how precarious your position is here? How much you've done since you arrived? You've touched my people more than I ever could."

I shook my head, surprised. "That's not true. They love you; they-"

He frowned. "It's not a bad thing, and I'm not upset. I'm just. . ." He threw up his arms in frustration. "I don't know what I am anymore. You confuse me more than anyone else I know."

Tears pricked at my eyes and I fought to keep them from breaking free. "I think I should go now."

I turned to leave, but he caught my hand. I refused to look at him. "Kit, I'm sorry." When I couldn't find the words to respond, he sighed. "I don't know why I'm upset. Well, I do; I just don't know what to do about it."

I forced the question past the knot in my throat. "Do about what?"

He pulled gently at my hand again and I turned slowly, afraid of what I would see. At the look on my face, he simply stared at me, his eyes wide. "Look what I'm putting you through," he said quietly, more to himself than to me.

The sorrow and regret in his voice broke my heart. "I'm fine," I lied.

He shook his head. "No, you're not. You've been through a lot in the past few days and I'm making it worse." He turned his head away. "I don't even deserve you as a friend, Kit."

The tears broke free, spilling down my cheeks. I stepped forward and hid my face against his chest.

Surprised, he froze, then put his arms around me gingerly as if he thought I would break. A finger of cold twisted about my legs and I shivered. He pulled me tighter. "I'm so sorry," he whispered.

"You have nothing to be sorry about," I said, my voice catching. "I'm just a little emotionally unstable right now and I'm blaming it on the bump on my head."

"Convenient," he replied into my hair. "But what excuse do I have?"

I hugged him tighter. "You have a whole country on your shoulders, and are doing a much better job than anyone I know has done at twice your age, but you give yourself no credit for it." My heart constricted. "You don't see the impact you have on your people. They love you more than you realize."

He was quiet for a long time. I listened to the rhythmic pounding of his heart. My own slowed. When he finally spoke, his voice was soft. "I care about you, Kit. I care about you more than I've ever cared about anyone or anything."

My heart skipped several beats; I stepped back to look at his face. He stared down at me, his eyes unfathomable. He reached out and wiped the tears from my cheeks with a gentle hand that shook slightly. "I didn't plan for this to happen."

"Me neither," I said softly.

His eyes clouded and he looked past me. "I never realized how much I didn't feel until I met you and saw how you brightened everything you came in contact with." He looked back at me and gave a half smile. "Even me." He pushed a wayward strand of hair behind my ear. "I didn't know how closed off I'd become. I guess. . ." he sighed and closed his eyes. "I guess I was as lost as Father the day Mother died; I just never knew it."

"You're not lost anymore?" I asked softly.

He shook his head, hesitated, then shrugged with a wry smile. "Let's just say not *as* lost," he concluded with a laugh. Then he fell quiet and I watched as the lightheartedness faded from his eyes and the laughter from his face. It made my heart ache to see him close off again. "But you're a Crown," he finally whispered.

Everything crashed down around me at that simple truth. "And you rule your kingdom," I replied, trying to keep the heartache out of my voice and failing entirely.

He opened his arms and I stepped into them. This time, the tears didn't fall. There was no reason for them, and we both knew it. We had a duty to our countries, and neither could leave our people without a ruler. We held each other for a long time, safe but heartbroken within our little bubble that would burst the second we let go. It was never to be, and the hardest part was accepting it.

I shivered in the cold night air and it seemed to bring Andric back to himself. "You really do need to sleep," he whispered. It sounded like goodbye.

"You, too," I said into his chest. "You work so hard."

"You make it worthwhile," he replied with a hint of a smile in his sad voice.

I hugged him tightly for a second, then stepped back. "I-I. . . ." Words eluded me as I looked at him, the starlight in his gaze, his dark hair unruly. He still had circles under his eyes and shadows beneath his cheekbones. There was no one to take care of him, and he always put himself last below everything else. I wouldn't be able to take care of him. My eyes stung. Without a word, I turned and fled the roof and the Prince who watched silently after me.

Chapter 20

Our trips through the city began to show more of the effects of the poverty-stricken country. Families whose homes fell in disrepair due to the lack of supplies abandoned their houses to move in with other family members. Prince Andric's stewards and staff carefully rationed food so that every family received just enough to get by, which sometimes seemed meager indeed. Medicine was of short supply, and I spent a lot of my time with Jesson making what salves we could out of his remaining herb stash.

We brought soup to the sick, helped mend broken roofs, repaired fences to keep the remaining livestock in, patched clothing, and carried food to those who couldn't travel to the castle for the weekly rationing. I admired the way the Antorans worked to keep their spirits up, but could tell that the thought of leaving their beautiful but barren land broke some of them, driving them to tears when they thought no one was watching.

The weekly dinners in the banquet hall were a special treat and gave us all something to look forward to. The week when Bown Voise was deemed fit enough to get out of bed was a happy one. Mylena and I spent a lot of time together preparing for the celebration; it heartened me to see the families of those who had lost loved ones during the battle preparing for it as well.

They created beautiful banners and reminders of their loved ones' accomplishments to be displayed in the banquet hall during the festivities. Everyone helped each other, and laughter made a pleasant harmony as we hung streamers and decorated the tables.

After the ride to save Bown, smiles were everywhere. I was greeted by numerous people each day who knew my name and at least one of the amazing versions of the tale of how I saved Mrs. Voise. It was amazing to me how twisted the story became, and my favorite was one of how I had killed not one but five lions with nothing but a sharp stick.

The Princes became favorites with the children, all of whom flocked close to hear stories of our countries below the mountains. They especially liked Landis' descriptions of the animals, for they seldom saw anything but snowshoe hares, foxes, eagles, and the animals that had bonded to various Antorans. Landis' description of a water buffalo had them bursting into laughter, and they couldn't get enough of Trevin's accounts of the giant sea snakes that sailors saw out in the ocean.

The girls, myself included, made dolls with the little children out of anything we could find. It was a competition among us to see who could be the most inventive, but I think the prize ultimately went to Brynna when she made a baby out of one of Cook Syra's big wooden spoons. When the cook saw the spoon dressed in a blue painted burlap bag with beads for eyes and curly yellow yarn for hair, she merely smiled and didn't have the heart to take it from the little blue-eyed girl who treasured it.

The night of the celebration came quickly, and everyone enjoyed the escape from daily struggles and the chance to dance. The dinner, though simple, was amazing, a true tribute to Cook Syra's abilities. Andric made her join us and everyone complimented the food and her staff until she beamed with pride.

After a dessert of honeyed oatcakes, the doors opened and Mr. and Mrs. Voise came in. Mr. Voise walked slowly, but smiled at everyone. I ran over and hugged them both. Everyone laughed and cheered. Men rose to pat Bown on the back while the women hugged Mylena.

When the enthusiasm died down, Mr. Bown said that he had a present for me.

"I'd be honored if you would accept this small token for saving my wife and I," he said, drawing something out of a small bag he carried.

My mouth fell open when I saw a beautifully worked, intricate chain on which hung a single claw that had been polished until it practically glowed. The claw was huge, close to the length of my palm. Looking closer, I saw that an image had been carved into it, the image of a fierce mountain lion.

"I don't deserve this," I said in awe.

Bown smiled. "This claw was from the lion that would have killed Mylena if you hadn't been there," he explained; his eyes glittered moistly. "We understand if you don't want to wear it, but it would honor us if you'd accept our gift. We weren't the only ones who worked on it."

"It's beautiful," I said honestly. "I would be honored to wear it."

Bown gave me a big smile before slipping the chain around my neck. I studied it. The black claw shone and was as smooth as a stone worn from years in a stream. The carved mountain lion had been inlaid with white sand and sealed over so that it, too, was smooth. The silver clasp the chain ran through was shaped like two paws with claws unsheathed. The tip of the big claw was coated in polished silver.

"We weren't diamond craftsmen for nothing," Mylena said with a warm smile that grew at my obvious admiration of the gift.

"Thank you," I told them both. I searched for other words to show how much the necklace meant to me, but came up at a loss in the face of such beauty.

"No, thank you," Mylena said. She threw her arms around me. Bown joined her, and then so did Mylena's closest friends followed by Bown's until I was squished in the middle of a huge, happy hug.

"Alright, then. Who's up for dancing?" Andric asked.

The crowd around us cheered and yelled, and the musicians scrambled for their instruments. The tables were moved out of the way and within a few minutes, the floor was full of laughing, merry Antorans. I made my way to where the other Crowns stood by the head table.

Trevin, still munching on an oatcake, gave me a toothy grin. "That's neat," he said with his mouth full, indicating the claw.

Landis picked it up and appraised it with a knowing eye. "Craftsmanship like that should bring them a fortune."

"Except they have nothing left to craft unless Kit kills another lion," Kaerdra said with a grin.

I laughed. "They'd better hide from me now!"

Behind us, a polite cough made us turn. Ayd bowed low, a small blue snow flower in his hand. When he rose, I was surprised to see him look straight at Nyssa. "For you, Princess," he said, his face slightly pale but his voice steady. "I would be honored if you would give me the pleasure of a dance."

I gritted my teeth, worried about Ayd's embarrassment when he was rejected; but to my astonishment, Nyssa blushed. "I would love to," she said. She smiled at us sheepishly and accepted his hand.

All of us watched, stunned, as the overjoyed Hawkmaster escorted her to the middle of the room where they twirled and melted in with the graceful pandemonium on the dance floor. I exchanged glances with Andric who stood near enough to be part of our circle but not too close that his presence might be an imposition. He grinned at me, then schooled his face to a wall of warm politeness once more, nodding at the citizens who came over to thank him for the wonderful evening.

Landis and Tisha joined the dance next, followed by Danyen and Brynna. I was even more surprised when Kenyen asked me to dance. I stuttered about how it was rude to leave Kaerdra by herself, but Andric swiftly stepped in and asked for her hand with a polite bow. Together, the four of us walked to the dance floor.

There was something special about the feeling in the castle that night, the way Antorans and foreigners laughed and danced without regard for rank, the hour, or the desperate times to come. It was as if everyone was determined to forget everything else and give themselves up to enjoying the evening. Nyssa danced two more songs with Ayd, then accepted the hand of a young farmer so shy he could barely meet her eyes. Not to be outdone, Kaerdra and Brynna were gladly escorted back onto the floor by two dark-haired brothers.

I danced somewhat gracefully with Kenyen, and only stepped on his toes once. He was a gentleman about it and blamed it on himself even though he danced with the same grace he used when wielding his sword. I sat out the next dance by choice and was swarmed by a group of younger girls and boys who begged me to tell them about the mountain lion. Young men and women drifted over to listen, and I found myself nervous at the attention. I had to school my talking so that I didn't rush and fall over my words.

The listeners leaned in as I described the snow and the shadows. I skipped the details about the Breizans because they were still children and deserved to live in the innocence of youth as long as possible. I told about finding Bown and how brave everyone was when an unknown danger attacked us. I spoke of the relief at finding ourselves safe again, then described the shape of the mountain lion as it jumped through the air.

My heart began to pound as I relived the sight of its reaching claws and the glint in its golden eyes. I described seeing Mylena in danger and the way my body reacted before my thoughts could even comprehend what was happening. I told them the lion's body felt like a battering ram when it crashed into me, and they laughed when I pushed away my fear of the memory by saying at least I was warm underneath its huge body.

I stopped at the point where the lion was on top of me and I could hear everyone calling but couldn't free myself, because that was all I remembered. I paused, then was surprised when a voice behind me took up the story.

"We ran over fearing the worst," Andric said. "We couldn't even see Princess Kit for the huge beast on top of her. It shuddered, and the tip of her sword stuck out of its back from where it had gone all the way through."

Several of the girls put hands to their mouths in horror, but they continued to listen eagerly to the story.

Andric sat down on a chair next to mine and leaned with an elbow on his knee, giving a dramatic air to the story. His voice caught the cadence of a practiced storyteller. "It took Captain Jashe, Falen, myself, and two of the other Princes to haul the lion off, and all we could see was Princess Kit covered in blood."

Another gasp, this time not just from the girls.

Andric smiled. "Luckily, most of the blood was from the cat." His face clouded minutely. "But she didn't respond when we waved smelling salts under her nose."

"What did you do?" a young girl, perhaps twelve, asked breathlessly.

Andric smiled at her. His voice lowered, "The men loaded her onto my horse and I rode until Tereg couldn't run any more. We switched horses at the base of the mountain; Horsemaster Drade's steed Sorn practically ran over anyone who dared to suggest any other mount. I could have sworn Sorn grew wings the way he flew over the ground that night. Bayn and Freis led the way, and the Princes rode close behind us. The others followed along much slower with Bown, Mylena, and the others who had been wounded during the fight."

I studied his face as he spoke. This part of the story was new to me, and he was well practiced at keeping his face expressionless of all but the emotions he wished to bring out in the story. I wondered, then, what he had really felt that night.

"When we reached the castle, Healer Jesson was already waiting for us, having been told of our distress by Hawkmaster Ayd whose birds had tracked us since the battle." His eyes glittered darkly. "My arms were about to fall off." I slapped him on the shoulder and everyone laughed. "But I wouldn't let anyone else carry her through the castle." All of us grew quiet. Andric continued, his eyes distant. "When she didn't wake up, I feared that she never would even though Jesson kept telling me she was going to be fine. I didn't leave her side."

He fell quiet, and I heard one of the girls whisper, "How romantic."

Andric didn't seem to hear her. He stared down at his hands, his expression unreadable.

I took up the story. "When I awoke, he was asleep in a chair next to my bed. I called his name, and at first I think he thought he was dreaming."

The girls giggled.

"It was the best dream," Andric finished. Everyone laughed, but he only looked at me.

A new song, a beautiful, slow melody, struck up behind us. Several of the older boys, inspired by the story, turned to the girls and asked them to dance. The girls blushed and accepted, giggling to each other. The younger ones, boys mostly, were sickened by this display and dispersed to root out snacks from the kitchen.

Andric and I smiled at each other, then he asked seriously, "Would you accept my hand for this dance, Princess Kit?"

The way he said it made my heart skip a beat. I knew I shouldn't accept. Our emotions were too near to the surface, and our hearts were caught in a situation we couldn't win. But it was one dance, and perhaps the only dance I would ever be able to enjoy with him. I would survive a thousand heartaches for the chance to be so close to him. I nodded and he smiled.

His hand was cool when I took it, making me wonder if my own was hot. He spun me in a slow circle as we made our way onto the floor.

"That's a beautiful necklace," he said after what seemed an eternity of silence and mixed emotions as we danced slowly across the floor.

I smiled slightly, glancing down at the claw. "It makes me feel tough."

"You are tough," he replied.

I looked up to see whether he was making fun of me or not.

He studied me seriously for a moment, then the smile that I loved tugged at the corners of his mouth. "You're too easy to read, you know," he said, stepping back to bow as the dance required.

"Oh, yes?" I challenged, "And that's a bad thing?"

He nodded, clicking his tongue. "An undesirable trait for a ruler; those who look to you for guidance must never know your true thoughts or else they'll see you as human."

I curtsied a second behind the other female dancers. "I'd rather they know I'm not perfect, that way if a mistake occurs, I haven't destroyed their respect in one fell swoop."

He laughed, a light, pleasant sound. He pursed his lips. "I can't say that I find much fault with your logic, except that in expecting to fail you might set yourself up for it."

I enjoyed his banter and grinned, up to the challenge. "Not setting myself up for it; more like preparation. Because I'm human, I know I will make mistakes. I just don't want to devastate an entire country because of it."

He raised an eyebrow. "Perhaps the Zalens will be getting an unexpected firecracker for a Crown Princess when you go home." His smile faltered.

A knot formed in my stomach and I pushed on quickly. "So how do you avoid making mistakes?"

He spun me around slowly as the other dancers did the same. "Oh, I've made plenty of mistakes." He winked at me. "It's just a matter of making the ones that no one will notice. I was hard put to explain the time I put a man in prison for stealing based on another man's account, only to find out that it was the other man who was the thief and had stolen a horse the first man was just trying to get back." He grinned. "The confusing part was when it turned out they were brothers and the horse had been given to both of them by their father, and so in essence, they were each stealing something that already belonged to them. Very confusing."

I laughed. "What did they do?"

Andric grinned. "Well, the second I let the first brother out of jail he punched the second brother, then they decided to trade the horse for a bull and a heifer of which they each kept one." He sighed dramatically as we spun around each other, then he concluded when we met up again, "It started all over again when the heifer got pregnant from the bull."

I laughed and tripped over my feet, but he caught me just before I fell. He held me close to his chest for a moment and stared down at me. Then he shut his eyes tightly. "It's too much," he said quietly.

"I know," I whispered, the pain in my heart evident in my voice. I longed to feel his arms around me like the night he held me, and missed the touch of his breath in my hair and the way his scent wrapped me warmer than any blanket.

He opened his eyes and attempted a small smile. "But I enjoy talking to you like this. If this is all that we have, at least it's something."

I nodded past the lump in my throat.

He picked up the dance where we had left off, spinning me around him again. We danced the remainder of the song in silence, hearts aching but reveling in the closeness of the moment.

Chapter 21

A knock sounded at my door. Glancing at the light filtering through the marble, I noted that it was late, sometime past midnight. Most of the celebrants had retired from the dance about an hour ago, myself included. I wondered who was knocking at the late hour.

To my surprise, Tisha, Nyssa, Brynna, and Kaerdra all waited expectantly when I opened the door. They wore their night robes with their hair either braided or pinned for sleep, but no one looked tired despite the hours of dancing.

"Mind if we come in?" Nyssa asked. She walked into the room without waiting for an answer.

The others came in at my motion and filed past me toward the bed. Without an invitation, they all climbed onto my bed and made themselves comfortable amid the plush blankets. "Come sit," Tisha said. She patted a spot by my pillows encouragingly.

"Fine," I complied with some hesitation. "But I have no idea what you're up to."

Brynna laughed. "Oh, it's not as bad as you think."

I crawled onto the bed and leaned back on my pillows. When nobody spoke, I spread my hands. "Alright, what's going on?"

They grinned, but it was Nyssa who spoke. "We need to have a serious talk about boys."

My eyebrows rose in surprise.

Tisha laughed, "Don't worry, we know all the mushy stuff. This is nothing like that."

"Yeah," Kaerdra put in. "Besides, you're the youngest Crown here next to Tisha. Don't think we'd come to you for that kind of advice."

"Good," I said, extremely relieved. "What is it then?"

Brynna moved closer on the bed. "At home, I have my nursemaid Krynn to talk to about boy stuff and all that."

"But here, we only have each other," Nyssa said. "And we have some major things to talk about."

"Like Ayd," Kaerdra put in with a knowing laugh.

Nyssa blushed, but nodded. "Yes, like Ayd." She sighed. "He's wonderful, isn't he?"

Tisha nodded. "I like his eyes; they're such a pretty color of blue."

"You have your Landis, so you can just back off my boy," Nyssa replied in mock seriousness.

Tisha laughed, "Don't worry. Landis and I are spoken for. We've made a promise to be wed a year from now, but our parents don't know we're that serious yet."

The girls oohed in excitement.

"And you're all invited to the wedding," she said with a little clap of joy as if she couldn't contain herself.

"Congratulations," Kaerdra replied with a big smile. The rest of us echoed it, bouncing up and down on the bed like little girls.

I found myself grinning and enjoying myself. I had never had sisters or close girl friends to gossip with, so it was an extra treat to find that these girls actually went out of their way to come talk. I was almost at ease when Kaerdra turned to me.

"Alright, let's have it about Andric."

My heart slowed.

"Yes, yes," Brynna said, scooting closer. "What's the deal with you two?"

"And how will your father react?" Tisha put in. It was no secret that the countries below the mountains held Antor in contempt for the stealing they had done and the rumor of their animal magic, but my father and Landis' father held the biggest grudges. I wondered now if it was because they wanted to keep their own raids secret from the rest of the rulers.

I sighed, feeling the weight of reality settle onto my shoulders. "Andric and I know it will never work out," I said softly.

"But you're perfect for each other," Brynna protested.

"And he obviously needs you," Tisha said, running her fingers through the ruffles on the edge of a pillow.

"But he was a thief, and I don't know if any of our parents will ever be able to forgive that," Kaerdra said gently.

As much as her words hurt me, I nodded. "Exactly. It would never work out."

Kaerdra then surprised me. "Who cares what the rest of the world thinks? You have to worry about yourself once in a while."

The other girls nodded and I stared at them. "But I'm a Crown. I can't just marry a Prince from Antor, hundreds of miles from Zalen. Neither of us can leave our people."

That sobered them up. "You're right," Nyssa said quietly after a few minutes. "I forgot that you're the Crown now, and Andric's father doesn't rule."

"But Rory will be alright," Kaerdra put in. There was an edge of stubbornness to her voice.

I looked at her in surprise, and was even more startled when a tear rolled down her cheek. "Kaerdra?" I asked, confused.

She lowered her head so that her face was hidden by her long blond hair. "I can't help it," she said. "I love him."

All the girls turned to stare at her.

"You love Rory?" I managed to say. Tears burned in my eyes.

She nodded again, then buried her head on my shoulder. "Oh, Kit. How do you stay so strong? He's your brother and you don't even know how he's doing."

I rubbed her back and blinked rapidly to keep the tears from falling. "My parents keep me informed," I said, leaving out the fact that their updates were very simple and sparse. "He's going to be alright; I just know he is."

"Is he getting better?" she asked. She turned to look up at me, her blue eyes rimmed with red.

I couldn't lie to her; instead I shook my head and tears spilled down my cheeks. "No," I whispered.

She turned her head and cried on my lap. The other girls gathered close, patting our backs and telling us that Rory would be alright.

I knew deep down that what they said didn't make a difference in Rory's condition, but somehow I felt better, as if just knowing that other people here shared my sorrow made it easier to bear the fact that my brother was sick to the point of dying and I didn't know from one letter to the next if the news they brought would shatter my world.

***

The next morning, Andric began breakfast by announcing that if everyone was ready, we could have the duel that night. The girls jumped up and down very unprincesslike and taunted the boys. The Princes and I exchanged worried looks, but I knew they would go easy on the girls. I also knew that the boys would be surprised when they saw how much the girls had learned in such a short period of time.

All of the talk during the day was of the coming duel. We heard it as we rode around the city delivering food, and when we stopped to help a kindly older woman move her few belongings to her sister's house down the road so that they could stay together.

"I hope you Princesses knock their socks off," she said in a feisty tone that surprised us. I was grateful the boys were out of hearing range. "We'll be cheering for you!" she said excitedly.

When we left the house, Tisha turned to me worriedly. "I didn't know that anyone would be coming to watch."

I shrugged, surprised as well. "I guess we can't blame them for wanting to attend. It should be highly entertaining."

"Hey," Nyssa said at my teasing tone.

We joked on the way back to the stables, and then met the boys near the forge where Smithy Hensas said to meet him for our swords. He had planned to hand them out earlier, but decided last minute that he would wait, saying that there were some 'final touches' that had to be made.

"He probably has to finish cutting yours out of paper so that it's light enough," Danyen teased Nyssa.

She slapped him on the shoulder. "Maybe he melted yours in the forge."

His eyes widened and she laughed.

"Not melted, nor paper," a deep voice said behind us. We turned to see Smithy Hensas and his craftsmen walking our way. They held the swords wrapped in hides so that we couldn't see them. "A bit anxious, are we?" the Smith asked knowingly at our furtive glances toward the hides. He smiled in amusement. "I can guarantee that each sword is to your satisfaction." His face darkened and he continued in a low rumble. "And if it's not, you'd better say it is." At our lack of intimidation, he grinned, showing more joviality than we had ever seen from him. He waved his arm toward us. "Men, present the Princes and Princesses of Denbria with their swords."

I stood last in line and waited almost patiently as the other Crowns accepted and unwrapped their blades. I could hear their oohs and aahs, and saw the pleased smiles on the faces of the Smithy's men.

When Bagan handed me my sword, his black bear shuffled up behind him and gave the weapon an appreciative snuff. Bagan bowed low and said, "You've already proven worthy to own such a blade. May it defend you well."

I blushed and accepted it, and was immediately amazed at how much lighter and refined it felt compared to the sword I used in practice, which was the same one that had saved me from the mountain lion. I was loath to part with it afterwards, and Smithy Hensas never asked for it back.

When I took the wrapping off my new sword, I could only stare. The blade was light silver in color, and polished until it shone in the last of the evening light. The hilt was gold, and wrapped securely in smoothed golden wire threads that fit my hand like a glove. Intricate etchings ran down the blade; the palm leaves of Zalen mixed with the stockier leaves of the Antoran trees and trickled down the blade to where a fierce mountain lion snarled at me, twin to the one etched on the claw around my neck. The bottom of the hilt was shaped like a dew drop, and the guards curved up toward the blade to protect my hand, rising in two graceful curves to catch unaware combatants so I could throw their swords aside.

The blade was lighter than I had imagined, but weighted well so that it rested securely in my hand. I swung and it whistled through the air. It was a sword like no other I had ever seen. I didn't feel worthy to hold it.

Smithy Hensas must have seen something in the look I gave him, for his smile grew even bigger and he nodded, a proud gleam in his eyes. Tanner Saren handed us the sheaths he had fashioned to fit each sword. His work showed the palm leaves of Zalen down the leather of my sheath, and I saw that the emblems of the other countries, the oak of Eskand, the sword of Tyn, the apple of Veren, the great ships of Faer, the hoof print of Maesh, and the dagger of Cren were emblazoned on each sheath and echoed on the blades. The others grinned at each other when they saw the mountain lion on my sword.

"I don't think any of us has a chance against the lion killer," Kenyen teased.

"That's fine," I told them honesty. "I'm really not planning on dueling. This is between you *real* Crowns."

They laughed at my inflection, then protested; but I refused to give in. "I've had enough dueling for a lifetime," I told them. "Besides, this way it'll be even and we'll have a good match."

"But we'll be fighting alone!" Tisha protested.

I laughed. "You'll have each other. And don't worry, Master Hensas is going to give everyone padded blades so no one will get hurt. It'll be fun."

The girls looked ready to back out of the duel. Smithy Hensas chuckled. "Now don't be gettin' cold feet. This crowd's been wanting a good fight for quite a while. They're just thrilled you volunteered for it!"

"Why did we volunteer?" Brynna wailed on our way back to the castle to get changed.

I wore my sheath strapped around my waist, and was amazed at how comfortable it felt to have the sword there. The hilt was cool to the touch, and I rested my hand on it as we walked.

The boys followed behind us comparing their blades and fighting against invisible foes in the snow. They seemed excited now that the duel was at hand, and I regretted my decision just a tiny bit to not go up against them and test my skills; the twins, especially, were well-known for their prowess with a blade. At least with the girls dueling the boys, it would all be just fun and games.

Chapter 22

The arena was next to the stables and covered against the snow. The sides were stacked with benches, some that were already there and others that had been roughly fashioned for the occasion. At Andric's invitation, I joined him near the head of the arena where his herald, a jolly man with a long, skinny nose, entertained the crowd with topsy-turvy stories until he had them rolling in laughter. Andric told me that the man had begged for the position when he became ruler, and Andric had given him a chance at a small luncheon in which the higher-ups of the country came to test out his mettle on the throne.

"I knew it would be a stressful meeting, so I told him that if he could lighten the mood, I'd hire him."

The herald turned and bowed at us, his eyes twinkling. "And here I am," he said with a flourish. He spun back and continued the story he was telling without missing a beat.

Andric laughed. "It was probably one of the best moves I made when I first took up the crown."

"The best," the herald put in smoothly before turning back to the crowd again.

We both laughed.

The herald announced each Prince and Princess with an amazing assortment of information about their home countries. The Antorans were impressed at his description of the Faerean ships, the Tyn horses, and the acres upon acres of crops that grew around Veren.

Then he started into descriptions of the rulers, the Crowns' parents, that had everyone laughing, the Crowns included. When he stuttered into an introduction of Kenyen and Danyen, his voice a low vibrato in an exact representation of their father's stately voice, they were laughing so hard they clutched their sides. With Tisha, he gave a hearty imitation of the Maesh King's sturdy walk, complete with a little hop at the end. She laughed until tears rolled down her cheeks. It was at his impersonation of Brynna's father, King Trand, sipping tea while he decided the fate of a poor prisoner in bonds that topped them all. Brynna was still laughing when she put on the padded armor to prepare for her first fight against Landis.

The duels went quickly, but it was obvious the Princes were surprised by the Princesses' skills. They thrust and parried fast enough to keep the Princes on their toes, and Kaerdra even took Trevin out of the running with a quick spin and a slash across his unprotected back. The Prince took the defeat gracefully and made his sister grin when he stated he was relieved they had used wooden swords.

In the end, though, it was Kenyen against Danyen, as everyone had known it would be. They fought swift and hard, two opponents who knew each other's every weakness and strength. It quickly became clear that the battle between them was one that had been fought often and without mercy; they laughed at each other's occasionally landed hits, but their stances were sure and the onlookers held their collective breath with every attack.

By the time Kenyen finally beat Danyen, the audience stood and roared for both of them, chanting their names in unison. Nobody cared who won; it was the chance to see such a good fight that made them cheer.

When the fight was over, Andric walked across the arena floor to give Kenyen the small dagger that was his reward. The audience cheered until someone yelled, "Show us what a true King's made of!" His voice wavered and I wondered if he had partaken of a bit too much old cider.

"Sit down, Dowld," another audience member yelled. "We like our Prince in one piece." Several cheers of agreement went up.

Andric was obviously torn. He glanced at me and I shook my head firmly. He looked back at the crowd and sighed, "Pity that he's already worn out from fighting his brother. It wouldn't be a fair duel with Crown Prince Kenyen already tired out, would it?"

Several people shouted that it wouldn't be fair indeed. I think they could see that Prince Andric wanted to duel almost as much as the crowd wanted him to.

He handed the dagger to Prince Kenyen and shook his hand. "To the best swordsmanship I've ever seen," he told the Tyn Prince. He turned to Danyen and handed him a smaller dagger I hadn't seen. "To a pair of brothers I would be honored to have as guests any time."

The audience roared and clapped, storming the arena floor to congratulate the brothers and commend the other Crowns. The older lady from earlier gave Kaerdra a tight hug.

Andric smiled when he reached me. "So," he said with a gleam in his dark eyes. "Did you shake your head because you were afraid I'd lose, or because you were afraid I'd win?"

I grinned. "Both, actually. If you won, you'd risk ruining the relationship you've created with the twins, possibly affecting the way the other Crowns think of you and any future alliances that would be greatly beneficial for your people. If you lost, it could affect the respect and motivation of the people who follow you. It's hard on citizens to see their ruler get defeated. It makes them human," I concluded with a grin, using his words against him.

He laughed and gave me a sideways appraising glance. "Wow, I didn't know you'd put that much thought into it."

I shook my head. "I hadn't," I confessed, "But it makes sense."

He nodded thoughtfully. "Yes, it does."

***

Trae's leg had mended and he was anxious to run. At my request for places to go, Drade offered to give us a tour of the country, at least as far as we could get in a day's ride. The others joined with more enthusiasm than I expected. They were tired of entertaining themselves within the castle walls. It had been too stormy of late to do much outside, but the weather had finally cleared and the winter sun shone brightly on the fresh snow, making it sparkle like a million diamonds.

I was surprised to see Andric come out of the stables with his horse Tereg and the five wolves following close behind. The younger wolves dove through the snow and chased each other in circles around the group, clearly excited for an adventure. Freis and Bayn watched with matching calm wolfish grins, nipping good-naturedly at them when they came close.

"They're a rambunctious bunch," Kenyen said as Tyd, the dark gray male, and Myn, the light gray female, raced around his horse. The horse set its ears back and stomped threateningly.

Andric nodded. "They keep us on our toes. There's enough energy in those three to keep Freis and Bayn busy for the rest of their lives."

"You mean you're not bonded to them?" Landis asked interestedly.

Andric shook his head. "I bonded with Bayn and Freis. The other three were cubs that we stumbled on when we were patrolling the border. Though we never bonded, they've been a welcome addition, though tiresome," he added with a laugh. His expression grew thoughtful as he watched them. "I never did find out what happened to their previous pack. Their memories are clouded when it comes to that part, and I think they were taken out by an avalanche or one of the other many accidents of nature."

"That's horrible," Brynna said.

I nodded. From what Andric had taught me about wolves, the other pack wouldn't leave their pups roaming about for no reason. Something terrible must have happened.

"So you can read their thoughts even though you aren't bonded to them?" Landis asked.

Andric nodded. "I think it's because they're still linked to Bayn and Freis. Wolf packs are like that. They share thoughts to communicate; that's what makes them such lethal hunters."

At everyone's surprised stares, he smiled. "A lot of animals are that way. Have you never wondered at the way birds can fly so close together but they never run into each other and always seem to have the same destination? Or the way deer can run as a graceful herd, turning at the blink of an eye without missing a step?"

Drade grinned and Sorn stepped up to take the lead. "Well, now that you've some food for thought, let's muse over the ride."

Andric rode beside Drade and they talked quietly about the land, noting changes from the last year and discussing what the future would hold. Both of them seemed saddened by the fact that they would be leaving, but accepted it stalwartly because there was no other choice. I did hear Andric mention that he planned to come back and check on things.

We stopped on a hill between two of the craggy rocks that seemed to be everywhere. Drade said they came from an ancient volcano, stating that one of the mountains around us had heaved molten lava centuries ago and it had cooled into the twisted forms. I know I wasn't the only one who looked up at the nearby mountains with a touch of uncertainty, hoping that another one didn't decide to erupt.

We were eating lunch when Trevin pegged Danyen in the head with a snowball. Danyen yelped and dove at Trevin, tackling him in the soft snow. We laughed as they rolled down the hill still wrestling each other. By the time they came back, they were covered from head to toe in snow, and acted like they had gotten it out of their system; but the second our backs were turned, they pelted us with snowballs they had gathered on their way up.

It turned into an all-out snowball fight. Tisha ran behind a scraggly tree where she packed snowballs for Landis and he protected her. Nyssa and Brynna shrieked and tossing powdery handfuls at everyone, while the rest of us took up positions behind the various rocks and trees, darting back and forth to take shots at unguarded backs before diving for shelter. The wolves galloped between everyone, nipping playfully and biting at snowballs tossed their way.

Kaerdra came over and pretended to be on my side before she smeared a handful of snow in my hair. I chased her around the side of the hill into an ambush set by Trevin and Kenyen. I yelled and ran back with both of them at my heels, only to be rescued by Andric and Danyen carrying armfuls of snowballs.

I took two of the snowballs from Andric's arms as I ran by, then spun and chucked them at my pursuers. The first one caught Trevin in the stomach and the second hit Kenyen on the side of the head when he bent to gather more snow. They both yelled in dismay, and were spattered with more snowballs from Andric and Danyen. I wondered where Drade was until he dove from the top of the hill and tackled our two attackers so that they landed face down in the snow.

We were all laughing so hard that we could barely stand. I fell to my knees in the snow, dropping the partly-packed snowball in my hands. Andric and Danyen collapsed on either side of me, their noses red and cheeks flushed. I fell back on the snow between them, laughing until my sides hurt. The wolves settled around us, panting with pleased wolf grins.

As we lay there, a snowball flew up into the air and fell toward me, a lucky toss by Danyen who was also lying in the snow where he had fallen. I was too tired to move and merely put my hands over my face, but Andric threw his cloak over me before it landed. I heard it splatter and laughed weakly, my sides sore. "My hero!"

"Saved from a fate worse than death," Andric replied with a chuckle as he collapsed back down next to me.

I turned my head to look at him, and was surprised to see him watching me. "Thank you," I said softly.

He gave me a little smile.

There was snow and leaves tangled in his brown hair, disheveled and unruly since it had pulled free from its warrior's tail. I reached over and freed a leaf. "You really should wash your hair once in a while," I teased. "Creatures might come to live there with all this vegetation."

"You can have that," Andric replied, his tone overly-generous. "It's my gift to you."

I sat up, laughing. "Then I shall treasure it always." I tucked it in my thick riding cloak.

Andric jumped to his feet and offered me a hand. I took it and rose to join him, then stumbled when the snow shifted under my feet. He caught me close to him and held me for a second. "Saved twice," he whispered in my ear.

He let go before anyone noticed, but winked at me charmingly behind Danyen's back as he leaned over to help the Prince out of the snow. My ear tingled from the brush of his lips against my skin, and I wondered how I would ever get along without the Antoran Prince.

Chapter 23

The group dinner a few nights later started out like the others, full of talk and laughter, stories from the week, and a simple but filling fare. Landis was entertaining everyone with a story of the day he and his father had gotten caught in a hurricane on one of their ships; then I heard Freis snarl.

Surprised, I glanced over. The wolf stood next to Andric, who was one seat down with Kenyen between us. Andric looked at her as well, but turned his attention quickly back to Landis so as not to seem rude.

An object whistled through the air straight at Andric. Before anyone could move, Freis leaped to the table in front of the Prince, knocking him off his chair. A sharp yelp sounded, followed by Andric's shout. I rose to my feet in time to see Andric holding Freis. My heart slowed. A thick black arrow shaft stuck out of her side. Guards swarmed around the Prince, blocking him from view.

Bayn snarled at the Prince's side, his eyes searching the crowd for the shooter; he kept glancing at Freis with his ears back and a whine in his throat. Andric looked around with wide eyes until he spotted me through the ring of guards. "Help," he mouthed, tears bright in his eyes.

His gaze broke through my shock. My limbs were freed and I could think. "I'll get Jesson," I shouted over the roar of the confused crowd.

He nodded and I turned and ran. I sprinted past the Crowns who watched helplessly, and through the other guards who began to search the onlookers for weapons. One of them shouted just before I sprang through the doors at the end; I only had to turn and show him who I was before he apologized and let me go.

My heart pounded and each step I took renewed the scene in my head of Andric holding the white wolf, blood streaming down her fur and her eyes glazing over. I ran straight through the side doors held opened by a wide-eyed young servant and darted across the snow in my dress and slippers. I had almost reached the door to the stables where I knew Jesson was tending to a foaling mare when the howl pierced the air.

My steps faltered and I stumbled to my knees in the snow, tears clouding my vision. There was no mistaking the sorrow in Bayn's voice. I was too late.

The stable door flew open and Jesson ran out. He saw me kneeling in the snow, glanced once at the castle, then his face went white. "Was that Bayn?"

At my nod, he put a hand to his head. "Prince Andric?" he whispered as though afraid to hear my answer.

I shook my head. "Freis."

"Freis," he replied, his voice somewhat stronger but still full of sorrow. "What happened?"

I couldn't think past the fog in my mind. I kept seeing the scene over and over again, the whistle in the air, Freis knocking Andric to the ground, the arrow protruding out of her white fur, the pain in Andric's eyes when he looked to me for help. I had run to get that help, but it didn't matter. Now he was there by himself, surrounded by hundreds of people but completely alone.

I pushed to my feet heedless of the snow in my slippers. "He needs us," I said, staring past the healer. I stumbled through the snow and heard Jesson fall in behind me, his own steps faltering.

When we made it back to the banquet hall, we found only chaos. People shouted to each other and milled about, wanting to help but uncertain where to start. Andric and his guards weren't there. When I made it to the Crowns, they saw the look on my face and pointed at the small side door that led to the hallway past our staircase. Jesson and I both went through it.

At my fumbled questions, a servant told me that the Prince was unavailable. His words struck a wrong note that helped clear my mind. "I am Crown Princess Kirit of Zalen. You'll show me where Prince Andric is," I commanded, finding strength in knowing that if I didn't reach Andric as soon as possible, I didn't know what would happen.

The servant straightened immediately and held a hand to his heart in salute. "Yes, Princess Kirit. Please follow me."

Jesson glanced at me sideways as we followed the young man dressed in Antor's black and green, but I ignored him. The only thing that mattered to me was Andric. When the servant ordered the doors to Andric's quarters to be opened, we pushed past him into an elegant sitting room. There, in stark contrast to the pandemonium below us, we found only silence.

Six guards stood at various positions around the room, two at the windows, two at the doors, and the other two standing helplessly to either side of where Prince Andric had sunk to his knees on the floor. Bayn sat next to the Prince, his dark head so low it almost touched the ground. The other wolves, Tyd, Kreen, and Myn, lay on the floor around them and didn't give us so much as a glance when we walked in.

I couldn't tear my eyes away from Andric. His head was bowed, but I could see tears falling to land in Freis' soft white fur. He held the wolf on his lap as gently as if she was a sister who had died. The wolf was someone he had spent his entire life with and had finally given up her own for him. The thick black shaft sticking out from the side of her ribs looked cruel and out of place. The sight of it reminded me that she wasn't sleeping; she was gone.

Tears welled up in my eyes and I fell to my knees in front of Andric. Bayn came out of it long enough to look at me. He touched his nose to Freis' fur, then shuddered. Another howl tore from his chest. He lifted his nose, his eyes closed tight, and voiced his sorrow long and low. The sound pierced me to the core, echoing and magnifying the feeling of loss there by a thousand fold. Even when it faded away to nothing, I heard his howl continuously in my mind.

Without lifting his head, Andric set a hand on the dark wolf's shoulders. His fingers convulsed into a fist, holding onto the thick fur as though it was a lifeline. Bayn turned his head toward his Prince, and Andric rested his forehead against the wolf's. They sat there like that for a long time, Andric's tears running down the wolf's nose, both of their eyes closed.

"I can't do this anymore," Andric finally whispered. I wasn't sure he knew I was there, but when he looked up, it was straight into my eyes. The pain on his face was so hard to see that I almost looked away, but I couldn't tear myself from his gaze. "I can't do it anymore."

I nodded, unable to speak.

Andric lowered Freis' body gently to the ground in front of me; her beautiful white fur matched the thick white rug that was stained with her blood. The Prince rose to his feet. I could see the helplessness in his eyes, the fury and pain that had no outlet. He gazed around, looking through the guards and Jesson as if they weren't there.

Without warning, Andric grabbed a huge glass vase of dried branches that stood near the door, then turned and smashed it against the fireplace. "I can't do this anymore!" he shouted, tears of rage mixing with those of sorrow.

A guard stepped forward to stop him, but I shook my head and he took his place back by the window.

Andric picked up an end table and slammed it against the wall. It broke into splinters, taking down a wall sconce with it. He turned and caught up a stone statue as long as his forearm and threw it against the fireplace. It broke into three pieces, tearing chunks of marble from the fireplace with its momentum. The Prince threw two armchairs out of his way to reach a second vase which he then smashed near the first.

Andric stumbled against the fireplace, his chest heaving. He leaned so that his forehead touched the cool stone, his disheveled hair hiding his face. "Why?" he asked, his voice full of agony. "Why?" he repeated louder. He growled, then pounded the stone with his fist, heedless of the pain.

I jumped to my feet and grabbed his arm. He tried to wrestle it out of my grasp, then gave up and fell against me, burying his face against my shoulder. "Why, Kit? Why did this happen? Why do I keep going? Why do I care so much?" He sobbed. "Why Freis?"

I smoothed his hair, blinking the tears from my eyes. "I don't know," I whispered. "But it's who you are."

He took a shuddering breath, then stepped back and turned away. For a minute I was afraid he would start punching the wall again, but his voice was defeated when he spoke, "Who I am? How do you know that when I don't even know myself?" He wiped the tears angrily from his face and turned back to look at Freis' body. "This is because of me," he said softly.

Bayn rose and put his head against Andric's leg. We were close enough that he brushed against me, too, and shared with me the images he showed the Prince.

I saw Andric and all of his wolves as they raced through the snow. Andric rode a horse and it was night, but they galloped heedless of the danger of unsure footing. The scene was through the wolf's eyes, and I gave a start when he glanced up at Andric and the form he was holding in front him on the horse. Me, lifeless, his arms tight around me. They were racing home after the battle with the mountain lion.

"Why her?" Andric's voice asked the wolf in the memory. "Why is she so reckless?" I could feel all of the wolves connected with him, sharing a conversation in their minds.

"Not reckless," a thought corrected him. Freis. The words were sounds, translated through my mind as though I had spoken to wolves all my life.

"How could I let this happen?" Andric pressed angrily.

The wolf nudged him again, her mind calm but also anxious as they loped headlong through the night. "If any of us dies to save another, it is a death of honor, of love. Love is what we live for and what we die for."

"What kind of love am I showing her if I can't even keep her safe?" he demanded. Sorn stumbled on a deeper patch of snow, then quickly regained his footing.

"You can't live in fear of losing someone," Bayn said, his tones deep and sure. "You can't be there at all times to protect those you care about. Danger is a part of life, and so is death."

Freis' softer tones agreed, a gentle harmony to Bayn's thoughts. "It's the way of the wolf you've known since you were young. We live for each other knowing the danger life carries with it."

"But she's not a wolf," Andric said. There was a gentler touch to his thoughts, but also one of frustration. He sighed, "I don't know my thoughts when I'm around her."

"She's close to a wolf," Tyd said.

"Close enough," Freis agreed. "She'll be alright; you'll see."

"I hope so," Andric replied.

Bayn glanced up to see the castle spires looming above the trees.

"She wouldn't be here if it wasn't for me," the Prince continued, his thoughts forced.

"None of us would," Bayn concurred. "But your purpose is ours. Fate, destiny, whatever you'd like to call it brought us all together to this point; the rest is up to each of us. None of us goes into it blindly. Kit knew the danger when she chose to lead the group, just like each of us knew the battle we would face when we found Bown. You can't save everyone, Andric, and you can't destroy yourself for those who slip through your fingers."

Freis continued where Bayn stopped. "You're in a position to do the greatest good, and you owe it to yourself and all of Antor to do that. Don't live in regret; live with wisdom from your memories, not sorrow. We believe in you."

Freis' last words, 'we believe in you', stayed in my head when I stepped back from Bayn. Andric stared down at the wolf, his face troubled and tear-streaked. "I don't think that belief was well-founded," he said quietly.

"It was and is," I said out loud. I felt Bayn's echoed agreement even though I wasn't touching him.

Andric walked slowly to one of the remaining chairs and sat down, his head in his hands. We waited quietly. After what seemed an eternity, the Prince took a deep breath, then rose back to his feet. He didn't say a word when he knelt by Freis and gathered her body up in his arms. We followed him out the door and down the stairs, past the people who still waited around the banquet hall and watched us quietly with sad faces when we went by, and out the door leading toward the wall.

252

We walked past the stables and down a rocky path to a clearing I had never seen before. Giant headstones marked the graves of the royal members and honored soldiers who had died in service to Antor. I was numbly surprised to see Jesson already there; I couldn't remember when he had left Andric's room.

A grave had already been prepared, attesting to the length of time that had gone by in Andric's quarters. The markings of an ice pick and a shovel could be seen on the sides of the hole, but the tools had been taken tactfully away. Two guards stood a short distance back to give us privacy. A thick green velvet cloak had been spread across the bottom of the grave. Andric knelt down and set Freis' body on the cloak, then rose quickly and turned away to hide a sob that shook his body.

The four wolves ringed the grave, their heads low. Bayn raised his muzzle and gave one last, long howl. The other wolves joined him this time, their voices mixing in a beautiful, haunting harmony that I knew I would never forget. When Bayn was done, he dropped his head and walked slowly back toward the castle. The others followed him solemnly; none of the puppyish capering that I was used to seeing from them lifted their steps.

I glanced at Jesson, uncertain of the customs in Antor regarding the loss of a bonded animal. He looked past me, his brow creased and eyes wet. I turned in the direction of his gaze and saw the Prince kneeling at another grave site; one hand rested on the feet of a beautiful white headstone that had been carved into the shape of an angel with her head bowed. He whispered softly; his lips moved, but his words didn't reach us. I desperately wanted to go to him, but I stayed where I was.

After some time had passed, Jesson walked over and asked the Prince something. When Andric didn't reply, the healer came back with deep sorrow on his face. He motioned to one of the guards who brought over a pair of shovels. When the guard bent to scoop from the pile of frozen dirt, Jesson shook his head and held out his hand. The guard gave him the shovel wordlessly. I reached for the other one. At the guard's stare, I frowned slightly and he handed it to me.

Jesson settled his own cloak around Freis' body so that it was covered completely, then we began to fill in the grave. We set the dirt in softly so that there was no sound of cold earth falling against the body that had been warm and alive such a short time ago. It took longer than I expected, but Andric didn't move from his mother's grave until we were done.

When we finished, we waited without pressing him. He finally rose and came back to us; we waited with him near the fresh grave for a long time. He eventually turned and patted Jesson on the shoulder, then seemed to notice me standing there.

"Thank you," he whispered.

"Can I walk back with you?" I asked quietly.

He shook his head. "I need some time alone, if that's alright. I just have some things I need to figure out."

I nodded, my heart constricting painfully as I watched him walk slowly over the snow. I shivered, suddenly feeling the cold. A hand touched my shoulder and I turned to see Jesson watching me.

"You alright?" he asked quietly.

I nodded, but the tears that filled my eyes said differently. I was amazed I wasn't out of tears yet after all I had cried, but they were persistent.

He nodded in understanding. "I need help with a foal if you have some time."

The thought of a warm stable and new life was like a balm to my aching heart. I nodded. "Yes, please."

Jesson put an arm around my shoulders and led me toward the stables where Drade met us with tears in his eyes. I remembered the horse he had lost on our journey to Antor, and realized he knew exactly what Andric was going through. Maybe that was why Jesson had invited me, so I could be prepared to help Andric through it the way the Prince had helped Drade.

The Horsemaster opened the door and motioned for us to go through, then followed behind us after securely shutting out the cold.

Chapter 24

This time, I was the one on the roof with the blankets when Andric finally left his room two days later. It was nighttime and cold, but Tyd, the small gray wolf, and Kreen, the young black one, kept me company. The wolves had all taken turns sitting with the Prince. It was Bayn and Myn's turn now. Tyd gave a short whine and I turned to see Andric push the door open, the two other wolves behind him.

He walked straight to me and hugged me tight. "I'm sorry," he said quietly.

"About what?" I asked, surprised. "You have nothing to be sorry for."

"This isn't how I pictured your stay in Antor, sword fighting, near-death experiences, sadness, loss, misery. . . ."

I cut him off with a frown. "I'm glad you didn't picture it that way, because that's not how it's been. You wanted this to be a learning experience? Well, I've learned more about life and leadership in one winter here than I have the rest of my life put together. I won't be the same when we have to go home."

He looked at me for several minutes, his face unreadable. "And that's not a bad thing?" he asked softly. "You've seen and gone through things you should never have experienced."

I shook my head firmly. "It's not a bad thing at all. Look at the Crowns now compared to who they were when they came here. It used to be that they wouldn't even give the time of day to someone who wasn't a member of a royal family; now, they dance with Antoran citizens and enjoy themselves." I gave him a frank stare. "If anything, it's us who owe you an apology. You never did have an ulterior motive for kidnapping us."

Andric turned away and put his bare hands on the cold marble of the parapet. "Maybe it would have been better if I did." He was quiet for a minute, then sighed. "Jashe tracked down the man who shot Freis. He's an Antoran who lives in one of the outlying towns."

My mouth fell open. "An Antoran? What are you going to do with him?"

"Nothing." Andric gave a slight, rueful smile at the look on my face. "He'll be forced to leave the country when the pass opens, but we'll all be following him shortly so it's not much of a punishment."

"Shouldn't he be in jail or something?" I asked, horrified. "Andric, he tried to kill you!"

"I know," the Prince replied. He looked out over the dark city. "But I can't imprison everyone who feels we're making the wrong choice to leave Antor. There're many families who are upset, but the majority agrees that we can't live by stealing for the rest of our lives. It's not a secure environment in which to raise the future generations, uncertain of where our sustenance and materials will come from. It would be more irresponsible to stay than to say goodbye."

I didn't agree, but I fell quiet, enjoying just having him near again. Being with the Crowns in the unsettled atmosphere of the castle since Freis was killed had nearly driven me crazy. I spent most of my time in the stables with Drade, Jesson, and the winter foal.

"He might feel it's wrong to leave Antor, but trying to kill someone is never right," I said quietly through teeth gritted against the other words I wanted to say about the man.

"I spoke to him for a long time," Andric said.

Surprised, I kept quiet.

"He apologized over and over again, saying that he was half-mad with starvation and worried about his family who was perishing of hunger. When I asked him why he didn't bring them to the castle like most of the Antorans, he said it was on principle and honor; he didn't think leaving was right, so he was trying to prove that we could survive without stealing." Andric's eyebrows lowered. "When he realized he was wrong, it was more than he could accept. I know how he feels."

I turned to him. "You still think you were wrong to bring us here."

He nodded. "I had no right. I'll accept whatever punishment the other rulers of Denbria feel is appropriate."

I shuddered, thinking of the anger that still showed through in Father's letters. The other Crowns had voiced the same thing, saying that their families were counting down the days until the pass opened so they could make the Prince pay for his actions. I wasn't the only one who would do what we could to protect Andric, either.

"You've got to admit that good things have come from this," I argued.

Andric turned to face me. "Like what?" he asked quietly.

"Like us," I whispered before I could stop myself. I blushed and turned away.

He caught my chin and turned my face back gently until he stared down at me. "But there can't be an us," he said softly.

"I know," I replied; pain laced through my heart. "But I don't regret the fact that I love you." My heart jumped when I said it, and I knew it was true even as the words left my lips.

Andric stared at me, his eyes widening slightly. "You love me?"

"With all my heart," I said. He looked at me for so long I finally turned away.

After a minute, he touched my shoulder. I looked back at him. "I love you, too," he said, gathering me into his arms. "You must know that I do, that the one thing I don't regret is having met you. You woke me up and reminded me why I do what I do." His voice broke. "You help me through this even when you don't realize it."

I held him tight and all the force of my body prayed for the moment to last forever. I matched my breath with his, my head on his chest as I listened to his heartbeat. For that moment, despite all of the heartache and hardship we had gone through, I was content to just be held in his arms and loved. The voice in the back of my mind kept telling me that I needed to be rational about all of this, but I couldn't deny the way my heart pounded stronger when I was near him, and the way I felt complete when he held me in his arms.

***

Antorans from all over came to express their sorrow at the loss of Freis. Everyone, it seemed, understood the deep bond between Andric and his wolves, and they hated to see their Prince in pain. The one good thing it did was open Andric's eyes to the fact that his people truly did love and care about him. At each expression of heartfelt sympathy, he returned his thanks and spoke to the person individually. When they left, I saw newfound respect and honor on their faces.

I wondered if Andric knew how much he strengthened his relationship with his people, but it was obvious he was just as taken by the effort they made to see him. Though I could tell he wanted to put what had happened to Freis behind him, he made a great effort to take time out for every person who came, and also asked them their concerns about the upcoming move.

It took most of his time, leaving us alone as the winter wound down.

"Is there anything we can do to make their leaving any easier?" Kaerdra asked one day as we dawdled in the breakfast room as a group, unable to find interest in any of the activities of the castle.

"I don't think so," Trevin replied.

We had practiced with them that morning out in the courtyard like always, but the atmosphere was growing more somber as the winter drew to a close. It was as if everyone knew the inevitable was coming, but no one wanted to talk about it.

"Yeah," Landis said. He put his hand on the glass of one of the windows and studied the print he left in the morning frost. "They're leaving their homes, occupations, and everything they know. How do you prepare a kingdom for that?"

"They're going to places where they don't even know they'll be welcome," Brynna said. "That would be hard."

"It doesn't have to be," Tisha said thoughtfully. She reached up to draw a beak and legs on Landis' hand print, turning it into a bird.

"How so?" Nyssa asked from the couch.

"Well," Tisha shrugged. "We know where they'll be going. Maybe if they knew there were places welcome to them, they'd feel better about going there?"

Kaerdra moved to sit on the arm of the couch next to her. "But how do we get our parents to accept strangers into their countries. They're scared enough about Antorans as it is."

"We just have to make it easier for them," I said suddenly, brightening up. The ideas came quickly as the spark Tisha started caught on. "Everyone's afraid of what they don't know, right? So we'll tell them what to expect; that way, they'll be less likely to reject the Antorans."

"Yeah," Trevin put in. "And maybe we can see how many people each country is able to take."

"And they can start building houses and stuff so that the Antorans have a place to stay when they get there," Kenyen said with growing excitement. "How would it be if we could tell them they all have places to stay already?"

"Where do we start?" Landis asked.

"Ayd can send out the hawks today," Nyssa said, happy for an excuse to go see him. She blushed when she realized we all knew what she was thinking. "Well, he can," she concluded sheepishly.

"Alright then, let's get started!" Tisha said.

I went to the door and asked Kimber to bring plenty of quills and paper. She grinned at the look of excitement on my face and ran to get the supplies herself instead of sending someone else.

By the time we finished, there were letters from each of us to our parents, as well as a group letter we wrote together and copied to send to each country so they had the exact same information about the Antorans. We kept it simple, knowing that if we could get everyone on the same page, it would be well worth the effort.

It was hard to keep the secret from Andric, but I managed as well as I could. He knew something was up, but he was busy enough not to ask, and by the time we met on the rooftop at night, we were too tired to do more than hold hands and watch the stars. He was happy for some peace and quiet, as were the wolves who laid at our feet and kept our toes warm. I was grateful for every moment near him because I didn't know how much longer we would be together.

When the reply to our letters arrived a few days later, we opened them with trepidation. Inside, we found mixed responses to our suggestions. Tisha's father was open to the idea of new citizens, but worried about the reception they would receive from his people. Kenyen and Danyen said that their father was interested in the idea only because he knew the Antorans were warriors and would add to his soldiers in case of war, to which we all laughed because there hadn't been a war in more than a decade.

Trevin and Kaerdra's parents were more reserved, telling them that there was not enough information to make a decision. The three groups against the idea were my father and Landis', who were completely firm in the opinion that the Antorans should stay on their own side of the mountains regardless of their condition, and Brynna's father, who was still furious that we had been kidnapped from his castle. Nyssa's father would band with Brynna's if it came down to it.

We realized we had a lot more persuading to do and got to work writing replies to each of the parents' concerns. The others helped Landis and I the best they could, but we both knew it was going to be a hard argument, especially since my parents still spoke to me like I was young and inexperienced.

When Landis read my letter, he bristled. "They don't give you any credit for what you've done here."

"I haven't told them much," I admitted. At everyone's stares, I blushed in embarrassment. "What was I supposed to tell them? That I've been training the other girls to wield swords when my father was completely against me using one of my own, that we barely survived a brush with Breizans on our way here and another one in which a mountain lion was nearly successful in squashing me flat, and that I'm in love with the Antoran Prince, the one person my father hates most in the whole world?"

Their expressions turned sympathetic when I said the last sentence. Several of the boys exchanged glances, but I could tell they already knew. Kaerdra touched my shoulder and I sighed, "It's alright; it'll just be that much harder. At the very least, we might have to ask the other countries to accept more Antorans for the time being."

"Don't worry, Kit, we'll help you," Tisha said confidently. "Maybe we can get our parents to talk to yours. It might help them accept the whole Antoran thing."

I turned to Landis. "Do you think your parents will let up?"

He shrugged, his expression doubtful. "It makes me wonder how much they were actually involved in the state the Antorans are in," he said quietly.

I nodded in agreement.

"Well," Nyssa said, grabbing a quill. "We have work to do, so we'd better get started."

We didn't go to bed until late that night planning for the worst but hoping for a positive response from our parents. We concluded that our last-ditch effort would be to tell them that as their Crown Princes and Princesses, they owed it to us to trust that we would never put our people in danger.

While we waited for the return letters, we tried to put it out of our minds by working harder around the city. There were houses to fix, walls to repair, food to distribute, and wood to cut from the remaining trees to keep everyone warm during the last days of cold weather. A fire started in one house and caught to the houses to either side, and it took an effort by the whole city to get the families settled elsewhere. I heard one of the husbands comment that at least they had less belongings to cart south, but his wife shushed him with heartache plain on her face. It made me more grateful for what we were doing to get them secure places to stay.

When the next letters arrived, our efforts were rewarded. All of the parents were tentatively on board except Landis' and mine. Tisha's father and Trevin and Kaerdra's surprised us by saying they were already making plans for building temporary housing and they were setting up supplies to get the newcomers off on a good foot. Kenyen and Danyen said their parents were asking citizens to make room in their houses until new ones could be built.

To all of our surprise, Brynna and Nyssa's parents got together for a conference and agreed that if they didn't listen to their children, it would cause more trouble than it was worth. They agreed to be open to their daughters' suggestions as long as the safety of the kingdom was always in their minds.

"Well," I said to Landis with a shrug after handing him my letter. "Looks like we have some work to do."

He nodded in agreement, his expression slightly deflated. "What do you do when they don't believe in you enough to trust you?"

I shook my head. "I'm not sure; help the others, I guess."

He brightened slightly. "At least there's that."

We agreed that we would keep trying, but didn't get our hopes up from the tone of the last letters. It seemed that our parents had also gotten together, but they came out with a different conclusion. They were fiercely against allowing any Antorans to cross their borders, and threatened to make an example of those who did. When Father mentioned that I wasn't experienced enough to ask him to make such a change, I refused the tears of frustration and hurt and turned my attention towards helping to answer the other parents' concerns.

Finally, we had enough answers and preparations completed to announce our intentions to the Antorans. We waited until the citizen dinner about ten days after Freis was killed. Andric sat quietly at the table, but we had been expecting his silence; counting on it, in fact. It gave me the time I needed to steel my nerves.

Finally, toward the end of the main course, I rose to my feet. At first, no one noticed, but Kenyen tapped politely on his glass to get their attention. I forced myself to stay standing when the tables fell quiet and all eyes turned expectantly to me. The atmosphere at dinner had been quieter than usual and the meetings more solemn since Andric's wolf was killed; the coming of spring and their imminent departure loomed in everyone's minds. They looked at me patiently, but without much emotion.

"As you know," I began; my voice wavered slightly and I hesitated. I questioned our decision to have me be the spokesperson, but the other Crowns had insisted, saying they wouldn't have come up with the idea if I hadn't been so accepting of the Antorans in the first place. I looked down at the Crowns' upturned, encouraging faces, then glanced at Andric. He watched me quietly with his brows drawn together. I took a deep breath and continued in a stronger tone, "We have enjoyed pleasure of spending our time in Antor this winter, and appreciate all that we have shared with you."

"Thanks for saving my life," Bown yelled out. Many of the Antorans laughed.

I grinned despite my nerves. "Yes, and all the near-death experiences."

They laughed again, and I felt them warming to me.

My smile faded as I continued earnestly, "You've been through so much more than any other group of people I have ever known, yet you continue to help each other keep going, to lift your neighbor up when things get rough. It's because of your spirit of love and devotion to each other that we decided we had to do something about your trek from your homes to our lands where your reception was to be hostile at the very least."

I glanced down at Andric again; he was looked out at his people, judging their reaction to my words. "We've been in contact with our families since we arrived here, and decided it was time to put that contact to good use."

I motioned for the other Crowns to stand up so I wasn't the only one taking the credit for the work that we had done. Trevin caught my encouraging nod and smiled at the crowd of listening Antorans. "Our parents, the royal Kings and

Queens of Denbria below the mountains, have agreed to welcome you into our countries with open arms."

He nudged Tisha so that she could take part in the miracle she had sparked. She smiled with tears in her eyes. "As we speak, houses are being prepared for you so that when you arrive, you have somewhere to call home."

A cheer, louder than we had expected, went up in a roar from the Antorans. Tears slid down cheeks and husbands hugged wives, giving view to the fears and worries they had kept locked away for so long, troubles that were now eased. They would not be turned away; they would be welcomed.

Cries of thanks and blessings were called out to us and I heard our names praised. I sat down, my heart heavy at the thought that at least two countries would be off-limits to these wonderful people. Someone grabbed my hand; I looked over to see Andric staring at me.

"Did you do this?" he asked; his eyes were bright and wet with tears that threatened to spill over.

I shook my head. "Tisha started it, but everyone's been working on it for over a week now." I faltered. "There're two countries where Antorans won't be welcome, though."

From my dark expression, Andric guessed it. "Zalen?"

I nodded. "And Faer. Landis has been working at it as hard as I have, but our fathers won't budge."

He squeezed my hand. "It doesn't matter." His voice was so soft that I could barely hear it above the clamor in the room even though we were only a seat apart. "I owe you everything, all of you."

I shook my head. "We owe you."

"Yes," Landis said as he sat down on the Prince's other side. "We've learned more this winter than you probably imagine."

Kaerdra took her seat between Andric and I. Everyone beamed with the joy that they were able to share. They told Landis and I that we should join in as well, that we had worked as hard as the rest and deserved to celebrate.

"All that matters is that my people have somewhere to go," Andric said in a voice tight with emotion. He rose to his feet and held up a glass of pumpkin milk sweetened with honey. "To the Crown Princes and Princesses of Denbria!"

"To the Crown Princes and Princesses of Denbria," the Antorans repeated in a cheer that echoed off the walls.

Chapter 25

Letters detailing the preparations that were being made for the Antorans and for our homecoming started to arrive every day. We answered them as quickly as we could; Landis and I helped the others in the absence of the multitude of letters from our own countries. I kept hoping that somehow our parents' attitudes would soften as the excitement that flowed from the other countries continued, but it never did. My parents wrote about how happy they were that the pass would be open soon, but they said nothing in reply to my pleas to change their minds about the Antorans.

Ayd came unexpectedly into the breakfast room about a week after we told the Antorans our plan. We were still eating following an especially intense training session, and everyone waved to him over our food. He grinned and held Nyssa when she ran up to him, kissed her soundly, then proceeded to my side.

"He wouldn't listen to me, Princess Kit," Kimber protested, running into the room. "I told him you were at breakfast and not to be disturbed."

"It's alright," I reassured her. "He doesn't disturb us."

The others watched him expectantly. Andric had joined us since the dinner to help with planning; he now watched the Hawkmaster with a hint of amusement in his eyes at Ayd's infatuation with Princess Nyssa and her returned affection. This was obviously something he hadn't seen.

I realized that Ayd was waiting for me. I turned to him and the sparkle in his eyes made me pause. The only thing that would bring it was good news, and undoubtedly something he had seen from Rush since he kept his word and never read our letters. What would Rush have shown him?

269

I accepted the letter he held out to me with shaking hands. I rose from the table and my eyes took in my name written in a hand I knew by heart, but one I hadn't seen in a very long time. "Rory," I breathed. I tore open the seal and my eyes flew through his brief letter, written faintly but still in his hand.

> Kit, I miss you so much and I'm finally getting well enough that Father might let me go at least to Eskand when the pass opens. I would have written earlier, but I had to be sure I was getting over this. I feel stronger now, and have finally convinced Mother she doesn't have to hover beside my bed day and night. She really needs a rest. But now I'm rambling. I just can't wait to see you again. I can't believe all you've gone through. Your letters helped me hold on. And I am stronger. You won't have to carry everything on your shoulders anymore. I need to say goodbye, though I don't want to go. It's amazing how quickly I still get tired, but I am getting better. The pass will be open soon, and I can't wait to see you.
>
> Love, Rory

Tears clouded my eyes and prevented me from reading the letter again.

"Is something wrong?" Kaerdra asked next to me. She touched my arm.

I shook my head and cleared my eyes. "It's from Rory; he's getting better," I said in disbelief; the reality still danced in front of me as I tried to grasp the fact that I wouldn't go home to say goodbye to my older brother.

"Better?" Kaerdra asked. Hope rang in her voice and her eyes shone.

I nodded and she surprised me by grabbing my hands and spinning me around while she laughed. "Of course he's alright; you said he would be! You never gave up hope!"

"I didn't, did I?" I said when we stopped. "I knew he'd get better. He just had to!" I looked around at the grinning faces that surrounded me, then glanced up at the Prince at the end of the table.

Andric's eyes met mine and it felt as if a bolt of lightning jumped straight from him into me. Hope warred with doubt in his eyes, fear tangled with possibility. The Crowns looked between us, but I couldn't tear my eyes away.

Andric opened his mouth to speak when the door flew open again.

"Crown Prince Andric," a soldier said breathlessly, "The pass is open and a large troop of soldiers is heading straight for us."

Andric stared at me for a second longer, then blinked and turned his head, breaking the spell. The guard repeated his words and Andric rose to his feet. "We'd better be ready," he said. Without glancing back at me, he left the room.

I looked at the other Princes and Princesses; they stared back at me. I shook my head. "We'd better get ready, too. This is going to be rough." We all knew that I didn't mean just meeting our families.

***

It was Andric's idea that we meet them on foot outside the city boundaries to lower hostility and prevent any of the Antorans from being inadvertently harmed. Much to Captain Jashe's dismay, Andric made the soldiers and the three younger wolves stay quite a distance back, well outside the range to protect him if he was attacked. Instead, Prince Andric walked forward with only Bayn at his side. The rest of us followed with foreboding that increased at every step.

It was easy to tell when our fathers and guards recognized us for who we were, because they spurred their mounts and galloped haphazardly across the snow-covered field that stood between us. My father took the lead, and before he reached us he held up a hand. The others slowed immediately, having obviously designated him as the leader of their expedition. Father and King Fasred, Landis' father, dismounted their horses and walked quickly toward us. The others waited behind them anxiously on mounts who looked exhausted from the trek through the mountains.

Father's eyes sought me out and I saw the relief in them when he found me unharmed. He looked at the others in turn, then his eyes came to rest on Prince Andric who stood before us.

I had never seen Andric look the way he did now. His head was bowed and he held his hands behind his back, his feet spread slightly apart as if he gave himself up to whatever method of punishment they chose. Royalty in Denbria were forbidden to bow to each other, giving one line or heir precedence over any of the others, but Andric's posture was the closest thing to pure submissive sorrow I had ever seen. Bayn sat silently beside him clearly under direction from

Andric, his eyes low even though the Kings strode toward them with possible ill-intent.

The corner of Father's mouth lifted in the slightest hint of a smile, then it disappeared.

"I deeply apologize for any harm my actions have caused," Andric said in a low, almost expressionless tone. "Do with me what you will."

My father's brow creased, then he motioned to me. "My first concern is to get my daughter safely home. We will address this at another time."

Andric nodded, his head still bowed. My father motioned to us, and the others ran past to their waiting fathers. Bayn lifted his nose and I brushed it with my hand as I passed, trying to send reassurance for him to pass onto Andric. I stepped into my father's arms and hugged him tightly.

"I was so worried," Father breathed into my ear, holding me as though he would never let me go again."

"I'm alright, Father. We're all fine," I tried to reassure him.

Heedless of my words, he held me back at arm's length so that he could look me over again. A frown touched his lips at the scar on my cheek from the mountain lion's claw. He brushed it with a finger.

"It's a long story," I said. "You'll hear it later, I'm sure."

He nodded. "You've grown taller," he said with a calculating eye. "And you've lost a bit of color from all this winter, but you look stronger. Is that your sword?" His tone was careful.

I nodded, but didn't know what else to say.

He gave me a small, weary smile, and I remembered that they had just crossed the mountains. "It seems like a lot has changed."

I shrugged and tried to sound positive. "Not so much; it was just a winter." The words sounded false to me; it felt like so much longer, and I knew by the expression in Father's eyes that he was thinking the same thing.

Father took a deep breath and smiled. "Well, let's get you out of here. We've got a long ride ahead of us. Your mother's been worried sick, and Rory threatened to ride here himself if we didn't hurry."

My heart leaped into my throat. In all the commotion, I had forgotten about Rory's letter. "How is he? I got his letter, but it said so little. He's getting better? Is he up and about?"

Father laughed and held up a hand at my onslaught of questions. "You'll see for yourself. He and your mother are meeting us at Eskand with the rest of the families who couldn't come along. We had to get a coach especially fitted for his accommodations, but he wouldn't consider staying home when we told him what you've been going through." He snapped a finger and Captain Rurisk rode forward with Father's horse, Megrath, and a dark brown mare on a lead rope.

The Captain swung down and gave me a deep bow before grinning. "It's a pleasure to see you again, Princess. We're anxious to have you back home."

"Thank you," I told him, touched at the sincerity in his voice. He held the mare's reins needlessly as I swung up onto her back. Father mounted his horse and I looked over to see that the others were already in their saddles and ready to head out.

Father turned his horse's head to take up the lead and my horse took a step to follow him, but I held the reins with a lump in my throat. I looked back at Andric who still stood with his head bowed as though he would never raise it again. I glanced at Father. He motioned impatiently.

I kicked my feet free of the stirrups and hit the ground running before anyone could stop me. "Andric," I yelled.

"Kit?" he asked, looking up in surprise.

I ran right into his embrace and my lips met his. A jolt of emotion passed between us and I could taste the salt of both our tears.

"Kit," my father said sharply.

I broke away from Andric and, stifling a sob, turned and ran back across the field to my waiting horse. Without slowing or using the stirrups, I swung onto the mare's back the way we had done so many times during practice in the courtyard. Father looked at me for a moment, but I stared straight ahead, afraid that his glare would make me shatter into a million pieces in my current state.

Without a word, Father kicked his horse into motion. I tightened my knees and my horse followed behind.

***

The night echoed with celebration and jubilee, though Father kept guards on duty in case the Antorans tried to kidnap us back. It was good to see the other Crowns smiling and laughing as though the winter in Antor had been nothing more than a brief vacation; though at times when they thought no one noticed, I saw contemplative expressions on their faces. When our eyes met, their smiles faded and they gave me solemn half-smiles as though they understood how torn I felt.

Ironically, we slept in the same cave on our return journey that we had used as shelter after the Breizan attack. Father was anxious for us to get home quickly, but felt that there was no need to push everyone as fast as their journey to Antor had been. When everyone else had fallen asleep but the soldiers on guard duty, Father confronted me.

"You kissed him?" he asked in a tone that resounded with shock and betrayal.

I couldn't answer him, and when I didn't, he got angry. King Tryst's temper was well-known throughout Denbria, and I think it was one of the reasons the other Kings and Queens followed him when they needed a single head to lead them. He vented his full fury now.

"I forbid you to speak of the Antoran Prince and your so-called feelings for him to anyone. I'll not have a daughter of Zalen falling for one of Antor's beast rulers." He grimaced. "You've been raised with far better standards than that."

I looked away and clenched my jaw against the argument that screamed within my heart. When Father took that tone, there was no changing his mind. My heart sunk into a black pit and locked itself away. I chose not to feel the pain and forbade my tears to betray me.

Chapter 26

When we finally reached Eskand, a welcoming party rode to meet us. Mother was with them, and I jumped off my horse and ran to meet her. She held me tight, her tears soaking into my hair.

"My daughter," she sobbed, "I'm so glad you're safe."

I returned her hug. "I'm alright, Mother."

"Yes, thank goodness you're back," she breathed.

Father came up behind us and put an arm around Mother and I as we embraced. I stiffened at his touch, but tried to ignore it, reminding myself that I had not seen him all winter and he was just worried about me.

The other Crowns came to greet their mothers, siblings, and relatives who expressed amazement that they had survived a winter away from the comforts of their castles. Everyone except Landis and I talked to our parents about the arrangements that had been made for the Antorans' arrival in a month when the pass had cleared enough for the citizens to travel safely through. I exchanged an unhappy glance with Landis, but our parents either didn't see it or chose to ignore our frustrations.

When I finally made it to our quarters in the Eskand Castle, I found my brother pacing his room like a caged tiger, forbidden by Mother and his healer to leave for fear that he would catch a chill and undo all of the progress he had made. A big grin spread across his face when I walked through the door. He picked me up and spun me around as if he had never been sick; but the hollow cheeks, pale skin, and quick weariness told on him. We sat on his bed shut away from all the commotion below to catch up on the long months we had been apart.

Rory merely smiled mysteriously when I told him of Kaerdra's interest in him. "We were pretty serious the last time I visited Cren for a hunting expedition with Prince Trevin. I'm glad to know she still remembers me."

I stared at him, surprised by his honesty on the subject.

"What?" he asked innocently. When I continued to stare, he grew serious. "You've been gone a long time, Kit," he said. He pushed a strand of hair behind my ear. "I can tell you've grown up in more ways than Mother and Father are ready to accept. Forgive me if I talk to you like a peer instead of a younger sister."

I smiled. "I'd rather you talk to me like that. I'm tired of being treated like a kid."

He nodded in understanding, then his eyes darkened. Without speaking, he ran a thumb lightly over the thin white scar the claw had left across my cheekbone.

I pulled the necklace with the claw on it out from under my shirt. His eyes widened when he saw it. "It's a long story," I said. "But the mountain lion was going to hurt a friend of mine."

"So they killed it?" Rory asked. His expression was puzzled as he studied the carving on the claw.

I shook my head. "I did," I said softly.

He looked up at me quickly to see if I was joking. When I didn't smile, his eyes grew even wider. "You mean to tell me that you killed this lion by yourself?"

"I had a sword," I said by way of an explanation. "Oh, look, they did it on here, too." I drew the sword that still hung at my side, something my parents pointedly overlooked.

Rory whistled. "May I?"

I nodded and handed it to him. He ran his finger over the scroll-worked mountain lion, then tested the weight of the sword. "This craftsmanship is unmatched by anything I've ever seen," he said, surprised.

I nodded. "Master Smith Hensas of Antor made it; I've never wielded a sword created like this for me before."

"Me neither," Rory said with a hint of envy in his voice. Something occurred to him and he turned back. "You mean to tell me that Crown Prince Andric let you guys have weapons while you were hostage over there?"

I sighed. "There's so much you don't know," I told him sadly. "But I've been forbidden to tell anyone."

"Father?" my brother guessed.

I nodded. "But it's fine. I'll deal with it in my own time."

He studied me for a second and then nodded. "You really have changed, sis. I've missed you."

"I've missed you," I told him sincerely.

He gave me another hug and I buried my face against his shirt. I missed Andric's windswept scent of the outdoors and the mountains, wilderness and freedom.

***

When we reached Zalen, the only thing I wanted to do was write to Andric; except every time I put my quill to the paper, the words wouldn't come. I didn't know how to write to someone I felt like I had shared an eternity with over the course of a single winter. So much had passed between us that hadn't required words, and now that words were required, they wouldn't come.

So I couldn't write, and lost myself instead working for my country the way Andric did for his. The only time that I couldn't push the thoughts from my head was when I tried to sleep at night. Away from everyone, the thoughts and emotions overwhelmed me and by the time I fell asleep, I had soaked my pillow in tears.

I hid my heartache during the day, though I often felt Mother and Father's worried eyes on me. Rory comforted me the best that he could, though I knew by his silence that Father had also forbidden him to talk to me about it. I think Father's theory was if no one mentioned Antor or Andric or anything about our winter, I would forget. I felt glad in a way that he didn't know any better, because it would hurt him to know how much I ached inside.

I spent most of the days with the healers, not just a bystander and a helpful hand once in a while, but a participant now. They appreciated my input and answered all of my questions; if they thought it strange that the Princess stayed away from the castle as long as she could each day, they didn't mention it and I could breathe in their silence. Animals seemed drawn to me, and even the injured ones were more at ease under my touch than that of the healers. The healers were more than grateful at my willingness to help calm an injured puppy so its wounds could be stitched after a fight with a bigger dog, or soothe a steer that had cut its leg on a fence pole. I couldn't talk to them even when I touched them, but they responded to calming thoughts and a soothing scratch on the head.

On the few stormy days when sleet fell in sheets from brooding clouds, or when the healers spent their seventh day each week gathering and drying herbs, I wandered around like a lost dog. One day of wandering found me at the home of a Zalen citizen whose neighbors were helping to raise a small barn for his pregnant mare. I knew the man by sight, one of the shipbuilders who raced horses like most Zalens. The horse was well along in her pregnancy, and by the way she stood solemnly watching the building process with her sides almost ready to burst, I could tell they were cutting it close.

I turned the sleek black mare Father had given me toward the group with a slight pang of what I recognized with some confusion as homesickness when I thought about how Trae hadn't needed to be guided; he had known exactly where I wanted to go.

"Can I help?" I asked as I dismounted. Luckily, most women in Denbria wore loose dress pants during the winter; it was considered acceptable as long as one wore a dress when weather-permitting. Otherwise, the stares I got would have been for my attire as well as the fact that I was a Princess asking to do manual labor.

When they realized who I was, everyone bowed as a group, some even kneeling on the ground still coated in late frost. My cheeks turned red. "Please, I just want to help. I get a little bored and enjoy working with my hands."

Most of them looked up in surprise, making me blush even deeper. "A princess not afraid to get her hands dirty?" A big man about the size of Bagan's bear rumbled. "I like the sound of that."

281

Several others laughed. The man who owned the land came over with his hat in his hands. "I would be awfully ashamed if you got hurt, Crown Princess Kirit."

I shook my head, my hair brushing against my back. I had taken to wearing it loose since we left Antor as a simple reminder of Andric. "Just Princess Kit, or Kit, if you please. Rory's doing much, much better now."

"I apologize," he said with a low bow. "And we are all happy to hear about Crown Prince Rory's recovery." He glanced up quickly as if afraid he had slighted me. "Not that you wouldn't make a fine ruler," he said quickly.

I raised my hand with a warm smile. "No offense taken. I'm just relieved that it gives me the excuse to escape training and spend time outside the castle."

"You helped the healers with my brother," A skinny young man with a shy smile said.

"I like healing," I told him with an answering grin. "It makes sense to me, unlike some of the shipping agreements we have."

They all laughed. The agreements were a mess, and nobody tried to straighten them out because the other countries were just as confused as we were, so no one could get mad at the other if some lines got crossed. It was a case of chaos turned to saving lives.

"Have you ever hammered before?" The landowner asked cautiously.

I nodded. "I suppose most of you have heard something about my trip to Antor." At their nods and looks of interest, I smiled despite the pang in my chest. "One of the first things we did there was to help to rebuild a roof that had caught fire. It was my first true taste of manual labor." I winced dramatically. "If you want to see something funny, just give nine Crown Princes and Princesses hammers and ask them to fix something. There were nails hammered in every direction but down."

They laughed and a young man a few years older than me asked, "Did their animals help?"

I saw sideways glances and hushed whispers, eyes averted so they didn't meet mine. I nodded, feeling bold. "Yes, they did. It was amazing to watch. A bear scraped bark from the logs, horses teamed together and pulling without needing their master to tell them where to go; there were even two crows that brought us twine and nails when we needed them."

The men listened wide-eyed with awed expressions on their faces. "Are they bewitched?" the landowner asked. He dropped his eyes as soon as he asked it.

I shook my head. "Not at all. They just have a special understanding with certain animals. The Antorans call it being bonded. They can even talk to the animals and the animals talk back in their minds."

"Wow," the first man said. He grinned at me. "Do you have more stories like that?"

Surprised, I nodded.

"Then you don't need a hammer," the big bear-like man replied. "You can tell stories while we work."

I laughingly agreed, though in the end I appeased both of us by distributing nails and other supplies.

Surprisingly, it helped to talk about Antor. The ache in my chest eased slightly when I told them about the mountains and the lions that lived there. They even got me to tell them about the mountain lion that tried to attack Mrs. Voise. Several crowded over and I took off the claw necklace and passed it around for them to see. I told them about my sword and the way it was made, though I had taken to leaving it at the castle because it got in the way when I was helping the healers.

The day went quicker than most, and by nightfall I was so tired that I fell into bed without any tears and gratefully sank into sleep the second I slipped under the thick blankets.

The next morning instead of going with the healers, I rode Fray, my graceful black mare from before Antor, around the city just to better acquaint myself with Zalen. The docks sat mostly empty, shipping and fishing still delayed due to the late ice storms. Usually by this time, Zalen and Faer had so many ships out in the ocean that the horizon was dotted with masts. Today, only a few of the younger captains dared to take their crafts to sea.

I rode along the beach enjoying Fray's smooth gait through the sand and the steady rush of the waves lapping at the shore. I guided the mare into a little alcove I had visited once with Father, and was surprised to see over a dozen young men and women with horses there. Gouges marked the sand along the beach as though they had been racing.

Curious, I drew near and slid down from Fray's back, leaving her reins loose so she could wander at her leisure. She would come back at a whistle her trainer had taught me. I took off my shoes and stuffed them in the saddlebag so that I could go barefoot like the others on the beach.

Most looked twice at the golden palm leaf emblazoned on my dark blue cloak, then they stared at me, wondering what they should do. I don't think anyone knew the protocol for dealing with a barefoot princess on the beach; I know I didn't.

Luckily, a boy stepped forward and grinned at me. I recognized him as the young man from the house who had been so interested in animals. "Good morning, Princess Kit. Do you mind joining us for a race?"

"Bad idea," a boy hissed behind him.

"You can't race with a princess," a girl argued. She held the reins of a dainty white horse that pranced in the sand.

"Don't worry," I told them. "I'm not going to race. I just want to watch."

Several of them turned back to their horses, tightening saddles and checking their hooves. "Good thing," I heard one of them say quietly to his companion. "I wouldn't want to face the wrath of the King when I beat his daughter."

My ears burned but I ignored the comment. As another race began, a loud whinny followed by an angry snort caught my attention. I turned to see a light brown horse with a dark dorsal stripe and a dark mane and tail kick up sand. He whinnied and reared; the two older boys who fought his lead rope jerked it hard enough to yank his neck painfully and bring him back to the ground in a cloud of sand. I walked toward them and stopped next to the tall rocks that surrounded the alcove.

The young man who knew me glanced back from where he had joined the group of onlookers and saw me watching; he scooted over to make room. "Danl," he said, offering me his hand.

"Kit," I told him even though he already knew that, but it felt funny not saying anything. I frowned slightly when the horse reared again and was brought with a crash back to the ground. "What are they doing to that poor horse?" I asked Danl quietly.

"Breaking him." By his tone it was obvious he didn't approve of the older boys' methods, either. "They've been at it since sunrise."

"Sunrise?" I looked closer. The horse definitely looked tired. Dirt-coated sweat streaked his sides and foam flecked his mouth. Each time the boys jerked him back down, he stood with his head held low and flanks heaving, but the second they stepped closer with a saddle, the horse reared back up again.

"Stupid horse," one of the boys shouted. He slapped its flank with the end of his rope. The animal kicked out and he barely jumped back in time to avoid its hoof. "Won't amount to anything this way."

I stepped forward on impulse. Danl grabbed my arm and I turned, surprised. At my look, he stuttered. "I just thought. . . well, that there's the Markam brothers and they don't take kindly to be'in told anything. I don't mean to presume," he said apologetically, letting me go.

I shook my head. I had heard of their father and his notoriously cruel way of training horses. They ran out of fear, not out of any respect of their riders or the joy of the race. Something about the spirit of the horse I watched called to me; I couldn't stand to see it broken the way the boys were trying to.

An idea hit me. "I'll ride it," I said. My heart leaped into my throat when I heard my own words.

Several of the onlookers glanced back at me incredulously, then turned away again as if I was joking. The horse whinnied, driving me closer. "I'll ride your horse," I said, my voice strong despite my suddenly watery knees. I had never broken a horse before, though I knew it should be done with kindness instead of cruelty. Father used the term gentle instead of break, and applied techniques that were surprising mild for someone with his known temper.

I felt distinctly out of my element when the two boys holding the lead rope turned to me. "What did you say?" the older one demanded. His eyes narrowed suspiciously when he saw who had spoken.

"I said I'd ride your horse if you let me," I repeated with false confidence. The horse snorted and rolled his eyes when I took a step nearer.

Both boys laughed incredulously. "Ride this beast?" the younger one said. He slapped the horse cruelly on the nose with the end of his rope. The horse reared and almost pulled them off their feet. They both yanked hard and brought it down again; it trembled and stood with its ears back.

"Fine, Princess," the older boy said, practically spitting out the title. "If it kills you, it's your own darn fault."

I nodded and stumbled back when they pushed past me, shoving the rope into my hands.

"What are you doing?" Danl hissed behind me.

"Improvising," I replied. I eyed the horse warily. The animal snorted and backed up, puffs of sand rising from his hooves. He jerked me with him because I was determined not to let go of the rope. Some of the onlookers laughed behind me, but I ignored them.

"Shhh," I said quietly to the horse. I took a step closer so the rope had a little slack between us. "I'm a friend," I said, thinking the words as I said them. I tried to project calmness and peace, though my heart pounded in my chest.

The horse stomped a hoof but didn't rear up when I took another step closer. I held out a hand palm up. "I'm safe," I told him. His dark eyes glanced from me to the onlookers; his ears flattened when he saw the two boys. "Don't worry about them," I breathed. "I won't let them hurt you." His ears went forward and my heart leaped into my throat. I took another step, then stared when he took one toward me as well.

I stretched out my hand, the rope lying forgotten between us. The horse touched my palm with his dark brown nose, the whiskers tickling my skin. He didn't send me images as Trae would have, but I felt an urge for the wind in his mane and sand under his hooves, the need to get away from fences and ropes and those who wished to hurt him.

"Let's go," I whispered softly.

He whickered quietly and pawed at the sand, his head bobbing up and down.

"I trust you," I thought toward him. I ran my hand down his neck. The small audience had grown quiet; even the two boys held their tongues.

The thought of trust was echoed back at me so strongly it made my head swim for a second. I put both hands against the horse to steady myself. "I guess the feeling's mutual," I told him quietly with a small laugh.

I hesitated slightly and glanced back at the young men and women, all of whom had now gathered to watch their Princess risk her life with the wild horse. Danl's eyes were wide and he shook his head as if to say I could back down if I wanted. I smiled at him and leaped onto the horse's bare back in one fluid motion.

The horse stood stock still as if surprised at my daring. I ran my hands down his neck. "I'm Kit," I breathed.

An image rushed into my head of the wind blowing through the fields, making ocean waves of the oats and corn rows. I opened my mouth in surprise. "Breeze," I guessed. He whickered again and pawed the ground; his head bobbed, and I knew we were on the same page.

"Let's get out of here," I said loud enough for the others to hear. I reached down and unclipped the lead rope that dangled uselessly on the ground. Before it touched the sand, Breeze leaped into a run faster than any horse I had ever ridden. I clutched at his mane and struggled to right myself, then leaned low across his neck with my hands tangled in his mane and my feet and knees gripping his sides.

We galloped out of the alcove to the dismayed shouts of the two boys and whoops of the others. I felt a slight twinge of guilt until I reminded myself that I had left Fray, so they knew I would eventually return.

The thrill of the ride filled me, partly from Breeze and partly from the release I felt as the wind tangled my hair and cleared my thoughts. We ran along the edge of the beach; water and sand flew up with each hoof beat. I sat up and let my body relax, swaying to the smooth gallop of the horse and gripping only with my knees and feet. The sun beat down on us, chasing the chill from the morning air. I leaned back and let it fall on my face as Breeze ran.

I didn't lead him or change his course; I merely let him run to his heart's content, a colt born for the thrill of the gallop who had never been allowed to stretch his legs. When he slowed to a trot and then a leisurely walk, I slid off and walked beside him, my hand on his neck and the cold water biting at my toes.

We headed south away from town farther along the beach than I had ever been. I enjoyed the cries of the gulls above and turned in time to see a sea hawk swoop down and catch a fish in its beak without breaking a beat of its wings. The warm air reminded me that the Antorans would be leaving their city in about two weeks. It was still cold up north, but soon the snows would clear enough for their journey.

I shied from the thought and Breeze stopped walking. He turned his head and looked at me. "Sorry," I told him. A thought occurred to me and I toyed with it. "I know someone who would really take to you," I said, reaching up to untangle a burr from his mane. I showed him an image of Drade and the way his horses lived.

Breeze snorted softly. He then showed me an image of a tiny stall barely big enough for him to turn around. The barn was dark but drafty and full of uncomfortable horses.

I frowned. "I won't let you go back there," I replied firmly. "My father will buy you. No one can refuse the King." For once, I was happy with the sway Father had over his people through the laws of the land and the firm hand he held. I could see how it would be an advantage among the less-tractable Zalens, though I had also experienced examples of other types of respect that were more powerful than fear and awe.

When the sun had reached its full height and began to descend toward the west, I turned reluctantly. "Time to go back."

Breeze showed me the stall again and shook his mane with his ears back.

"I promise I wouldn't take you there. You have to trust me." At his wary eyes, I touched his side. "You still have some energy left in there?"

He reared up, then crashed back down hard enough to spray me with saltwater and sand. "Alright, alright," I told him with my hands up. "You win. How about a run back to the cove?" He pranced when I swung on and waited for me to get settled before he took off again.

The ride back felt shorter to both of us. The rocks of the cove quickly came into view and Breeze slowed. He acted as docile as a lapdog when he trotted into the sheltered beach. I noticed the crowd had grown. Several other young men and women waited, and by the looks on their faces, they hadn't believed that the Princess of Zalen had ridden off on the Markams' crazy horse. I noticed two of Father's guards standing as inconspicuously as two well-muscled, heavily armed men in blue and gold could. I had seen guards several times over the last two weeks, but thought I had lost them that morning. Word got around quickly.

With a sigh, I slid off Breeze and walked toward the waiting group. Fray whinnied a greeting and nuzzled my shirt with her soft black nose. Breeze walked strictly behind me, his breath hot on my neck.

"Thanks for riding my horse," the older Markam boy said with a hint of sarcasm. He glanced at the two guards who stood in the shadows of the rocks. "I'll take him now."

"I'm buying him from you," I said firmly.

"He's not for sale," the younger boy snapped back angrily. "He's for racing."

"Then I'll be the one to race him," I told them both. "He'll only run for me."

"Liar," the older boy said. "If a girl can ride him, I can ride him."

A heavy hand rested on his shoulder and he turned to find one of the guards immediately behind him. "You just called the Princess a liar," he said in a deep voice that echoed around the alcove despite the soft tone he used.

"I-I didn't mean it," the boy stammered.

"It's alright," I said. I took a step forward. At the guard's calculating look, I smiled wryly. "I'd like to see him try. If he's going to call someone a liar, he'd better be able to prove it."

The guard must have seen something in my face because he smiled slightly and stepped back to join his companion at the edge of the group. "F-fine," the boy stuttered. He turned slightly and glared at me outside of the guards' view.

I merely gazed back, unaffected. "But if you can't ride him, I get to buy him from you."

"Fine by me," he spat out. "Wouldn't want a stinkin' horse I can't ride, would I?"

I turned and patted Breeze on the nose, giving him an image for the briefest second. He breathed softly into my hand and one ear flicked back. I stepped away to join the onlookers.

"That was amazing," Danl said.

"Yeah," a girl next to him agreed breathlessly. Her tawny hair was twisted into two braids that rested on each shoulder. She grinned at me.

"I've never heard Blays stutter," a younger boy with black hair that hung over his eyes said excitedly.

"Awesome," another girl grinned. She gave me a nod. "They need to learn a lesson in sportsmanship."

"And chivalry," a tiny, red-haired girl piped in, making everyone laugh.

Blays glared back at us, then turned his attention to the horse. As though he was a different animal entirely from the one I had seen when I first reached the alcove, Breeze didn't even flick an ear when the younger Markam boy hoisted his brother onto the horse's trim back. Blays sneered at us in triumph before Breeze reared and turned at the same time, dumping the young man into a heap on the sand. Blays sat stunned for a moment, then let out an angry yell. He jumped to his feet and ran at Breeze, his fists raised.

I ran forward and shouted in my best commanding voice, "Don't you dare touch him!" Andric would have been proud at the steel of my tone.

Blays turned on me. "You think you can make me look stupid just because you're a princess?" he asked, closing the space between us.

He threw a punch and I moved without thinking. I grabbed his right arm, ducked under it, and spun to the left in a move I had performed many times in Andric's courtyard during practice. Blays ended up in another ungraceful heap in the sand.

By that time, the guards had reached us both. The bigger guard set a hand on the boy's shoulder, impeding his efforts to get up. "If I were you," the guard said dangerously, "I would stay there for a while." The other guard took up position on my right hand side as if worried about another attack.

I frowned. "I didn't want that to happen. It's your cruelty and temper that make you look stupid, not me." Blays' ears turned red and I knew I had humiliated him. I tried to backtrack. "Let me buy the horse. He's no good to you, and my father could use another good runner."

"How much will you pay for him?" Blays grumbled.

"You know the horse is hers if she so much as asks," Danl reminded him from the crowd.

I shook my head. "I won't take anything that doesn't belong to me. My father won't either. I'll buy him fair and square and give you double what he's worth."

Blays' eyes widened at that and his hateful expression disappeared. I realized then that his fear wasn't so much from the guards, humiliation, or the horse; it was fear of what his father would say if he came home without the animal. A hefty purse would make things easier on him.

"So it's settled," I said. It was a statement, not a question.

The guards backed off and Blays rose to his feet. "He's an expensive horse," he said stubbornly; his younger brother hurried to his side.

"I figured he would be," I replied levelly.

I turned to one of the guards and was relieved to see him pull a purse with Father's crest on it from his belt. I never carried money with me, so I was glad Father had sent them prepared.

With the exchange of gold for the horse, both of the Markam boys' attitudes lightened. I stayed with the group for the rest of the day. Boys and girls raced several horses up and down the beach, but Breeze, Fray, and I merely watched. Regardless of what they said to persuade me, I knew it wasn't a good idea for a princess to race against her countrymen. The conversation I'd had with Andric about sword fighting came to mind, but I shied away from it.

I rode Fray home to give Breeze a chance to get used to his new surroundings; he followed like a well-mannered steed. The guards rode home on either side of me. I was glad they had been there and told them so before we parted ways near their barracks.

"You handed the situation well," the smaller man said.

"We were there for backup, just in case," the bigger guard stated with a twinkle in his eyes. "But I'm glad to see that our princess can take care of herself."

"It didn't go like I planned, but I'm just glad Breeze found a new home." I patted him on the neck. Fray snorted and butted me with her nose for some attention of her own. I laughed and rubbed her forehead.

"Breeze, huh?" the first guard asked. He nodded. "It fits him. He's a beauty."

I frowned slightly. "I don't know how I'll explain it to Father. I wasn't prepared to bring a horse home."

The big guard chuckled in deep bass tones. "The King knows good horseflesh when he sees it. He'll understand."

"I hope so," I sighed. Four stable boys appeared at the door, staring at the new horse. I patted Breeze's side. "He'll go with you without any problems," I told them. "Please see to it that he has a big stall that opens to one of the corrals so he can run."

"Yes, Princess," one of the boys replied. He gave a curt bow and put a hand on Breeze's halter. The horse followed him without any problems, and Fray was led close behind. Both guards watched the horses for a moment with thoughtful expressions on their faces. I bid them a goodnight and walked slowly back to the castle.

Chapter 27

I slept better that night, crying only when I dreamed of Andric and woke to find that he wasn't there. Father didn't bring up the horse at all when I went down for breakfast. He and Mother exchange anxious glances at my ongoing lack of appetite, but they didn't say anything. Rory was absent, having departed on an early morning ride to see the city before the sun came up. I could tell Mother was glad he felt good enough for such a journey, but worried he would strain his returning health.

After a quiet breakfast, I rode down to the beach to find the alcove empty, and when I reached the docks I knew why. Masts had been spread across the white beach and were dutifully scrubbed with sand to rid them of old plant life and caked salt from the end of last season. Sailors swabbed decks and scurried up and down the ropes as black dots in the distance, heedless of the expanse of water lapping far below their tenuous purchase. I sighed and Breeze turned away. So much for making friends.

I rode down the beach until we were out of sight of the sails, then slid off Breeze's back and sat on the sand. It was chilly, but the sand was warming with the rising sun. I knew without thinking that it wasn't friendship that had driven me to the cove again. It was for a diversion. Every day that dawned warmer brought a reminder that the Antorans would be departing soon. My heart ached and I wished I knew what day they had picked, but I was still unable to write anything. Though I had sat for more than an hour late the night before wanting to write to Andric and tell him of Breeze, the words eluded me, creating only a swirling mass of memories that haunted the place behind my closed eyes.

I wished the other Crowns were around, then laughed wryly at myself when I remembered my first feelings about them at the palace in Eskand. How things had changed.

I forced myself to get up and rode Breeze into the city. I tracked down the healers and noticed the relief on the face of a guard who was following them and trying to be inconspicuous about it. To push down my pain, I took a page from Andric's book and forgot myself in helping others.

***

Twenty-seven days had passed from the day we left Antor. The ache never stopped, I just became more able to live with it. At least, so I thought until Rush flew through one of the windows open to the morning sun and landed on our breakfast table.

I stared at him and my heart started to pound. There was a letter fastened to the harness on his back. I could see the seal, the mountain ranges with the diamond overhead proclaiming it from Antor as much as its messenger did.

"Take it," Rory urged. My parents, their two head stewards, the maids, and the runner all stared at the hawk as though it had flown out of a storybook.

But I could feel anxiety from Rush. "It's bad news," I said quietly. My hands shook as I unlaced the harness and took out the letter. Andric's handwriting was unmistakable. The single word, "Kit", was written across the front. With foreboding, I broken the seal and stared at the brief letter written in Andric's flowing hand. With each word, my heart slowed until it felt like it was barely beating. Tears came to my eyes.

"What's wrong?" Rory and Father demanded at the same time. Mother rose and stood behind me; her hands rubbed my arms in a soft, reassuring way.

"He's dead." I stared at them in disbelief. "Andric's father is dead. He found his way to the roof and stepped off." My tears spilled over as the image of the lost King came to my mind. I saw his son comforting him and promising that he would find his Queen again someday. 'He just couldn't wait for someday,' Andric said amid telltale tear splotches that disturbed the ink. 'He said that he could see her, then he stepped off before I could stop him. He was staring out at the ocean.' The writing became more faint. 'I couldn't reach him in time. I couldn't even save my own father.'

A sob escaped my throat and it became impossible to read on through my tears. I stood up quickly and my chair screeched in protest against the varnished wooden floor. "I've got to go to him. I should have been there."

Father and Rory rose also with concern on their faces. Father tried to protest, but I wouldn't hear him. I turned back to Rush. "Tell him I'll be there soon," I said and thought at the same time. The bird clicked his beak once, then lifted his great wings and vanished through the window as quickly as he had appeared. I felt the stares of everyone in the room and ran out before they could question me.

By the time I reached my rooms, full, harsh sobs tore at my chest. I pulled on the riding pants I had worn yesterday, a silk shirt, my boots, and my thick cloak. A sudden impulse made me grab my sword from where it hung on the back of the chair by my bed; it was comforting to strap it about my waist, a familiar weight to hold me down when all I could see was Andric's pain-filled handwriting.

I couldn't believe I had left him knowing all that he was going through. He held together an entire kingdom, filling them with a hope that was as full of pain as promise. He took care of everyone, his own father even, but no one took care of him. He blamed himself for everything that had happened. He had been lost at the end when I kissed him. I had seen it in his eyes, the defeat, the weight of his people looking to him for guidance, the fear of failure. What would he do now by himself and so truly alone?

A soft cough made me turn and stare. Father, Mother, and Rory stood in the doorway dressed as if ready to ride. At my wide eyes, Father nodded. "We're coming with you. It's about a week early yet, but preparations can be made to leave within the hour."

"P-preparations?" I stammered out in confusion. "What preparations?"

Rory winked at me. "It's a long story; you'll hear it all on the ride."

I shook my head wildly. "I can't wait an hour. We've got to go now; it's too late already."

Father held up his hands. "Alright, alright; the servants are already saddling the horses. I'll have Captain Rurisk follow behind with more men and supplies; they'll meet us at nightfall. Your mother will be leaving later; she's got more to prepare than we do."

I looked at her, unable to comprehend what they were talking about. "Mother, you're coming?"

She nodded with obvious concern at my nearly hysterical tone. "It'll be better if we show you." She put an arm around my shoulders and led me out of the room and down the stairs, Father and Rory right behind us.

We met Rurisk in the courtyard with a dozen men attired in Zalen blue and gold already standing by their saddled horses. Father went over to speak to him while Mother led me in the opposite direction.

Mother's greenhouses, her pride and joy created by Father so that she could grow her exotic plants in perfect temperatures, had been disassembled and were now being bound into manageable piles. I stared, but couldn't understand what was going on. My mind was a whirlwind of chaos and emotion, and nothing sunk in past the intense need to reach Andric. "Mother, you're greenhouses," was all I could say.

She smiled. "They're meant for a higher purpose than sheltering my prize roses. And we'll build more on a grander scheme when we get there." She gave a truly girlish grin. "It'll give me the chance to make a few choice improvements that have been driving me nuts."

"What higher purpose?" I asked.

"Taking care of your Antorans," Rory said from behind me. He had his dark red horse, Ragen, and Breeze on lead ropes. Breeze nuzzled my shoulder, forcing me to rub his forehead. I obeyed numbly. "We're taking all of this there," Rory continued. At my stare, he frowned and spoke slower. "Instead of a whole country running south, Father thought it would be better for us to bring what they needed to them."

My mouth fell open. Father was the one who started this?

Rory laughed and handed me Breeze's reins. "You can stand there gaping like a fish, or you can lead this expedition." He swung up onto his long-legged horse. "I'd recommend the latter."

I gave Mother a quick hug with my mind still reeling from shock. She whispered for me to be safe, then I mounted Breeze and hurried to the front of the small group of soldiers that waited for us. Father saw the expression on my face and shook his head with a slightly embarrassed expression. "There'll be time for words later. We need to get going."

I nodded and fell in behind him, hoping that eventually something would start to make sense.

***

King Fasred and Prince Landis rode out to meet us with another small group of soldiers, strengthening our numbers to almost forty. "The rest will come with the Queens," the King said, greeting my father with a fist to his heart.

"It's good to have you," Father said warmly, returning his salute.

Landis grinned at me. "Tisha wanted to come, but she's busy with wedding preparations."

I gasped. I had completely forgotten that they set the date for a month out, far sooner than anyone had expected. "Congratulations; I'm sorry I haven't said anything earlier. I'm so happy for you," I said in a rush; embarrassment colored my cheeks.

Landis grinned cheerfully. "You've had a lot on your mind, Kit. We understand as long as you promise to be there."

"I promise," I said sincerely.

We fell in behind our fathers. Rory and Landis caught up on the time they had spent apart and my thoughts bounced around like a hundred grasshoppers.

***

We camped the first night on the border of Zalen in tents that had already been set up by Father's outriders. Though my whole being urged for us to keep going, my muscles ached as if I had never ridden a horse before. I sat reminiscing about another night in which I had felt much the same way, my heart pounding with unknown danger and adrenaline, my mind rushing and refusing to slow, and an overwhelming number of possibilities and scenarios haunting me.

Father sat down beside me and put an arm around my shoulder. It was awkward at first, because we weren't a very physically affectionate family, but he kept his arm there.

"Thanks, Father," I said quietly past a tight throat. I forbade the tears to come again.

"King Fasred and I felt like we had some making up to do," he said. His brow creased. "The Antorans have been through rough times; some of which could have been prevented, but others that we helped along with our greed."

"But you're making it up now," I said. "That counts so much more than you can imagine."

Father nodded with a small sigh. "That's what happens when you let ignorance and fear take over. We were all so afraid of what we would find in the Antorans that we convinced ourselves they were savages. It was easier to ignore the old treaties and trade agreements than to work with them, or so we told ourselves."

I frowned thoughtfully. "But you've learned that they aren't savages?"

Father's eyes tightened with a hint of humor. "Crown Prince Andric and I have been conversing through letters."

I sat up in surprise and stared at him. "And?"

He smiled. "Let's just say we've come to an understanding."

I didn't know exactly what he meant, but I didn't press it. It was enough that he seemed more open-minded now, and enough to give me hope, though I barely dared breathe lest the hope flicker out and I feel the pain again.

We both sat for a long time by the fire until Father mentioned that we should get some sleep because we needed to ride out early.

"The earlier, the better," I told him.

He nodded. "We'll get there, don't worry."

On impulse, I hugged him tightly. "Thank you, Father."

He patted my back. "It'll be alright, darling. I promise."

Chapter 28

If nonstop riding, brief glimpses of sleep, and more nonstop riding could still feel like the journey took forever, this definitely did. Even though I ached every morning and barely slept when we stopped, I was up before everyone else and ready to go. I felt like we couldn't get there soon enough. I didn't know if it was the fact that Rush never returned, or that we all seemed to feel foreboding in the air the closer we got, but it took forever to cross the mountain range. Regardless, we were not expecting what we found on the other side.

When we passed the wall our first small group hid behind after the attack of the Breizans and the avalanche, Captain Rurisk rode ahead with four of his men to scout the trail; they rode back a few minutes later to tell us that they heard the sounds of battle echoing through the pass. We galloped over the last stretch, then stared below.

At nightfall it should have been hard to make out anything in Antor besides the castle basking white in the moonlight; but tonight, fires lit up the sky. Houses burned below us and people screamed in terror; we could only stare as another house went up like a torch, the flames quickly burning through the thatched roof. Then I heard the shrieking.

My blood ran cold and I drew my sword so quickly it rang in the night. Everyone turned to stare at me. "It's Breizans," I said in a tight voice.

"Breizans?" several men echoed around us.

"Are you sure?" King Fasred asked quickly.

I nodded. "Positive. We've fought them before."

I glanced at Landis. His face was white, but he nodded. "It's them."

"Alright," Father said. He motioned for everyone to pull back. "We aren't rushing into this blindly. That'll help no one."

I fell back grudgingly and slid off Breeze's back to join the Kings, Princes, and Captains in a circle. "We need to hurry," King Fasred stated. "It looks like they were hit unprepared. Anything we can do to give them the advantage might save the city."

Father nodded. "We'll split up, half to the castle and the other half to the city to save what we can of the Antorans there." He indicated members of the group. "Rurisk and I will lead our men through the city. Fasred, you've got the castle." The King of Faer nodded.

"We need someone who knows the lay of the land to lead both parties," Rory said. He nodded at Landis and I. "Landis, lead your men; Kit will lead ours."

"Kit?" Father repeated in shock.

Rory ignored him and turned to me. "Can you do that?"

I nodded, adrenaline racing through my veins. "Yes, but I'd rather lead the troops going to the castle."

Rory's eyes softened slightly. "Right. You ride with King Fasred. We'll take Landis and meet you there."

Father just stared between us, unable to argue. He had to trust his son's judgment in this as much as he hated to admit it.

"See you at the castle," I told them. I ached for us to be on our way as soon as possible.

"Take care of yourself," Rory said. He patted me on the shoulder, then pulled me in for a short hug before he turned back to his men. "Let's make it quick; people are dying down there."

King Fasred and I ran back to our horses with his men on our heels. We were riding down the mountainside before Father and Rory finished speaking to their soldiers.

We swept to the side, riding around the outskirts of the city toward the castle wall. I knew the hardest part would be storming the gates, and hoped a side passage would be easier to access. The others followed without question; out of the corner of my eye I saw swords drawn and looks exchanged as the shrieking drew nearer. Then the first shadows leaped out at us.

The rider on my left flank screamed as he was torn off his horse. Two riders stopped to help him before they realized that his throat had already been torn out. They tried to ride back to join us, but foul, shrieking Breizans stepped out of the darkness to surround them. I motioned and we turned in a tight circle, thundering back to save the soldiers.

My sword bit into flesh for the first time, severing a hand that swung a jagged-toothed axe toward a soldier. The owner of the hand screamed and tried to attack me, but Breeze lashed out with a hoof and sent the Breizan flying against the wall. King Fasred cut down another attacker, then wheeled his horse to stop a third from slicing his horse's hamstring. I leaned down to catch another Breizan across the back before he could leap onto an empty horse. He gnashed his teeth at me even as he fell bleeding to the ground.

The two soldiers quickly turned their horses to join us as we spun and headed back toward the gate. "Stay close," I shouted. "Fighting as a group is our only advantage against them."

We thundered along the outside of the wall but kept a good space between it and us, fearing that Breizans would leap from the wall onto our horses. Fortunately, we reached the gate without losing any more soldiers. Two men ran over and forced the lock with their knives, then swung it wide for everyone to enter. We galloped through with our swords held low, ready for attack.

It came like a hurricane. The Breizans battered us against the wall, but we held our own against them, surviving by sheer skill and speed against the savage onslaught. Teeth bared and stained with crimson ripped at our horses' sides, but our animals showed true battle spirit and rose on their hind legs to lash out with hooves, then dropped to give us the advantage of a quick lunge.

Eventually, only bodies littered the light skiff of lingering snow and stained it red. We didn't dare let ourselves rest; I was afraid that the men would realize what we were up against and flee. I saw the same fear echoed on King Fasred's face as he did a quick check of his men. "We've survived; let's keep going," he said to me. I nodded and led the way again with the King close behind.

Short, hard battles made the going slow as we crossed to the castle doors. Breizans were everywhere, attacking citizens from Antor and our soldiers alike. There were animals I recognized fighting beside their humans, Bagan and his black bear and Drade with more than half of his horse herd thrashing the Breizans in their path. I even spotted the white deer from my first day in Antor. The little blue-eyed girl was nowhere to be seen; I prayed that she was alright.

When the Antorans saw us, they fought quickly to reach us and clear a path to the castle. "There're more inside," a young man told me breathlessly. He held onto my stirrup to catch his breath. "We hid those who made it in time in the safe room in the bottom of the castle. Prince Andric's men are fighting to keep them safe."

"Where's the Prince?" I asked him quickly.

He shook his head. "I don't know. He was hurt in the first wave and I haven't seen him since."

King Fasred must have seen the look on my face because he urged his horse to my other side and grabbed Breeze's bridle. "We'll get there; follow me." He took the lead and sliced our way to the open castle doors; our soldiers kept a tight wall around us. We dismounted as soon as we reached the doors and ran inside. I sent a thought to Breeze and he led the other horses to fight against the Breizans that tried to come in after us.

We met chaos at every corner. Though a few skirmishes were fought along the massive hallway, it was obvious by the clamor that the majority of the battle was occurring further down the stairs to the safe room. My heart screamed for me to find Andric as quickly as possible; I wondered if I was already too late.

I ran to the stairway that led up to the royal quarters and turned to face the men that followed me. "I've got to find Andric," I told King Fasred. "I'll join you again as soon as I can."

He nodded, his eyes kind and calm despite the battlefield frenzy around us. "Four of my men will go with you; take care of yourself."

"You, too," I said earnestly. I turned to go.

"Princess Kirit?"

I looked back to find the King still watching me. "Yes, Sir?"

The expression on his face surprised me. "You've done your country proud," he said, putting a fist to his heart in salute. "I'm honored to follow you into battle."

I opened my mouth, but couldn't think of a reply. He gave me a nod, then led his men toward the sound of battle. I took a deep breath to calm my pounding heart and ran up the stairs, the four soldiers following close behind.

It felt like a dream to run down the hallway with the clashing of swords and screams of agony echoing around us. The white marble and drifting moonlight lit the castle in eerie shadows that moved as we ran past and made me jump. But I knew our destination by heart and didn't falter. We surprised a nest of four Breizans which we dispatched swiftly, then I burst through the doors into Andric's quarters.

They were empty. I could feel it the second I walked in, but I searched anyway. Fresh blood stained the carpet by the fireplace and discarded bandages on a table. I bit my lip and turned back. "He's not here," I said, faltering. He was supposed to be here. I had counted on that, survived on that; and now he was gone.

"He may be fighting with the troops below, Princess," one of the older soldiers said gently.

I stared at him for a minute and willed my mind to work past the panic. He nodded encouragingly and I knew he was right. Andric would never leave his people to fend for themselves. No matter what shape he was in, he would be there fighting for them.

"Thank you," I told him sincerely; I turned to face the door with my sword still drawn and stained with Breizan blood. "Let's go."

We ran back down the first set of stairs, then I made a quick judgment call and took us along the other hallway so we would come through the back stairs instead of meeting the battle head on. The soldiers followed me without question, something I appreciated. There wasn't time for second-guessing or doubt in the midst of battle. We cut through the few Breizans who stood on the stairs and stormed through to the bottom hallway and the heart of the fighting.

More Breizans than Antorans filled the wide hallway that fronted the safe room, and the Breizans were winning by sheer strength of numbers and ferocity. Wounded and dying Antorans lay everywhere. The floor glistened dark red and was littered with weapons and body parts. The metallic smell of blood washed over us as if we had stepped into a butcher's kitchen. Everywhere I looked, Breizans with bared teeth streaming blood tore apart the brave soldiers who dared to stand between them and the doorway.

Time slowed. I could see King Fasred and his men at the other end of the hall striving valiantly to fight through to the Antorans. Toward the middle, I saw Father, Rory, and Landis surrounded by their soldiers. Father had a gash across his forehead and Landis limped with Rory's help as they fought to protect each other and take out as many of the Breizans as they could.

I glanced toward the door in the middle of the hallway that led to the safe room and saw Jashe, Jesson, and Ayd. My heart stopped beating entirely.

Andric leaned against the door, his right hand clutched across his stomach while he fought mercilessly with his left. He parried a brutal blow from an axe and slid sideways across the door from the force of the attack. Red streaked the burnished wood behind him. The Breizan with the axe shrieked in rage and swung again. This time, Andric's sword flew from his hand. He fell behind the frenzied crowd that fought between us.

"No!" I screamed. I leaped off the stairs already swinging my sword before my feet touched the ground. Breizans rose up around me, but I only had eyes for the last place Andric had been. My attacks brought me closer and closer to him, and though I barely knew it, the four soldiers kept pace behind me and protected my back.

I reached the middle of the hallway, then couldn't make any more progress toward Andric and the others. There were just too many Breizans. Despite the skill with which we fought, the savage horde beat us back by strength of numbers.

I heard a yell of agony and my heart slowed when I recognized Captain Rurisk's voice. I turned toward it and gasped when a slice of fire ran up my arm. I thrust quickly and stopped my attacker before he could land another one. My arm throbbed, but I couldn't feel any pain through the adrenaline that pounded in my veins.

A grunt came from behind me and I turned again. One of the four soldiers that had stayed faithfully beside me clutched at his shoulder, his sword arm useless. The Breizan that attacked him grinned fiercely, his sharp teeth edged with red. He slashed again and cut deep into the soldier's leg. I looked around wildly. The other three soldiers fought to defend us from a rush of Breizans storming down the stairs. The Breizan near the soldier raised his sword to finish the soldier's life; a gleam of wild excitement glittered in the Breizan's eyes.

I pushed my own attacker to the side and lunged in front of the soldier, catching the full brunt of the blade's blow with my sword. My arm went numb, but I managed to throw the blade away with a turn of my wrist. The Breizan looked shocked, then angry. He snarled and prepared to leap at me, but I stopped him with a quick slash across the neck in a move that had been drilled into my by Andric's training. The Breizan gasped and collapsed with his hands at his throat.

I threw the soldier's arm around my shoulder, heedless of the blood that stained us both. "We need to fall back," I yelled above the clamor. The other three soldiers nodded in acknowledgment and began backing toward us. The wounded soldier and I did our best to clear a path so that our backs could be against the wall for better defense.

I barely missed a swipe at my stomach, then lunged and my blade sunk deep into a Breizan's chest. He grabbed at the sword, but I yanked it free and spun, chopping off his head. I fought to keep the contents of my stomach in place, afraid one moment of weakness would be my last. But as I took a quick glance around the hall, I knew the truth. We were losing this battle, and losing it quickly. If something didn't change, the Antorans behind the door would be easy prey for the bloodthirsty horde.

I looked around desperately, searching for something, anything, that could help us. My search came up empty and I fought down the despair that rose in my throat. Everywhere I looked, soldiers fell to the ground. Antorans were scarce; their bonded animals fought valiantly but were scattered through the room.

My thoughts suddenly cleared with one single idea that sounded sharply above the chaos. We had to take what made Antor different and use it to defend itself. "I need a second," I shouted to the soldiers. They didn't ask questions, they merely closed in the space so that I stood against the wall, protected by four blades against the onslaught.

I didn't know what I was doing, or if it was even possible, but I knew I had to try. My heart hammered in my chest. I closed my eyes and reached out. At first, my thoughts wandered tentatively through the room. I touched the minds of the animals there, but shied away from the angry, mindless roar that made up the black thoughts of the Breizans. I felt a few of the animals and their bonded humans look over at me in surprise. I ignored them and pushed farther.

Suddenly, it was as though the battle fury caught my thoughts like wildfire. I saw the main floor of the castle, then out the door to the bloody courtyard where battles were still being fought. I made it out into the city, but that wasn't far enough. My limbs started to shake, but I pushed again and gave all my energy to it.

Minds awoke, reached out, and embraced my thoughts. Animals of all kinds and a few bonded humans living outside the city heard me. "Help us," I pleaded. "Antor is under attack."

A yell sounded close to me and the sound of it echoed in my mind. Something shoved me hard against the wall and the connection broke. I opened my eyes with a gasp; a wave of nausea flooded through me. I turned my head in an effort to staunch the feeling and looked into the glazed eyes of one of the soldiers who had fought beside me and defended me when I was at my weakest. A spear stuck straight through his body and into the wall. The soldier's effort to push me away and save my life was what had broken my concentration.

Tears welled up in my eyes, tears of rage, frustration, fear, and anger at the hopelessness of the battle we fought. I yelled wordlessly and leaped at the Breizan that stood admiring his proficient kill. He kicked out before I could reach him and caught me in the ribs just below my sword arm. I rolled along the ground, aware enough through the blind fury that filled me to keep my sword up so I didn't roll over it.

I couldn't feel the cracked ribs when I leaped back to my feet and dove at him before he could get set. We fell into three more Breizans fighting a desperate Antoran soldier. Ready for the distraction, the Antoran dispatched them quickly, then turned and helped me with mine.

My chest heaving, I looked closer at him. "Ayd!"

He pushed a strand of sweat-damp blond hair out of his eyes, leaving a streak of blood across his forehead. "Hello, Princess Kit," he said with a quick bow and then a slice at a Breizan to my right. "I'm surprised you've joined us."

"Don't think we'll be here very long," I said quickly. I turned to catch another Breizan in the chest before he could take a slice at me.

"Death in battle is a warrior's fate," he replied.

Despite the fighting around us, I was surprised to hear the bitterness of his tone. I had never heard Ayd be anything but positive, and somehow that made me even angrier. I let out a growl that would have made Bayn proud and, with a crouching spin, sliced behind the knees of the Breizan Ayd battled. He fell backward with a howl of pain. "Living through it would be better," I said through my teeth.

Ayd nodded, his eyes full of pain. He grabbed my arm before we could be attacked again. "Give Nyssa my love."

I shook my head. "Give her it yourself. We're going to make it through this."

He shrugged helplessly, indicating another swarm of Breizans coming down the stairs on either end of the hallway. "How?"

I gritted my teeth against the prickle of tears and refused to let them come. "I don't know." I ran forward to help one of the soldiers when a massive rumble sounded above us.

I looked up in time to see three huge bears gallop down the stairway battering Breizans out of the way like they were saplings. Behind them, four elk thundered down the stairs with their antlers held low. Breizans screamed as they were skewered and thrown aside with a shake of the animals' heads. More animals poured down the other side led by two massive moose with several of Drade's horses behind them. Hawks and eagles flew low overhead, diving down to peck and claw at the faces of the Breizans who attempted to attack the animals. Several ferrets wove between hooves and feet and bit at unprotected legs.

Bayn gave a deep howl; a quiver ran through the room when it was answered in force from above before more than a dozen wolves loped down the stairs. Rush flew past and showed me with a brush of his wing across my cheek that the courtyard was full of animals fighting to defend Antor.

Hope hit me and the thread of energy that I was holding onto, the very last bit left from my contact with the animals, left me as though it had been cut through. I fell back against the wall and slid down it, willing my grip on my sword to stay true.

I didn't have to worry. At the first sign of my exhausted state, Ayd and the two remaining soldiers moved to protect me. I could see brief glimpses of the fight through their legs, but it was already dying down. The animals were swift and merciless in their execution; they flowed down the stairs until the hall was filled with more four-footed creatures than two. I watched them in a daze, unable to do more than stare when a wolf brought a Breizan down in front of Ayd's feet and the life blood spilled from his throat.

"Kit," someone shook me gently. "Princess, it's over."

I opened my eyes slowly. My head pounded. I put my hand to it and pushed myself up slowly with my back against the wall. I willed my knees to hold and stood still for several seconds. Then I blinked and looked around.

Ayd stared at me anxiously, three soldiers with him. I was glad to see that the two remaining soldiers who had come down the stairs with me were still alive. They both gave respectful nods. I smiled back at them wearily.

"You were right," Ayd said with a grin. "We made it!"

Everything flooded back in a rush. "Andric?" I asked. I pushed away from the wall and stumbled toward the door where I had last seen him. Ayd caught me before I could fall and pulled one of my arms over his shoulders.

A crowd of Antorans and soldiers circled the door. Ayd helped me push through it. People saw who we were and gave way. A lone figure sat against the door, his head on his knees and his knuckles stained red. His brown hair was tangled and matted with blood.

I let go of Ayd and fell to my knees. Weariness flooded my entire body; I struggled to remain alert. "Andric?" I forced out.

He raised his head and his brown eyes stared straight into mine. "Kit?" he asked in soft disbelief.

I nodded, a small smile coming to my lips.

His eyes creased at the corners. "I heard you, but I thought it was in my mind." He rubbed his eyes with a blood-stained hand.

"It was in your mind," a voice said.

I looked over to see Drade step forward from the crowd. He bent down and gently lifted one of Andric's arms over his shoulder. "She called to them, all of them."

"Who?" Andric asked weakly. He winced and held his side with one hand as he was helped to his feet.

"The animals," Drade said. He met my eyes, his expression one of awe. "She called them to help us."

Strong hands slid under my arms and legs and lifted me up as though I weighed less than a sack of flour. "You wielded that sword true, Princess," Smithy Hensas said with a hearty chuckle that was touched with relief. "No one could have done it better justice."

"No other sword would have held up so well," I replied sincerely. I still held it in my hand. I wasn't willing to put it away just yet. The blade was covered in blood and had a few nicks along one side. "I've damaged it."

The Smithy grinned. "It's fixable, as is the city. We'll recover from this battle."

"With as much help as you need," Father's voice said from behind us.

Smithy Hensas turned and Father's face fell when he saw who was in the burly man's arms. "Kit?" He ran forward.

"I'm alright, Father," I said. The Smith lowered me down so I could stand. I wobbled a bit. Father reached forward to steady me, his eyes anxious. "Really, I'm fine," I reassured him. "Just tired."

I looked back at Andric and saw that he, too, was weaving where he stood. Several soldiers stood around us in various degrees of injury. "Has anyone seen Jesson?" I asked.

Several members of the group chuckled. "He'll be very busy," Drade replied.

Prince Andric took a deep breath and let go of the Horsemaster so that he stood by his own power. He lifted his chin, his eyes catching the light with a faint glimmer of his confident self. "Jashe, Drade, divide the company into two halves." His voice strengthened. "One half to help the injured to the great hall and the other half to gather the dead from all sides. We'll burn the Breizans outside the eastern wall so the wind can carry their ashes to sea where they belong."

"And the others?" Jashe asked.

Andric's eyes were full of sorrow when he looked back at the door behind him. I gasped when I saw Falen's still body there, a slain wolf by his side. "We'll help their families bury them. Antor is a country in mourning."

Chapter 29

Despite my protests, Father and Andric saw to it that I went directly to the Great Hall to get checked out. I felt like a little girl being hustled about and made a fuss of, but my loved ones were safe and that was all that mattered. Rory, King Fasred, and Landis found us there. I must have looked worse that I thought by the glances they exchanged.

King Fasred sat on the edge of my cot where I waited for one of Jesson's assistants. I wasn't in a hurry because there were so many others with wounds far more serious than my own, Andric's included. The Antoran Prince stubbornly insisted that he wait for the others to be cared for first; he was too busy helping the Antorans from the safe room to worry about getting patched up.

"I've never seen anyone fight the way you did," Landis' father said with a smile.

"The Antorans are good teachers," I replied. Captain Rurisk and I exchanged hidden smiles from his cot a row away where he was having a nasty slash across his ribs stitched.

"Well, your bravery and willingness to put others above yourself is outstanding. You'd make a fine leader."

I smiled at him. "I'm just glad I don't have to worry about it."

Rory laughed and squeezed my shoulder. "Maybe I'll step down and give you the position."

I punched at him playfully, then winced at the twinge in my ribs. "Don't you dare. I'm not leadership material."

"I'd argue against that," Father said, his voice funny. I looked back at him and he shrugged. "Who would have thought my little girl was so dangerous?"

"I did," Landis said. We all looked at him and he grinned. "The first time she danced with Trevin, I knew we were in trouble."

Everyone laughed, and I blushed at the memory. A wave of weariness swept through me again and I settled back on the bed. Father knelt next to me. "Are you alright, sweetheart?"

I nodded, fighting to keep my eyes open. "Just tired, really, really tired."

Father patted my hand. "Sleep, darling. We'll help out with the others and be back before the healer gets here."

I nodded, but watched him and Rory with a slight twinge of worry.

Something must have shown on my face because Father reached out and smoothed the hair from my forehead. "What is it?" he asked gently.

"I'm afraid of bad dreams," I admitted softly, the all-too-real images from the day crowding my mind.

Father smiled fondly, then looked up and nodded at someone behind me. "I'll leave you in good hands," he said. He rose, ruffled my hair, then left with Rory, Landis, and King Fasred.

"Still having trouble with nightmares?" a familiar voice asked. A thrill of warmth ran through my veins at the sound.

I gathered my strength to roll over and look at Andric, but he set a hand on my shoulder. "Stay," he said quietly. "You need to rest." He walked around the cot and pulled another one close so that he could sit next to me.

He looked as awful as I felt. His cheeks were pale and sunken with dark circles around his eyes as though he hadn't slept in weeks. I suddenly remembered his father and tears came to my eyes.

Andric's expression tightened with concern. "What is it?" he asked quickly.

"Your father," I said, my voice tight.

Pain washed through his eyes and then vanished as swiftly as it appeared. He took one of my hands. "He's in a better place now. I wish I could have stopped him, but I couldn't." His voice dropped lower. "It's not something I can deal with right now."

I nodded as tears pooled on the blanket that served as a pillow under my head.

Andric gave me a gentle smile and reached over to wipe the tears away. He winced at the movement and gritted his teeth as though fighting back a gasp of pain. I sat up quickly and my head swam. "You need the healer," I said.

Andric shook his head. "It's not that bad; I checked it already. I can wait." He motioned for me to lie back down.

I shook my head. "Only if you do, too."

He sighed, saw that I wouldn't give in, and nodded. "Alright, but I should be helping my people."

I smiled at him and settled back down on my pillow. "Trust me, Andric. You have two Kings, two Crown Princes, several Captains, and enough soldiers to keep this place running for months. No one will begrudge you a bit of sleep after all you've done for them."

Andric settled down on the other cot, then turned and watched me, his eyes narrowed thoughtfully.

"What?" I finally asked with a slight blush.

He gave me one of his true smiles. It made him look younger, less exhausted, as though he didn't have any walls or pain. I wished I could see that smile on his face forever. "I was just thinking how lucky I was to have kidnapped you."

I laughed, then winced at the sharp pain that responded. Andric reached out and I took his hand. "It's the other way around," I told him. "I'm the one who was lucky to get kidnapped."

He lifted an eyebrow. "You sure about that?"

I smiled but remembered not to laugh. "Pretty sure."

He grinned again, his eyes closing with weariness. "As long as you're sure," he said, his voice soft.

I listened as his breathing settled into a steady rhythm. His grip loosened and his hand fell to rest on my cot. I put my hand over his. "I'm positive," I whispered.

Chapter 30

It was a good thing the wedding was outside; they wouldn't have been able to accommodate all of the people and animals otherwise. It felt like a dream to walk under trees strewn with flowers and ivy, lit with lavender scented candles and tied with white and yellow bows. The setting sun lit the clearing in hues of orange, pale pink, and gold. Dancers spun to the sweet chords of stringed instruments flowing across the meadow. Light peals of laughter were a sweet harmony to the calls of evening birds and the chirp of crickets beginning their songs to the night sky.

I breathed in, enjoying the heady scents of the candles mixed with the exotic flowers from Mother's greenhouses that had been spread along the table tops. Closing my eyes, I tried to hold the scene in my mind so that I could remember it forever.

"Waiting for someone?" a voice teased in my ear.

I spun with a wide smile. "Just you," I said, putting my arms around Andric's neck. The movement pulled at my ribs and made me wince. I tried to hide it, but Andric's shrewd eyes took in everything.

"Still a bit sore from your triumphant battle?" he asked. He lowered my arms and brought me close to his chest.

I ran a finger lightly down his side and smothered a laugh when he, too, winced. "And you're not?" I teased.

He stepped back and grinned at me. "It's best to keep you at a distance. You're dangerous."

I laughed, ignoring my ribs' protest. "Oh, I'm the dangerous one? You brought half the animals in Denbria."

He gave a thoughtful smile. "You think they came for me? It's not my fault your calling them to our aid also implied some invitation for them to stay on. Half the Antorans are now bonded with some sort of animal." His smile turned sly. "And I hear it's spreading."

I turned to see where he indicated. Hawkmaster Ayd and Crown Princess Nyssa sat under a tree with half a dozen curious children around them. Rush stood on Ayd's glove while a young snow hawk waited on Nyssa's covered knee. She ran her fingers through the soft feathers on its head and it nuzzled her cheek gently. She laughed, then turned to Ayd. He kissed her soundly; the children whispered to each other and giggled.

"Well, they're not the only ones," I told Andric. I pointed in the opposite direction and watched his eyes widen in surprise.

Mother and Father had finished dancing and were making their way to one of the many tables surrounding the clearing. Rory sat at the one they headed to, with Kaerdra at his side. Between them, a beautiful red and brown bobcat kitten toyed with a feather from Kaerdra's hat. Kaerdra laughed and picked up the kitten to cuddle it under her chin. Rory jumped in surprise, then bent down and caught a little red fox that had been playing under the table. The kitten wriggled free and jumped down. After a second of squirming, the fox was put down to join it.

"How do your parents feel about that?" Andric asked in surprise.

I shrugged and indicated for him to keep watching. The fox and kitten ran around the table and charged straight at Mother and Father. Father laughed when they circled his feet, their little growls of mock fury audible in the air. He bent down and caught one in each hand. "Now, now," we heard him scold gently. "If your humans are going to get married, you'll have to learn to get along."

Andric and I laughed, the surprise on his face now matching the shock on my own.

The scent of roses drifted to my nose and I thought of my handmaiden back at Antor. "How's Kimber getting along?" I asked.

Andric grinned. "She runs the greenhouses like she owns them." He laughed. "And thanks to your arrangement, she practically does."

"She's a good friend."

He nodded. "And she's good at what she does. I've never seen a girl who's happier."

I grinned. "I don't know about that."

He smiled down at me, his dark eyes aglow with the sunset. My heart skipped sideways in my chest at the warmth and happiness in them.

The notes of a familiar tune struck up. I smiled at the song we had danced to at the dinner for the Voises. The young Antoran King held out his arm. "Shall we?"

I nodded and accepted his escort to the center of the meadow. I could feel the weight of the mountain lion claw where it hung around my neck under the light gold dress.

"You still wear it, don't you?" Andric asked, guessing my thoughts.

I nodded and touched its shape under the fabric. "It means a lot to me."

"Me, too," he replied.

I frowned slightly as he spun me in a slow circle. "What do you mean?" I asked when I came back around to face him.

He stopped dancing. "Well," he hesitated, then dropped his eyes to my fingers entwined with his. "That was the moment I realized I couldn't live without you."

I stared at him, speechless.

He continued. "I almost lost you, then. It was my fault you'd been in danger, and I vowed to get you as far away from me as possible if you survived." His brow creased.

"And?" I asked.

His mouth twisted into a wry smile. "I realized after you left Antor that I also couldn't live with you so very far away, in possible danger from attacks, avalanches, or. . . ."

"Or?" I pressed, my heart quickening.

"Or other boys," he admitted finally. My mouth dropped open and he reached up to close it with a gentle finger. "I might not deserve you, but I vow to try."

My breath caught with the implications. I glanced back at Father and saw that he was watching us with an arm around Mother. He smiled at me.

"I've spoken to your father," Andric continued, "And though he's not exactly thrilled about the idea, he only gave me two conditions."

"What conditions?" I asked breathlessly.

He smiled, his deep brown eyes crinkling at the corners. "That you loved me, and. . . ." He sighed, and I could see the second condition wasn't to his liking, but he would accept it. "That I wait until you are at least eighteen to give you a chance to be sure."

My heart dropped slightly, but I put my arms around Andric's shoulders anyway, heedless of the pain in my ribs. "I do love you," I whispered in his ear. "I love you more than I've ever loved anyone or anything in my life. And I'll wait for you until I'm eighteen."

Andric held out his hand and I gasped to see a beautiful silver ring on a finely wrought chain sitting on his palm. He smiled at me, the smile that chased away all thoughts of sadness, and all of the trials and tragedies we had been through. He was truly happy. "For you, my Kit." He stepped behind me and clasped the chain around my neck.

I looked over to see satisfied smiles on Mother and Father's faces. Rory stared at me while Kaerdra grinned; she leaned over and whispered something in his ear. He laughed and turned back to her, tickling her with the feather.

Andric took my hand and spun me gracefully to face him. I set my head against his chest and danced slowly to the music. "I'm very glad I kidnapped you," he whispered quietly into my hair.

"I love you, my thief prince," I replied.

He laughed and spun me again, his eyes sparkling in the candlelight.

About the Author

Cheree Alsop is the mother of a beautiful, talented daughter and two amazing twin sons who fill every day with light and laughter. She married her best friend, Michael, who changes lives each day in his Chiropractic clinic. Cheree is currently working as a free-lance writer and mother. She enjoys reading, riding her motorcycle on warm nights, and rocking her twins while planning her next book. She is also an aspiring drummer and bass player for her husband's garage band.

Cheree and Michael live in Utah where they rock out, enjoy the outdoors, plan great adventures, and never stop dreaming.

Made in the USA
Charleston, SC
05 September 2012